When the phone rings between midnight and sunrise, it's usually nothing good. The call that Mike received that night was no exception.

He picked up the phone to hear a firm voice tell him "Get your arse out of bed, you've got work to do."

"Er…what? What the fuck?"

"You're going to fix it, or I'm dead, which means you will be too."

"Fix what? Who is this?"

The reply came between breaths as though the caller was performing some heavy task.

"The Judy. It's a mess. I bricked the fucking Judy!"

# Dark Streets

Andrew Ravenscroft

**Marinagh Publishing**

First Print Edition

Dark Streets Copyright © 2014 Andrew Ravenscroft

ISBN: 978-0692244142

Quotation on p.210 from Faust by Johann Wolfgang von Goethe.

Editing by Karen Barrett-Wilt
Cover Photo and Design Copyright © 2014 by Mary Musker

Published by Marinagh Publishing, LLC

For my father,
who I suspect knows a thing or two about
London's underworld.

# CONTENTS

# 1
# The Wind in the Door

"Where the fuck is the Judy?"

They were seven glum faces trying hard not to catch his eye. A semicircle of misery, all but one of them trying to look alert instead of scared shitless, literally on the carpet in front of the boss.

He stared at them through thick, black-framed glasses. No one spoke. The hand of the vintage analog clock on his desk was the only thing that moved.

Tick - 10:17.

"Am I making this too hard? I thought it was a simple enough question: adverb – verb – noun. Where – the – fuck – is – the – Judy. Question mark." His eyes stabbed at them one by one. "Hello? Does anyone here speak English?"

He turned his back and stared out at the orange glow of London and the dark wide ribbon of the Thames disappearing into the west. "I don't fucking believe it."

They stood in silence, watching his bulk outlined in the window.

Tick – 10:18.

He turned to face them again. "I'll make this very, very easy. If it's not back here by daylight, you useless bastards will have a lot more than the dole office to worry about. Get out there and fucking well find it. Yes? Are we clear?"

Nods from the crescent of pale faces.

"Then fuck off."

The men filed out quickly, except for one. A tall man with close-cropped, steel grey hair, he stood almost at attention as if waiting for a more formal dismissal. He watched the boss with calm steady eyes.

Tick – 10:19.

The boss sat down and ran his fingers over his bare skull, as though sweeping back a mane of hair long since gone. His gaze wandered across the objects on the mahogany desk: the pile of papers, the black rotary phone, the clock, the gun.

"Who is it, Nick?"

"Hard to tell, Harry."

"There aren't many with the bollocks to try something like this. What about the Poles? They've been a bit bolshie lately, and they have the tech."

"After the kicking we gave them in Hammersmith? I don't think so, Boss."

"Fair enough. Bermondsey Kasuals?"

"Out of town. Cup semi-final."

"Then that leaves the triads."

"Not their style. The 24K are mainly designer drugs. The Sun Yee On don't do tech."

"No, but they do bear a grudge. Wei has been lying low since the shootings, but he has a long memory. Plus he's an evil bastard." He glanced around the dark paneled walls of the suite, his gaze skimming over the gold-framed paintings that adorned them. He nodded. "Yeah, I reckon its Wei."

He looked down at the gun on his desk. "What's he up to, Nick?"

"I'll give him a bell, boss."

"Very funny. All right. Get the rest of the lads out on the streets while you see what you can dig up on Wei."

"Alright, Harry."

The boss tilted his head towards the door and Nick turned to leave. "Nick?"

He stopped, looked back over his shoulder. "Yes, Harry?"

"I want this sorted fast. If I don't get some answers by morning, I'm calling Martin, understand?"

Nick nodded and left the room.

Tick – 10:20.

The gang was waiting by the lift. Nick stepped in and they followed. He swiped an icon on the console, the doors slid shut, and the lift dropped. A spiral display of hundreds of green lights blinked out one by one in rapid succession, marking their progress as they descended from the top of the Coronation Tower to the parking levels below. In the spotless mirrored surface of the lift doors, a miserable-looking group of men in rumpled clothes stared back at them. No one said a word.

The lift stopped, the doors opening up on the soft light of the parking garage. They stepped out, casting quick glances at each other as they gathered in a grim crescent to hear Nick's instructions.

"I don't think I have to tell you that the boss is very unhappy."

One of the gang, a stocky dark haired man with a crooked nose, spoke up.

"I think we got that, Nick. What's pissing us off is why we have to go and find the Judy. Thought it was supposed to be able to take care of itself."

There were nods of agreement.

"I know no one's thrilled about it, Billy, but you heard the boss."

"Seems to me whether we find it or not, we end up on the shitheap."

"It's worse than that. If we don't have it back by morning, he's bringing in Martin."

The group became a mass of tilted heads and nervous shuffles and their eyes roved the concrete ceiling, the floor.

A young and sharply dressed man in the middle of the group spoke:

"Who the bloody hell's Martin?"

There was a subtle movement and the others were suddenly a half step further away from him.

Nick gave him a long look.

"Pete, you know the old saying: There are no stupid questions, just stupid answers?"

"Yeah?"

"Well, the first part of that saying is complete bollocks. Shut it and pay attention." He addressed the group.

"If we don't find it fast, we're in even deeper shit than we are now, so let's get moving. Dave, find out why we lost the trace. Col, check the building. Larry, talk to some coppers, see if surveillance picked up anything; it left the building somehow. Chopper, Billy, see what the other gangs are up to. Pete." He paused. "You're on CPP; try not to get the boss any more pissed off than he is already."

"Bodyguard? Why am I the bleedin' bodyguard?"

"'Cause the Judy's gone, and you've already demonstrated that you don't know how to ask intelligent questions."

Nick looked them over, one at a time. "You find anything, call it in. Yes, Pete, what?"

"What are *you* doing, Nick?"

The rest of the group was now a full step away.

Nick walked over and leant his face down into Pete's. "None of your fucking business. Now, get your arse into gear."

The group dispersed among the parked cars. Nick watched Pete as he walked around him and stepped back into the lift, his eyes on Nick the entire time. He swiped the icon for the rooftop garden level. The steel doors slid shut like a pair of razor blades cutting off a final glimpse of his scowl.

Nick peered at his reflection in the doors for a moment, taking in the lines written across his face, his creased brow, then turned and walked away down the rows of parked cars. The garage echoed with the squeal of distant tires as the gang headed out.

He stopped at a dark blue car. The onboard security recognized his chip, and the interior lights came on as he opened the driver's door and got in. His phone rang as he shut the door. He knew who it would be before he answered it.

"Yes, Mr. Wei?"

The voice at the other end spoke in a clear, polished tone: "I did not hear from you as scheduled, Nick."

"Yeah. There's a problem."

A pause.

"I heard that from other sources, but I wanted to hear from you."

"It's nothing serious, I'm sorting it out."

"When can I expect delivery?"

"Tomorrow?"

"Too late."

"It's the best I can do just now. Things are complicated. I'm working on it."

A longer pause.

"I no longer have confidence that you can deliver, Nick. I have made other arrangements to get the information."

"Other arrangements? Give me a bloody chance, here."

"I'm giving you a chance, Nick. I'm giving you a chance to run. Our business relationship is over. Get out of London."

"Oh, come on."

"Wheels are turning. If you are in their path, they will crush you. Goodbye."

The call ended. Nick gripped the phone as if about to throw it.

"Jesus Christ."

He brought the phone back down to his mouth.

"Xander," he said, and it called a number.

The voicemail that took the call was lengthy but the message that Nick left on it was very concise.

"Your friends have gotten us into some deep shit. Call me."

Nick ended the call and tossed the phone onto the passenger seat.

"Fucking useless toerag."

He looked in the rear view mirror as he hit the starter. The engine fired up and he backed out quickly, turned, and sped off up the ramp towards the streets of London. He tried not to notice the muted repetitive thumping coming from the boot.

Tick – 10:32.

# *2*
# The Exhibition

Xander couldn't believe how well the evening was going. Zelley had done his usual classy job, and the exhibition was a roaring success. The gallery was fabulous, all the critics who mattered were there, and the food and wine were on the tastefully expensive side. He could never get past the thought that even as he dispensed his patronage, Zelley was somehow mocking him, but tonight he was beyond caring. Drunk with wine and success, he swayed as he walked into the gallery bathrooms and over to one of the stalls.

A good number of his pieces already had buyers at prices that even he considered vastly inflated, and others were being hemmed and hawed over. Someone had already bought Work/Out, a man-sized water bottle filled with his sweat, and a Japanese entrepreneur was seriously eyeing Stain, an outline of his body in the pose of a crime victim, etched in his blood instead of chalk.

*Yes,* he thought, *a really fabulous night. Outstanding, in fact.*

Then he leaned over the toilet bowl and vomited profusely.

He hadn't realized he'd been overdoing it, but he'd lost track of the number of times one of the impeccably dressed waiters had refilled his glass. Some indeterminate time afterwards, he had felt the beginnings of the slide from a hitherto magnificently drunken high into his present state.

The descent had been rapid, until he finally reached the point where he realized that his voice might have been rather too loud and forceful.

Like faint signals from a distant world, the strained smiles of his entourage had eventually registered and he'd dialed back his volubility before it became obnoxious; as far as he could tell, at any rate. He'd been contemplating re-joining the fray when his stomach settled the matter for him and sent him to the bathroom.

He vomited again and sprayed red wine over the white porcelain where it clung like so many drops of blood.

*Good god, this is bizarre. Out there, people are dropping serious money on my work and here am I, throwing up 30-year old grapes. If only I'd had my masterpiece ready for tonight. 18 years and almost done. Almost done. That would really have knocked their socks off.*

In a moment of wild enthusiasm he entertained the thought of walking back into the gallery, making a big announcement and inviting everyone to his place to view it. Yes, that would be something. He'd sweep them up like the Pied Piper and lead them all dancing through the streets of London to his home where he would guide them to his top floor studio and his work of genius.

Then he heaved up some more Bordeaux and thought better of it. His nostrils burned from the wine and vomit. It would be all he could do to make a presentable exit.

He stared at the mess in the toilet and contemplated scooping the mass of red-tinged, semi-digested hors d'oeuvres out of the bowl and pocketing it for use in a future project. Instead he fumbled his phone from his pocket and took several photos.

*Waste not, want not. I could be the Jackson Pollack of vomit.*

He laughed out loud, then slid the phone into his pocket and flushed the toilet. "Sic Transit Gloria Mundi," he declared as the mess spiraled down the bowl.

He cleaned himself up, shoving his face into a washbasin of cold water for as long as he could bear it. Then he mopped the water from his skin with some paper towels and took a hard look at himself in the mirror.

*Not looking good; seriously disheveled, in fact. I have to get out of here quickly, but I need to say goodbye to Zelley. Can't afford to upset mein host.*

He left the bathroom, swaying dangerously to one side of the hallway, adjusting his gait as he did so to make it look as if he'd meant to do it, then swaying over to the other side. The net effect was that of a sailor crossing a deck in a storm.

He approached the gallery entrance. *Thank God.* Zelley was talking to an attractive brunette at the doorway, so he wouldn't have to navigate the crowd.

*Just walk up, say thanks very much, exchange a few bon mots, and head for the exit.*

Zelley looked over at him as he approached and shot a beatific smile in his direction.

Xander didn't know how long he could hold it together, and it felt as though the downward trajectory that he was on was steepening, so he launched right in.

"Ah, great event," he spouted, "thankssomuch. Feeling a bit peaky and must dash."

"Really?" Zelley eyed him with arched brows. "Shame. Hope you feel better in the morning."

"Mmm. Yes. Well, best be off." He looked earnestly at Zelley. "Be off then." He gestured vaguely towards the exit. "Must go. Thanks for everything. I'm jus' going. Call you tomorrow."

He half-nodded to Zelley and the brunette, tipped his head back as he made what he thought was a controlled turn, and set off down the hall. Overcompensating for a list to the left, he almost walked into the doorpost. He stepped extravagantly to one side, then wandered erratically to the exit.

Zelley's last sight of him was the mane of his hair through the glass exit doors dropping quickly out of sight as he missed one of the outdoor steps. The brunette turned to him with a big smile. "Quite an exhibition."

"Isn't he marvelous?" Zelley finished his champagne and put down the glass. He held out his arm for her to take. "Come, Sam, there's no more entertainment to be had here. Trotsky has left the building. Let us see what other marvels are on offer in this city of ours that never sleeps."

# 3
# What Shadow Walks Below?

Every city has a time of rest when it draws breath and restores itself for the coming day. London is no different. The streets are never completely quiet, but they slip into a dream state in which only ghosts and shadows move among the ancient empty thoroughfares.

Wrecked John curved his way across the road, the double helix of the Coronation Tower spiraling up into the sky behind him. The streets were lit, albeit dimly, but he navigated as much by feel and instinct as by sight. He'd long ago given up trusting what his eyes delivered to his brain. For this journey, in any case, he didn't have to rely on anything other than instinct. When the random summons came all he had to do was let his feelings lead him.

He walked past the Crick & Watson, an old pub that had been one of his regular haunts back when it was the Red Lion. It had become trendy after it had been tarted up in glass and chrome and renamed, and he didn't bother with it any more. He glanced in at the darkened windows and was unsurprised to see a drawn ghoulish face staring back out at him.

After a few moments, he realized the face was his own, and he continued on for a few more streets until he came to a corner dominated by a converted warehouse building, now a collection of high-end flats. He turned and wandered down a narrow brick-walled alley that trended south but whose meandering course mapped the winding path taken by centuries of feet. As he drifted down the alley, the kinks and turns screened him from view front and back, and the close proximity of high buildings on each side made him difficult to see from above. The ever-circling police drones would have a hard time picking him out, even with their keen eyes.

His path was scattered with empty beer cans, old matted-down cardboard boxes, broken glass, and syringes, the detritus of the hopeless. Moss patterned the brickwork, which was punctuated here and there by rusting iron doors with concrete frames mottled with wet stains. The tarmac underfoot was cracked and uneven with occasional bare patches of earth. It was a path less travelled by the everyday Londoner.

Wrecked John didn't pay much attention to his surroundings. Since everything that reached his brain was in constant flux, they weren't much more to him than backdrop, and as long as they didn't change too suddenly, he was happy to let them float across his faded retinas. It gave him a vacant look, which observers often mistook for a lack of awareness of what was going on, a misapprehension that had kept him alive more than once.

He stopped at an iron door, no different from the others, and leaned against it. It swung inwards and Wrecked John disappeared into the greater darkness. The door eased shut behind him.

Lights came on, illuminating a stairway going down. Squinting a little as his pupils adjusted, he shuffled down the stairs. At the bottom he opened a door and stepped into a tiled room. In the middle was a marble mortuary table with a drainage hole in the centre and a large circular operating light hanging from an overhead mount. Off to one side was a ceramic sluice sink with curved taps and steel work surfaces. Along the walls in two directions, a half-pipe drain radiated from a metal grille set in one corner. There was a red-painted door in the opposite wall. John walked in, sat on the slab table, and looked up at the operating light above his head. Slowly he keeled over onto his back until he was lying full length on the table. He closed his eyes and waited.

He drifted off into a doze, until a click from the direction of the red door brought him back to his normal amorphous consciousness. He felt rather than heard someone approach and the subtle change in temperature and the shadow across his eyelids as the person stood next to him. Something was placed on his chest, the shadow left, and the door clicked again. Wrecked John lay there for a while, breathing slowly. Part of him wanted to just lie here forever in the silence of this hidden space near the beating heart of the city.

An impulse brought his hand to his chest and he took hold of the object. It was a small, round bag, and the contents shifted slightly beneath his touch as he closed his fingers. He sat up, opened his eyes and looked at the bag. It was white with a piece of tape stuck to the side. John peeled off the tape and held it up to his eyes. On it was written: KEVIN – THE EYE AND PYRAMID. He weighed the bag in his hand, estimating the contents, then put it into an inside jacket pocket.

Sliding his backside off the slab, he walked to the door through which he'd come and headed up the stairs. As he reached the top step the lights dimmed and went out. The breeze from the iron door swinging toward him brought a smell of rust and stale vomit. He stepped out into the alleyway and the door closed soundlessly behind him.

Wrecked John turned to his right and resumed walking in the direction he had been going before his detour, trailing his fingers along the rough wall for guidance. The brickwork and concrete frames and iron doors drifted by in the darkness as the narrow crooked path led him back to the orange glow of the London streets.

# 4

# I Bricked the Judy

When the phone rings between midnight and sunrise, it's usually nothing good. The call that Mike received that night was no exception.

He picked up the phone to hear a firm voice tell him: "Get your arse out of bed, you've got work to do."

"Er…what? What the fuck?"

"You're going to fix it, or I'm dead, which means you will be too."

"Fix what? Who is this?"

The reply came between breaths as though the caller was performing some heavy task.

"The Judy. It's a mess. I bricked the fucking Judy!"

"I don't know who the hell you are but I'm hanging up."

"Doesn't matter; I'm there."

"What? You're where?"

"How do I open it?"

"Eh? You don't. Fuck off!"

The call ended. A few seconds went by, and then there was a bang from the hallway. The voice called from down the hall: "Never mind. I'm in."

"Jesus!" Mike grabbed his taser, rolled out of bed, and threw himself against his bedroom door.

"Get out of my flat or I'm calling the law!"

"You try to call the law you'll be dead in five seconds. Get your arse out here now. I'm not fucking kidding."

The motion detector had kicked on the lights. Mike snatched a glance into the hallway.

He'd seen some odd things, but this was as weird as it got. There in his hall stood a tall lean man in a long grey coat, a large gun in his right hand and a quivering blonde under his left arm.

Mike gave a short, hysterical laugh.

"It's not fucking funny. Look at this shit." The tall man dropped the blonde. She lay on the ground, left hand quivering spasmodically, fingers tapping on the wooden floor. One side of her face was fixed in a wide grin, the other completely expressionless.

The man's eyes looked at him, hard. "Fix it."

Mike stepped into the hall and stared at the semi-naked figure on his carpet. "What's wrong with it?"

"It's broken. Fix it."

Mike looked at the gun in the man's hand, and then at his front door. There was a large hole where the biometric lock used to be and through it he could see a dark blue car that he didn't recognize. The row of houses opposite was darkened, silent. If anyone had heard anything, they didn't want any part of it. Nothing moved between the widely spaced streetlights.

*So much for the neighbours,* he thought. *Even the junkies took the night off.*

The gun moved.

"I'll have a look. Shut the door and bring it."

The man pushed the door shut with a foot, and put the gun inside the grey coat. He picked up the blonde and followed Mike as he led him through the hallway and into a back room.

Mike flipped switches. Lights came on. The room was furnished with a lot of machinery.

Large hand-built cabinets held solid-looking electronics and screens and on one side of the room was a long workbench. A drum kit squatted in a corner.

"Put it over there." Mike pointed at the workbench.

The man lugged the twitching body over to the bench and laid it down.

Mike tapped a couple of screens, and icons flashed and dissolved. Programs and subroutines started running somewhere inside the many boxes of electronics. He reached for a handle on a large oval silver box that stood by the work table.

The man's right hand moved inside his coat.

"What's that?"

Mike paused.

"The fridge."

The tall man nodded. Mike pulled on the handle, reached in, and removed a carton of orange juice. He drank from the carton, and then looked at the stranger, who took his hand out of his coat.

"Why me?"

"You came recommended. Scruff."

"Really?" Mike made a mental note to sort Scruff out later. "And what's your name?"

There was a pause.

"Nick."

"Right."

Mike put the juice back in the fridge and walked over to the figure twitching on the bench.

"What happened?"

No reply. Mike turned around.

"I need something to work with. What happened?"

"I hacked it."

"You? *You* hacked it?" Mike laughed. "Looks like that went well. All right, Nick The Hack, what have you tried so far?"

"What do you mean?"

"To fix it."

"Reboot."

"How did that go?"

"Not good. Started that spazzy twitching. Now it won't even shut down."

"Outstanding. What did you use to hack it?"

"A package."

Mike raised an eyebrow, held out his hand.

Nick reached into an inside pocket and brought out a coin-shaped piece of plastic a few inches in diameter.

Mike took it, and weighed it in his hand; it was heavy for its size. He looked at both sides. Other than an on/off strip and a single OLED, it was featureless.

"What was this supposed to do?"

"Access some useful information."

Mike put the package down on the bench.

"I assume it's not your synthetic. How long before it's missed?"

"Too late for that. It'll be enough if it's working before morning."

"I'd better get going then."

Mike sat in front of a screen and swiped some icons. Then he opened a metal drawer in the desk. A thick pane of glass covered the top of the open drawer; he lifted it and put the hack disk inside.

He felt Nick looking at him.

"It's a microwave," he said with a sigh.

Nick raised an eyebrow.

"I don't know what this piece of shit does. First sign of trouble, it's fried."

He swiped the on/off strip on the disk and shut the microwave door.

Through the glass they watched the OLED blink rapidly for a few seconds then settle into a steady glow.

Mike watched his screen. A frequency meter wavered up and down as status bars popped up. On one of them text and icons scrolled past, some in English, and some in Cyrillic characters.

He swiped a couple of icons and a progress line on one side of the screen displayed a scan in progress. It moved slowly left to right, a green bar absorbing a red one. Mike sat back in his chair.

"So far, so good."

He looked over at Nick.

"This is going to take a few minutes. Cuppa tea?"

Nick frowned, looked like he was about to say something, then nodded.

Mike went out into the kitchen. Nick watched him from the doorway as he filled the kettle and rinsed out a couple of mugs. Mike was glad to get away from the tapping of the synthetic's fingers. It disturbed him. It was like being around someone with brain damage.

At first it had sounded random, but there were repeating rhythms and sequences in it that caught Mike's ear. Here in the kitchen he could barely hear it, but he found himself following it as he gathered his thoughts. He hadn't had a minute to think about what was going on since Nick had burst through his door and making the tea gave him a chance to consider his options.

His main worry was about what would happen if he couldn't get the synthetic functional. This Nick character was clearly a serious piece of work. As the kettle boiled, Mike wondered about his odds if he tried to alert the police. They didn't look good. Even if they bothered to come out to his neighbourhood, it didn't seem like there was much they could do to prevent things turning nasty. He had no doubt that Nick would shoot him before the law could do anything to intervene.

He'd met some characters in his time, but this one was of a different stripe. There was a determination about the man that made him seem particularly dangerous. For now, Mike decided, he would go with the flow and continue to try to figure out how to fix the synthetic. He'd patched up bad cases before, and maybe this one would turn out to be not too much of a disaster once he got inside.

Steam gushed from the kettle and Mike poured the boiling water over the teabags and waited for the tea to brew. He looked over at Nick. The man hadn't moved, seemingly hadn't blinked. Mike decided that he needed to keep things moving so using a spoon he squashed each teabag against the side of its mug and then dropped it in the rubbish bin.

"Milk? Sugar?"

"Yes."

Mike shrugged and dumped some milk and sugar in the tea, gave it a quick stir. He carried the mugs back to the workroom and gave one to Nick.

"Here you go."

Mike sat down at the screen. The scan had finished. He peered at the results.

When he was done he tipped his head back and looked at the ceiling

"Bad?" Nick asked.

"Yes. Very."

Mike swung round in his chair.

"It's mostly Russian. Some sort of chainsaw hack."

"That doesn't sound good."

"No, it's not. It's designed to load fast and do whatever it's supposed to do before countermeasures can figure out what's happening. On top of that it has a high rate of focused data transmission; probably squirted a lot of code into the synthetic. It's a serious package. Designed to chop through firewalls and hit the memory banks. Which it looks like it did, hence the fucked up twitchy shit." Mike looked at the synthetic's fingers tapping away at his workbench.

"How do we fix it?"

"Well, wipe and reload is always easiest. Can we get to the backup?"

"No."

"OK, then we wipe and load a generic core set. I can preserve the memory and it'll end up functional, but you won't get any of the fancy stuff – personality quirks, special programming, all that."

"Not good enough. I need the whole thing back. What else?"

Mike shrugged. "Hack it. Dangerous. Unpredictable. May have unintended consequences."

"Like what?"

"You ever see someone do too many drugs, too often? Burned out?"

"I know a few people like that. What else can you try?"

"That's all I've got."

There was a long pause.

"Do it."

Mike looked at Nick.

"You know, if you take it back and let whoever owns it wipe and reload, it'll probably be right as rain. If I go in and things don't go well, which they probably won't, it may totally fuck it up."

"It doesn't look too chipper as it is. Do it."

"All right. It's your funeral."

Nick stared at him.

"Figure of speech."

Mike stood up and went over to the body on the workbench.

Nick took a swallow from his mug and winced.

"Crap tea."

# 5

## Close Personal Protection

Pete stepped out of the lift. The doors slid shut behind him, and he stood for a few moments in the silence of the reception area. He scanned the room, taking in the muted lighting behind the desk, the soft darkness in the corners where the surveillance cameras watched from within their glossy black globes.

He counted silently. One, two, three, four, five. The door to the boss's office opened. "Come in, Pete."

He crossed to the entrance and stepped inside, walking with a practiced casualness to a respectful distance from the boss's desk where he stopped, folded his hands in front of him and waited.

The boss sat looking at his screen. Pete, in a stance that passed for standing to attention, glanced about the room taking in the dark paneling, the paintings in their gilt frames, the blinds on the window, the desk, the phone, the gun. The boss was in no hurry. Twice he tapped the screen, each time resuming his motionless contemplation of whatever he was looking at. After he tapped it for a third time he stood up without looking at Pete, turned and walked across to the window. He stared out at the city.

"How long you been with us now, Pete?"

Pete coughed, then replied: "Few weeks, boss."

"How are you liking it?" the question was open enough but there was something else there, a dark shape circling in the shadows.

Pete picked at his cuffs. "Bit bored, to be honest, boss. Thought there was going to be more action."

"Where were you before you joined us?"

"Sorry boss, I thought Col had shown you my file, I…"

"I've seen your file. I want to hear it from you."

Pete looked at the broad back, the thick round head tilted a little to one side, the frame of the glasses just visible.

"Right. Special Forces, five years. Tours of Taiwan, Afghanistan, Korea. The usual. Honorable discharge. Six months on a beach in Brazil. Then courier work for high value shipments, mostly tech stuff – Middle East, China, Europe. Got bored with all the travel. Three months in London picking my nose, then I met Colin through a mate. And here I am"

The boss nodded, a barely discernible motion of his head.

"Why are you here?"

"I'm sorry?"

The boss turned slowly around, the orange city light gleaming on his glasses.

"I don't like to repeat myself, Peter." Pete felt the dark shape circle closer, like a wolf in the shadows just beyond the firelight.

"Same reason as everyone else. Yours is the best outfit in London. A man's got ambition, this is the place to be. At least, that's what I heard." He edged closer to the darkness and whatever was waiting there. "Haven't seen much evidence of it yet, though."

The boss took a step forward and leant into the light.

"Have you not, Peter? Have you not?"

He walked out from behind the desk, his slow steady steps carrying his bulk almost gracefully, like a boxer stepping up to weigh in before a fight. The boss stepped past Pete, nearly brushing his shoulder, until he stood behind him.

Pete didn't turn around, but he tipped his head slightly to one side to keep the boss in his peripheral vision. He turned his left hand over in his right at chest height as though he were examining his fingernails and kept it there, an inch, a split second away from reaching inside his jacket.

The boss's voice came from behind his right ear. "You married, Peter?"

"No."

"Girlfriend?"

"Nah"

"Boyfriend?"

"Unattached at the moment, actually."

"Unattached. A lovely word. That's a good thing in this business, Peter, a good thing. Attachments are a liability. You never know when they're going to blow up on you."

Pete felt the boss take a deep breath.

"If you like, I'll tell you a little story about that. There's this bloke I knew, had a live-in girlfriend. He'd been in your line of work for a long time. Getting a bit long in the tooth, truth be told. Anyway, he was looking at settling down, retiring from the business. Perhaps make it all legal with his other half. Too late for kids, but maybe he could get out of the game and have a different sort of a life. A normal life.

"Trouble was, his timing was off. His girl was moving on. Got involved with someone else. Worse, it was someone this bloke worked with; someone on the same firm. All a bit messy, know what I mean?

"Might have turned out all right, except he goes and proposes to the girl. Down on one knee, all that. Of course, then it goes all pear-shaped. She can't marry him, but she can't tell him why not. What can she do? She turns him down and kicks him out. Doesn't tell him what's going on, of course, but she tells him she can't live with him anymore. Off you go, mate.

"Well, you can imagine what's next. Bloke in our line of business. He starts to unravel a bit. And then, well Peter, then he loses it."

The boss walked back into Pete's field of vision. Pete lowered his hands to his waist. The boss continued his slow, measured pace back to the window and the view of London beyond and stood there in silence, his bulk black against the orange glow.

Pete felt the silence pull the question out of him.

"What did he do?"

The boss's shoulders shifted a fraction, his head lowered a little.

"I don't know yet."

He turned around, walked up to his desk, and looked Pete in the eye.

"I'd like you to do a little job for me, Peter, one you're very suited for as the new kid on the block. There's someone I'd like you to check out."

"Sure, boss. Who?"

Without breaking his gaze, the boss reached over and turned his screen so that it was facing Pete.

The face looking out from the screen was gaunt, unsmiling, with cropped steel grey hair. It was Nick.

# *6*
# Mind the Gap

In the darkness beneath the curve of a railway bridge in Whitechapel, Larry stepped up to a battered steel door and punched a code into the metal keys of the old-fashioned security lock. There was a click, and he pulled the door open and stepped inside, closing it behind him.

He switched on his torch and followed the beam down the musty corridor. At the end there was a spiral staircase and he descended quickly, his footsteps tapping out his progress.

At the bottom he came out onto a long narrow railway platform.

Larry flashed his torch on the semi-circle of discoloured white panels that made up the curved walls and ceiling of the tunnel, the yellow ribs of the supporting frame showing at ground level through gaps in the paneling. Beyond was the trench where the narrow gauge railway tracks disappeared into the darkness.

Down the platform he went, past a row of dented grey lockers to the door of a small office. He shone his light into the narrow space, illuminating the glass door at the far side, the compound plastic desk, the ancient computer equipment, the chair and the man sitting in it.

"Evening, Larry."

"Inspector 'Odges."

"Fancy a drink?"

"Don't mind if I do."

Inspector Hodges pulled open a desk drawer and took out a bottle of Scotch and two glasses. Larry walked over and put the torch on the desk, the light shining sideways onto the opposite wall. He leant on the table with one hand while Hodges poured the drinks, and then picked up a glass with the other hand.

"The King," said Hodges, raising his glass.

Larry nodded. "The King."

They each took a large swallow of the Scotch. Hodges looked at the glass, turned it in his hand, eyeing the liquor in the reflected light of the torch.

"Been a little while, Larry. What's on your mind?"

"It's like this, 'Odge. Something 'appened tonight to the boss's Judy. About three hours ago it disappeared, right in the offices over at the Corkscrew. Went off the radar like someone flipped a switch. Nothing on the tracker, no sign of it in the building. Boss went mental. Called us all in and read us the Riot Act. I've never seen 'im so pissed off, and I've been around 'im long as anyone."

Larry drank again. Hodges waited, eyeing him with interest.

"I mean, I get it. It's 'is latest toy, and they're not cheap, but this was something else. You'd think the world was coming to an end the way 'e unloaded. Anyway, 'e sends us all out to find it, and tells us if we don't get it back by morning we're all in the shit."

Hodges gave a wry smile and poured out more Scotch.

"Wish I'd been a fly on the wall. You lot stood in a line getting told off by Harry like a schoolmaster with a bunch of useless schoolkids." He laughed.

"Thanks a lot, 'Odge."

"Well, you have to see the funny side."

Larry grimaced, drank again.

"So what do you reckon set him off so badly, then?"

"Don't know. Some of the lads reckon he thinks we did it out of jealousy."

"You what?"

"Well not that, exactly. Anger, being pissed off, you know?"

"Not following, Larry."

"The Judy. It's a walking Swiss Army Knife. Does everything. It's like a computer that can fight. All sorts of extras."

"Bit more help?"

"It's a replacement, innit? Who needs a mob when you've got one of those? 'Ow long before the boss decides 'e doesn't need us lot on the payroll?"

Hodges laughed out loud. "London's hardest put on the dole by a robot." He laughed again.

"Yeah, very funny."

"Looks that way from where I'm sitting" Hodges took a quick swallow from his glass. "So what do you want, Larry?"

"Wondering if you picked anything up. Anything on the scanners, the drones?"

"What're you offering?"

"Jewelry robbery in Deptford last Monday."

Hodges pursed his lips, nodded. He finished his drink. "We picked up a data squirt from the tower about 9:30. Heavily encrypted, but we identified it as Russian. And it was incomplete. Broke off after a few seconds."

"Not much to go on," said Larry, "Could 'ave been anything."

"The transmission was bounced off a drone circling the tower. It looked like a normal legal commercial drone registered to a company called East End Exports. The lads at West Drayton did a bit of digging and it turns out that East End Exports is just a front, a shell owned by a chain of offshore companies. We followed the chain down some very devious paths until it circled around and led us back to London. All the way back, as it turns out, to London China PLC."

"Wei."

"None other."

Larry scratched the back of his neck.

"I don't get it. Why the Russian connection?"

"I couldn't care less. That's your problem." Hodges put the bottle and the glasses back in the drawer. "The Deptford heist?"

"Kasuals. Billy the Fish. 'Ave a butcher's in the storage room at the back of his chippy in New Cross."

Hodges stood up, pushed back his chair.

"Thanks, Larry. I'll be off then. See you later."

"Can we make it somewhere else next time? I'm not particul'y fond of the tunnels. That pack of dogs is down 'ere somewhere. You know, the ones that escaped from the labs. Glow in the dark, they say."

"Yeah. They also say that one of them has three heads," Hodges laughed. "I'll see what I can do." He turned and left through the door opposite.

Larry picked up his torch and headed out onto the platform. There was a thin cold draught coming down the tunnel. He walked back towards the spiral staircase. As he reached the bottom he thought he heard a noise off in the darkness beyond the circle of light from his torch. Without looking back he went up the steps three at a time and ran down the corridor to the metal door.

He popped it open, dashed through, and slammed it shut behind him. He punched in the lock code and it engaged with a firm click. Larry stepped away from the door and stood panting beneath the bridge. He looked around. He was alone in the night.

"You silly bugger," he laughed, and he switched off his torch and walked over to his car.

# 7
# She's Not All There

Mike rolled the synthetic over on its front and restrained it with wrist and ankle clamps attached to the bench. After that he hard-cabled it through its lumbar port. The fingers of the left hand continued their incessant twitching, the knuckles making only a light tapping sound on the bench.

He prepped a machine next to it, loading some triage software. Then he connected the cable from the synthetic to the machine.

The triage app ran queries against the Judy's core operating system and returned status readings. A fully functional synthetic would light up the display. The one on the bench was mostly dark. Technically the thing was almost brain dead.

*Things are not looking good at all,* Mike thought.

The synthetic had been seriously compromised, and bringing it back was not going to be easy. He waited for the current state copy to complete and ran a full diagnostic against it.

It didn't take long to reveal the extent of the problem. As he'd thought, the hack had disabled the main firewall and antivirus countermeasures and then attempted to access information in the synthetic's memory banks.

At some point in the hack attempt, though, a further defensive program had fired and shut down most of the synthetic's core functions. Hence the catatonic state it was in when Nick had dragged it across his threshold: it had initiated a defensive crash to try to prevent the data hack. The thing had shut itself down rather than give up the information. Mike wondered what information was worth enough to wreck an expensive synthetic.

There was something else in the readout.

He turned to look at Nick.

"What haven't you told me?"

"What do you mean?"

"There's no governor."

"And?"

"Apart from that being impossible?"

"What are you talking about?"

"The behavioural inhibitor; the master program override, the governor."

Nick looked surprised. "It's missing?"

"Actually, it doesn't look like there ever was one."

"What does that mean?"

Mike pushed back from the bench, stared at the body.

"It means someone was ready to break a lot of laws. Look, it's a long way past my bedtime so I'll summarize. You put a hack into this synthetic that loaded malware that tried to do some major rewriting of the personality programming. That's pretty bad because to do that it had to get past some really fucking hardcore firewalls, so we know we're dealing with some heavy shit. What makes it a bit of a clusterfuck, however, is that there's no governor on the synthetic. No governor, no behavioural restraint, of course, but also no last line of defence for the cortex. Even if I can fix the changes the malware made, it won't make much difference unless I figure out what damage there is to the cortex."

"So do that."

"A full analysis and rebuild will take me 6 hours."

"You've got half that."

"That's impossible."

"There you go again. Are you saying you can't fix it?"

"I'm saying I'd be mad to try."

"And I'm saying you'd be mad not to." Nick let his coat fall to one side so Mike could see the gun in the holster. "We'll both be dead if you can't." Nick smiled. "You first, of course. Oh, one more thing. While you're about it, I need you to find and extract a file from the Judy's secure memory for me." He handed Mike a piece of paper with a long string of digits written on it.

Mike took it, glanced at it, then back at Nick.

"Anything else?"

"No, that'll do it."

Mike and Nick looked at each other for a long moment.

"Right then. Give me a minute, will you?"

Mike scooted back in to the bench and started swiping icons on the screen.

The phone in Nick's pocket rang. He left the room and took the call in Mike's hallway.

"Yes?"

"How's it going, Nick?" The voice was like sandpaper against his ear.

"Not much to report yet, Harry."

"Where are you?"

"South of the river. I'm following up a few leads on Wei's recent activity"

"Anything promising?"

"Nothing worth mentioning just now"

"Right, right." There was a long silence. "Find something for me, Nick. Find it soon. Whoever the fuck did this is going to pay."

"Yeah Harry. I'm on it."

Harry hung up the call.

Nick stared into space for a moment, and then walked back into Mike's work room.

"Get a move on."

# 8
# A Light in the Dark

In the satin black comfort of his meditation room on the highest private floor of the Shard, Mr. Wei sat in darkness looking out at the city. Down in the streets below, the night life had bloomed and died as it always did, surviving only as a few small fading blossoms in the hidden cracks and corners of the metropolis. Wei had sat, as he did most nights, watching with a proprietary interest.

The obsidian river separated him from the tall slender double helix of the Coronation Tower rising like a corkscrew from the site of the old Tobacco Dock, and beyond it the shorter towers built in prior decades. His gaze took in the broad view of the city that his room afforded, but his focus was on the suites at the top of the tower, and the narrow slatted blinds of one particular window through which the lights had shone all night.

On any other night but this one, that window would have been dark. The only illumination would have been the aircraft warning lights atop the tower's transmission antennae. Tonight, Wei knew, his old adversary had a lot on his mind, and so the oil had burned long past midnight. As he thought about the scenes that might have played out behind those blinds, he afforded himself a thin smile.

Motionless figures stood on either side and directly behind Wei, tall and slender, nothing but a trio of smooth silhouettes against the lights of the city. The rest of the room was empty but for his chair, a screen set into the wall, and a leather-paneled door.

For a long time nothing in the room had moved but now the door opened and a man entered. From his perspective the room looked like an art installation; a moment captured in time, motionless forever as the city lights came and went beyond the picture window in a semi-random pattern of white, yellow, red, and green. He closed the door behind him and waited, becoming part of the tableau.

Navigation lights on the river marked the progress of a boat as it crawled from the gothic turrets of Tower Bridge, past the dark hulk of HMS Belfast, until it reached London Bridge. The lights blinked out as the boat passed beneath the low arches spanning the Thames.

Wei spoke. "Where is Nick Turner?"

The man at the door bowed as he answered. "We don't know."

"Find him." Wei turned his head to look at one of the motionless figures standing in the room.

"Find him, and have him killed." He returned his gaze to the view through the floor-to-ceiling windows, to the light burning near the top of the tower. "What of our alternative course of action?"

"The delivery was successful. We await the connection later today, but I have concerns about the plan."

Wei tilted his head slightly. "Speak."

"The dealer is a burnout. A derelict. Why use him as a vector?"

Outside in the night there was the faintest glimmer of dawn, a fractional lightening in the cold North Sea beyond the Thames estuary.

"There is often more to the view than meets the eye. There is that which is visible to the world and that which moves beneath the surface. He is a creature of the underworld. He comes, he goes, and he is not remembered. Sometimes the certainty of completing a journey is not the most important thing. Sometimes it is more important that no trace of the journey ever exists. This is also why Turner must be eliminated."

The man at the door took a deep breath.

Wei anticipated him: "Yes?"

"I wonder why we do not simply use the agent you planted in the tower? It is both more reliable and unlikely to leave a trace."

"The cuckoo chick must conduct itself as do the other chicks until the host bird is away."

"I don't understand."

Wei sighed. "The time is not yet right. Do you think that I put my options in place with the intention of using them all?" Anger crept into his voice. "You see one corner of the board and think that you know the game. I have placed many pieces on the board knowing that not all will be useful. Those that are not useful may have to be sacrificed. See that you are useful. Kill Nick Turner."

The man bowed. He turned, opened the door, and left the room.

Before he could close the door behind him Wei spoke one last time, as if to the air.

"Go with him."

The three tall, slender figures that had been standing around Wei moved as one, gliding through the darkness of the room with sure-footed precision. They slid through the doorway and it closed behind them.

He turned his attention once again to the city. Dawn was paling the sky over London. The warning beacons atop the Coronation Tower blinked less brightly. In the room with the slatted blinds, the light had at last gone out.

# 9
# Wake Up Call

Xander awoke on top of his bed still fully dressed. The inside of his mouth was coated with tannin and bile and it tasted foul and acidic. He opened his eyes to a room that was not quite dark. Inside his chest, his heart was thumping hard and fast, but his head didn't hurt as badly as he'd expected. He rolled out of bed, crawled over to the window, and pulled himself up to look out at the city. London had begun its diurnal metamorphosis.

Off to his left the darkness was thinning. He could see the pinpoint lights of the first long distance flights from Malaysia and India on their glide path into Heathrow. The planes descended out of the approaching dawn in their long straight lines.

*Here you come,* he thought. *Canned blood and bone.*

He visualized the thousands of numbed bodies as they floated down through the sky, at once in motion and in suspended animation, waiting for the seatbelt lights to set them free.

He thought of the planes as metal dashes, like a Morse code message in the sky spelling out zero over and over again, while four miles above them circled the dots of smaller unmanned machines filled with glass and wire and meaning.

A bare mile above the city, the passenger planes would drop down over Hammersmith and Richmond to skim the rooftops of Hounslow and finally touch the runway in a puff of white smoke.

Xander looked back down at the city. The warning lights atop the Coronation Tower blinked reassuringly in the distance, a minor constellation hovering above the dirty yellow haze. He stood and looked at them for a while, his head empty until the pressure in his bowels reminded him that there was work to be done.

He was close to finishing his most ambitious project. Eighteen years in the making, it had been a strain to keep quiet about it for this long: a strain on his relationships, a strain on his own tendency to boast, a strain on his personal habits.

Now that the day was nearly here, he didn't want it to be over. The persistence of his vision over all that time had bred in him some habits that he could hardly bear to think of letting go. In many ways, the discipline he had exercised to create this work had become a part of him, and the thought of giving that up made him nervous.

Still, here he was. This might be the day when he added the final touches.

He reached up to scratch his scalp through the thick mass of his hair then stopped himself. He took off his clothes and threw them on the bed, then walked over to the bathroom and turned on the shower. While he was waiting for the hot water, he urinated in the toilet and then set a small timer to five minutes. He stepped into the shower and scrubbed himself with a nylon brush. The water drained slowly and pooled around his feet, gradually covering him up to his ankles.

As soon as the timer sounded, he turned off the water. He dried himself as he stood in the shower, and rubbed his hair vigorously with a white towel. Then he stepped out of the shower and put the towel into a white plastic bin.

Leaning back into the shower, he again turned the water on, lifting the showerhead off its holder and stretching it out on its long metal hose. He rinsed the sides of the shower stall, then turned the water off and waited for it to drain away.

Reaching down, he pulled a fine mesh filter from the drain hole. The hair he had scrubbed from his body was matted on top of the mesh. He put the filter next to the sink.

Next he shaved his face thoroughly with an electric razor. Then, still naked, he left the bathroom with the razor in one hand and the hairs from the shower in the other. He walked through the bedroom to a large studio space. The walls were covered with canvasses; some were finished works, others just scars of color on large white squares. Sculptures posed here and there, and over in one corner was a life-size glass statue of a man filled with debris.

Xander walked over to it and stood looking at his hollow doppelganger. It was a perfect likeness, cast from a body mould, the face looking slightly upward and the arms spread wide in a crucifixion pose. With the exception of a thin sliver at the top of the skull, the statue was filled with white and grey powder, run through with many clumps of black hair, and peppered with other unidentifiable organic objects, some brown, some yellow.

He stood up on a small pedestal in front of the statue, and put the matted hairs from the shower on top of the open head. Then he removed the blade from the electric razor, held it over the statue and tapped the side. A fine dust of beard hairs drifted down to join the pile in the statue. He gave the top a close look and stepped down off the pedestal.

During his literal period about twelve years ago, he had tried to use only cells from the part of his body that corresponded to the same place in the statue. Unfortunately that had proved too difficult. Cell death does not distribute itself evenly across the body, and some cells had been more readily available than others. Hair, for instance, had been available in greater volumes than dead skin. Nails too. Whenever he'd had a nosebleed or a cut finger, the blood had gone in there, as had his appendix and several teeth, but for the most part the statue was filled with hair scrapings, peeled skin, and the dead cells that his mesh filter had captured.

He looked at the top of the thing and sighed. Not enough. Close, but not enough.

He went back to the bathroom and put the razor on its stand. Still naked, he went out through the bedroom and down three flights of stairs to the ground floor hallway and the adjacent kitchen. Motion sensors turned on the lights. The kitchen was rich with the smell of coffee. He poured himself a cup from the still-spluttering carafe and went over to the patio doors where he sat down in a large leather armchair and watched the dawn reveal the shape of his garden, the first birds stirring on the lawn.

His phone rang. A low female voice identified the caller: "Nick Turner."

Xander picked up the handset from the side table.

The voice in his ear was fierce. "Where the fuck have you been?"

Xander winced and held the phone a little further from his ear. "Ah. Hello Nick. I am guessing from your tone that all is not well."

"Dead right it's not well. Did you listen to my message?"

"I have just woken up from a rather long night. What's wrong?"

"That piece of shit software your mates supplied didn't work. Not the way it was supposed to. It crashed the Judy. I've spent half the night sorting out the fucking mess."

"I'm very sorry to hear that. Were you able to get the money?"

"No, I do not have the money. You're not listening. The hack didn't work. There is no money. No one gets paid."

Xander put down his coffee and scratched his groin.

"They will not be happy. The software was very expensive. Who is going to pay for it?"

"That's a bloody good question. I don't have the money, and I don't have a plan B. You'll have to call your mates and tell them the deal's off."

Xander put his free hand to his head. "You should tell them."

"Why me? They're your mates."

"This is big trouble, Nick. We will need to watch out. They are dangerous people."

"Yeah, well right now, I'm dangerous people. They gave me a piece of gear that didn't work, I've got one of the nastiest Triads in London breathing down my neck, and any minute now Harry is going to start smelling a rat. I'm in some fairly deep shit here, Xander, and I'm not in the mood to deal with a bunch of incompetent morons who think they're owed something. Tell them what happened and tell them to stay out of my way."

"Nick, you don't understand, they will punish me, they'll come after you…"

Nick cut off the call.

Xander put the phone down on the table. He looked out the window for a few moments, his thoughts racing. A bird on the patio was pecking viciously at a worm.

"Shit!"

# *10*
# Beat Generation

Mike stepped away from his workbench. Nick looked up, raised an eyebrow.

"You're finished?"

"As finished as I can be."

"And now?"

"We reboot and see what we get."

Nick nodded.

Mike tapped some keys. The synthetic jerked on the workbench. There was a barely audible humming noise, then silence.

The fingers of the synthetic's left hand beat one last repeat of the sequence that it had been tapping out when it first was brought into Mike's apartment, then stopped. The eyes opened and it looked from side to side. The lopsided grin was gone from its face. It tried to push itself up and was halted by the wrist and ankle restraints.

It looked at Nick.

"Why am I here?"

"You had a malfunction, Cassie. I brought you here to have it fixed."

"Who is this man?"

"A specialist."

It looked at Mike.

"There is a seven hour, twenty nine minute and fourteen second gap in my memory."

"I had to do some editing." Mike said.

The synthetic lay still for a moment.

"There is no audit trail."

"No."

"How did you do that?"

"I'm a genius."

"It is not possible."

"It's not easy."

The synthetic switched to Nick.

"Where's Harry?"

"Waiting for you back at the tower."

"What really happened?"

An odd expression flickered across Nick's face but his voice came out steady.

"Told you. Software problem. Nothing to worry about. All better now."

The synthetic's hands lifted suddenly, testing the restraints. Nick looked at Mike with widening eyes and Mike tapped an icon on his screen. The synthetic slumped back down, eyes looking straight ahead.

"Nice work, mate. Better wipe the last couple of minutes, eh? You don't want it remembering you and trying to find its way back here."

"What are you going to do with it?"

"None of your business. I'll need to be able to start it up from a safe distance, though."

"All right. I'll give you a remote. As long as you have line of sight you can be streets away."

Mike busied himself with the final clean up on the synthetic then detached the cable from its lumbar port. After he'd undone the wrist and ankle restraints he pulled a small storage drive from the stack of equipment on his workbench and handed it to Nick.

"Your file."

Nick took it and put it inside his coat pocket. When he brought his hand out again it held a blank cash card. "Here you go. Sorry about the dramatic entrance last night; I'm under a bit of pressure. This should cover the front door damage with a bit left over. Access number's taped to the back." He put it down on the bench.

Mike looked at it but didn't pick it up.

Nick heaved the synthetic off the bench and put it under one arm as he had the night before. He walked to the front door, Mike trailing him.

At the door Nick stopped and looked Mike in the eye.

"This ever gets out, you know what'll happen."

"I'm not stupid."

Nick nodded, turned and walked off into the street and the gathering dawn, the arms and legs of his burden flopping with each stride.

Mike shut what was left of his front door and walked back down to his workroom. He tidied up a bit, then sat down at the bench and swiped an icon. The rhythmic tapping of the synthetic's fingers stuttered from the speakers. He listened to it repeat over and over for a few minutes, his right knee bobbing up and down as he followed the staccato beat.

"Cool."

# *11*
## Different Worlds

Samantha awoke with aches and shivers, and only vague memories of the night before. She rolled over on her side and squinted at the figure standing over by the window. The steady rumble of London came through the glass. It was late morning, and the traffic was thick.

"Zelley?"

The figure turned and walked over to the bed.

"Hello, my dear. How are you feeling this morning?"

"Horrible." She buried her face in the pillow and said in a muffled voice "What did we do last night?"

"The usual: everything."

She looked up and watched Zelley's lean form walk with halting steps out of the bedroom and into the living room. She gave a quick laugh.

"You look like you feel as rough as I do. Must have been a hell of a party"

She sat up on the bed and rubbed at her eyes. Slowly she got up and walked across to a dressing table where she took a quick look at her face in the mirror and winced. There were dark patches under her eyes and her hair was a rat's nest.

"Oh God," she said.

She turned and walked into the living room. Zelley was over at the kitchenette on the far side with his back to her, making tea.

Samantha slumped onto the sofa. "How much did I take?"

"Too much. As usual." Zelley's voice was clipped.

"Don't be a bastard this morning. I can't take it. I'll be all right in a bit and you can be as mean as you like to me then."

A spoon clattered on a saucer as Zelley picked it up and stirred the tea.

"Why do you think I want to be nasty to you?"

"Oh, you know. You probably don't mean it, but you're just such a bastard sometimes. You're always getting on at me about the drugs and shit when I'm having a good time."

He brought a cup of tea over and put it on the table. He looked down at her.

She met his gaze and wrapped her arms around herself.

"Your idea of a good time is starting to get old, Sam. I don't think you can stop. I don't think you know how to stop. You need to get some help and slow down a bit."

He stood motionless as she looked at him with wide eyes.

"See? You've started on me. I'm sitting here feeling like crap and you've started on me. It's not like you're a bloody saint, is it? You're just as bad. You go out and overdo it just as much as me."

"No I don't, Sam."

"Yes you bloody do! What do you think the difference is then?"

"I can stop."

"Oh, like you think I can't? Like you're all right but I'm some sort of addict? You self-righteous bastard. I can give up. I can stop taking it any time I like."

"I'd like to see you do that"

"Piss off."

"I was quite sincere. I would like to see you give it up."

"Well I can if I want. I'll do it any time I want, when I want to."

She reached for the teacup, knocking it and slopping tea into the saucer. Withdrawing her hand, she looked at him, her gaze firm.

"Sam, I think we should stop seeing each other for a while."

She looked at him in horror.

"You fucking bastard. You don't believe me. I can do it, I can do it."

"That's no longer the point."

"What's that supposed to mean?"

"We've been over this again and again for months but nothing changes. I'm sorry, Sam, I'm going."

"Just like that? Just like that you're going to walk out?" She looked at him, hard. His face was expressionless, carved in stone. "Well fine, get out then! Go on, just get out!"

He turned and picked up his coat. As he did so, his arm gave a strange jerk.

She stared at him as he put on his coat and looked back at her. His arm jerked again and he took a half a step backwards.

A chill ran through her body. She stood up and walked over to him, not once taking her eyes off him.

Right in front of his still, lean frame she stopped and stared at him, then screamed: "Oh my God! Oh my God! This isn't even the real you! Get out get out get out!" She pummeled him in the chest with her fists, then backed away, shaking her head from side to side. "It's not you. It's not the real you."

In his seat at a monitor on the other side of town, Zelley clicked off the microphone and sat back in his chair.

# *12*
# English Psycho

"Pete. Pass the HP."

Pete handed the bottle over to Colin and watched as he upended it over his fried breakfast. Colin started forking food into his mouth, and Pete watched him for a minute then turned and stared through the condensation-glazed window of the cafe.

He was feeling the edge that comes from staying up all night and downing countless cups of tea. 'Wired-and-tired,' he'd heard Chopper call it, and that was a man who knew a bit about being wired. The clatter of dishes and murmur of conversation from the other tables in the café was a familiar backdrop, and it helped to take the edge off a bit.

*At least there's one place in London without music going all the fucking time,* he thought.

As Colin chewed his way through his breakfast, Pete entertained himself by watching a dog digging about in a gutter across the way.

Finally Colin finished off his last mouthful of fried bread and looked up at Pete. He put down his knife and fork and sat back in his chair, looking with satisfaction at the white palette of his plate, smeared with swirls of brown and yellow and red. He scrubbed a back molar with his left index finger, and then peered at the finger for a few moments before scraping the nail against his lower incisors.

Pete took a last swill from his mug of tea, put it down and turned back from the window. Colin raised his eyebrows.

"Look, I know Nick thinks I'm a prat, and I haven't been with the outfit long, but I'm not a fucking moron. Why does he treat me like shit?"

Colin smiled a patient grin, leaned back in his chair.

"Look at yourself. You're a flash git, Pete. Flash suit, jazzy tie, handmade shoes." Colin made a show of looking him over. "Expensive wristwatch. Only posers wear watches these days. You invite people to give you shit. Like I said, you're too flash."

"The boss is flash. The boss wears expensive gear. Look at that office. Cost a bloody fortune."

Colin laughed.

"Yeh, but the boss is the boss. He can walk around in silk pyjamas if he wants 'cause he's top dog. You? You're a nobody."

"Thanks a lot."

"Just pointing out the obvious."

Pete fell silent for a bit then changed the topic.

"So what's this business with the Judy? The boss is pissed off, I get it. I had to listen to him shouting down the phone most of the night. What I don't get is the story with this Martin bloke. What's he all about that gets everyone bricking it?"

Colin gave him a long look before he spoke.

"All right, I'll tell you. I first heard about him not long after he left the Paras. He and Nick served together and were mates for a long time. He was a bit of a legend in Colchester, was Martin. Got into a lot of bother."

"So he's a bit of a nutter?"

"Nah, he's not a nutter. More of a psycho." He took a sip of his tea.

"Sorry to sound a bit dim, but what's the diff?"

Colin tipped his head back and contemplated the ceiling.

"Nutters tend to be thickos who don't know what they're doing when they get into a fight. When Martin gets violent he knows exactly what he's doing." He looked back at Pete. "Problem is you never know what's going to set him off."

"Such as?"

"So – this was years ago – he's in London with Nick after they left the Paras and he runs into this Irish fella who decides he's going to have a bit of a laugh. The Irishman gets introduced to Nick and Martin at a party and Martin, nice as you like, asks him what he's doing in England.

"'Oh,' says the Irishman, 'I'm just a poor working man here to see what the *craic* is, maybe get in a bit of labouring on a building site or suchlike.'

"'Really?' asks Martin, 'I've got some mates in the trade. Give me your number and I'll ask if there's anything they can do for you.'

"So the next thing, the Irish fella and his mates crack up and start grinning all smug-like, so Martin looks at them and says, 'What's up?'

"'Ah,' says the Irishman all smiles, 'I'm just messin wit' yer.'

"'I don't get it,' says Martin, and one of the Irishman's friends leans in and says, 'Yer man there's a PhD. He's just having a bit o' fun.'

"'Really?' says Martin, quietly. 'That's fucking hilarious.' And then quick as you like, he drops his pint and he's got the Irishman by the hair and he waves a gun in front of the man's face just long enough for him to see it before he sticks the barrel under his chin.

"'I've got problems y'see,' he yells in the Irishman's ear. 'I've got that PTSD and some things just set me off, and I think I'm gonna fucking top someone!'

"Everyone's backing away really fast, thinking Martin's lost it and all anyone can do is stare at the gun pointing at the bottom of the Irishman's chin.

"'Jesus Christ!' someone yells, 'The psycho's gonna fucking kill him!'

"And just then, perfect timing, just perfect, Nick steps forward and says, calm as you like, 'Nah, your man there's really an ex-Para and he's just messing wit' you.'

"Quick as a flash, the gun's gone, Martin's smiling happily and reaching for another pint like nothing happened, and the Irishman's stumbling for the door with his mates in tow screaming bloody murder."

Pete sipped at his tea. "Would he really have topped the bloke?"

"I don't know. He might've. But that's the point. One more smartass comment from the Irishman and he might have been dead. You just never know with Martin."

Pete looked out into the alley.

"So what's the story? We're supposed to work our asses off because the boss threatens to call in some hard man? You think I give a shit about Martin?"

"What I think doesn't matter. You're missing the point, my son. The boss isn't telling us he'll bring in Martin to make us work harder. There's something else going on. There's something about losing the Judy that's new."

"What's that?"

"Something I've never seen before." Colin ran his hand over his mouth. "The boss is worried."

Colin's phone rang. He picked it up.

"Yep?" He listened for a minute. "Right. On our way."

He stood up and took his coat off the back of the chair. "Let's go. The Judy turned up in the West End this morning. The boss wants us all at the office pronto."

Pete looked skyward. "Well that was a lot of fuss about nothing."

"Maybe – I don't think this is over yet."

"Why not?"

"There's something wrong with the Judy."

"What?"

"Don't know, but it doesn't sound good. C'mon, let's go."

# *13*

## Deny Deny Deny

They met in the large lounge adjacent to Harry's office. The room was decked out as an expensive imitation of a nineteenth century men's club with leather upholstered sofas, mahogany furniture, wood paneling, oil paintings. There was a bar at one end, a snooker table at the other.

The late afternoon sun was filtered to a tolerable level by the auto-tint glass in the great viewing window. It afforded a spectacular view of the wide park filled with trees, statues and fountains that sat atop the Coronation Tower and which sloped down to end at an infinity pool that stretched across the width of the tower. Beyond that, the spires, columns, and turrets of London, ancient and modern, filled the lower half of the visible horizon. No one in the lounge was admiring the view.

Harry sat back in an overstuffed armchair, looking around at the gang scattered around the room. Cassie was over by the bar, standing perfectly still while everyone else glanced nervously around the room or fidgeted with their ties.

Harry coughed. All eyes turned to him.

"Nick. Bring the lads up to speed."

"As you already know, the Ju-," he paused "Cassie dropped off the network not long after midnight last night with no trace until this morning when Dave's lads picked up a signal from the West End. They found her sitting in a café on Old Compton Street, brought her back here, ran a load of tests, and found nothing wrong with her."

Cassie turned her head to look at Nick.

"Except for one thing. Dave?"

"Except for a seven hour gap in her memory. Between 12:47am and 8:16am, when she came back online. We've been over and over it, and there's nothing. No data, no audit trail, nothing. It's like she was completely shut down, and I mean completely. Even when they're not doing anything, synthetics have background programs running; there are log files and processing activities. Here, though, we've got a complete blank between those two times, which is a bit of a problem."

Pete leaned in to the conversation, "Why is that a problem?"

Nick gave him a look.

"It's a bit obvious isn't it?" said Dave.

Nick chipped in, "Not for Pete."

Dave suppressed a grin. "We have no idea what happened during that time frame. Her existing memory banks and programs are all intact except for that gap, and there's no evidence of any data compromise."

Pete sighed. "I say it again: so what's the problem?"

"There might not be one. Maybe nothing happened while she was gone. Or something was done to her by someone who really knows their way around a synthetic, someone who can cut through the security systems and get back out without leaving a trace, except for a memory gap."

"Who's got that kind of know how?" said Nick.

Dave shrugged. "Not many. MI-5, the Tongs, maybe the Russians"

Colin piped up, "How are we even going to find out? If someone can cover their tracks that well, they're not going to be easy to find."

"Good question, Col." Harry gave a broad humourless smile. "And I expect you lot to have an answer by tomorrow." He looked at each of them in turn. "Right. Meeting over."

The group started heading for the door. Nick rose from his chair.

"Hang on a minute, would you, Nick?"

He sat back down.

Harry signaled to Cassie and she went behind the bar and started pouring him a drink. Nick watched her as she took a glass, filled it with ice, picked up a bottle of Scotch and poured. The whole time she was doing it her eyes were fixed on him.

"What's up, boss?"

"Nick, how long we been working together?"

"Dunno boss. Fifteen years?"

"Fifteen years." Harry nodded.

Cassie walked out from behind the bar. She was still watching Nick. He could see that the glass was filled to the brim as she walked over and placed it on a side table next to Harry's chair. She didn't spill a drop.

"You remember that time Susan caught me?" said Harry.

Cassie walked back to the bar and stood watching.

"Hard to forget."

"Those were the days, eh?" He reached for the drink and nudged the glass, spilling a little. Shaking the drops off his hand, he reached for the glass again. He picked it up and took a sip.

"Had to talk fast to get out of that one. Do you remember what I told you about that at the time, Nick? What to do if you ever got caught?"

Nick's gaze drifted to one side until he was looking at Cassie again. He found her cold eyes still fixed on him.

"You said to deny it."

Harry put down his drink.

"That's right, Nick. Deny, deny, deny. Doesn't matter if she walks in on you doing the secretary on the sofa. Always deny. Puts 'em off-balance, see? When someone loves you like that, trusts you like that, they want to give you the benefit of the doubt. They don't want to believe the evidence of their own eyes, because most of all they don't want to believe they've been betrayed. It's a hard thing to deal with, Nick; maybe the hardest thing. I don't know what I'd do if someone did that to me."

Harry took off his glasses, rubbed his eyes. He looked at Nick and their gaze met for a long moment. London rumbled faintly in the background.

Harry put his glasses back on and picked up his drink.

"So, what have you got to tell me, Nick?"

"About what?"

"About Cassie."

"Cassie?" Nick shifted in his chair. He gave a little laugh. "Well, I'm not shagging her, if that's what you mean."

"No, that's not what I mean."

"Ah." Nick rubbed the side of his nose. "Nothing to tell, boss."

"Nothing to tell," Harry repeated. "Right then."

"How about you, boss? Anything you should be telling me?" Nick's mouth was set.

Harry stared at his drink, and looked as though he was about to say something. Then he shook his head and downed his drink all at once. "Best be off, then, eh Nick?" He nodded at the door.

Nick stood up. "Suppose so."

"See you, Nick."

"Bye, Harry."

As he walked to the door and left the room, he felt the two pairs of eyes follow him the entire way.

# *14*
## 123God

It was a nothing day on Portobello Road. Beneath a pale grey sky, street traders hawked their goods to the late morning shoppers gathered beneath the Westway flyover.

As Mike walked down towards the overpass, he could see Scruff on the other side, working at his stall. Viewed from this distance, hunched over his boxes of bootleg albums, he looked like a shambling mound of hair. A handful of punters were flipping idly through the contents of the boxes.

Mike walked over and stood looking down at him, waiting to be noticed. Apart from his hair, there wasn't much to Scruff, just a wiry old rocker in a worn denim jacket. He'd been a fixture on the Road – a nexus of information and goods, much of it rare or illegal – for as long as Mike could remember.

Scruff was sliding an LP into a protective sleeve. The psychedelic cover showed a semi-naked woman, looking to the skies as fire flowed from her fingertips, two large yellow cats standing in front of her. He slipped the album into one of the cardboard boxes and looked up.

"Oh hi, Mike. You look knackered. 'Sup?"

"Not much Scruff. The usual. You know – up all night with an armed psychopath."

"Oh." He gave a lopsided grin. "Nick phoned you up then, did he?"

"Sort of. He was on the phone for about 30 seconds, then he walked through my front door."

"Blimey. That's a bit rude."

"Why did you point him at me, Scruff?"

The shorter man's features rearranged themselves and he looked as though he was about to burst out laughing. It was his contrite look.

"Sorry, Mike. He's very persuasive and I owed him one. He sorted out some bother I was in with a ragga gang last year. He's a bit of a fixer."

"Yeah, well he had me up most of the night doing some fixing for him. Do me a favour, Scruff. Next time you feel the need to settle your accounts, think of someone else."

"Sorry, mate." Scruff's face brightened. "I think I'm even now though."

"Not with me, you're not."

Scruff's right hand disappeared up to his elbow in his tangled mass of hair as he scratched his head.

"I'll see what I can do to square things up, mate. Anything you're looking for?"

"Not at the moment. I'll let you know."

"Right. See ya, then."

Mike nodded, turned and walked on down Portobello Road to the Albion. Like the rest of the area, the pub had been in a down cycle for a decade now and was a bit rough around the edges. This suited Mike and the ragtag bunch of musicians he mixed with just fine since it meant a decent pint and no tourists.

The door juddered as he pulled it open and stepped into the pub. It really was nothing special: a worn brown bar counter, nondescript carpet, dinged wooden tables and stools. There was something strange being played over the pub sound system and it threw Mike off for a minute. It sounded mid-way between ambient noise, like a group of people chatting quietly in a corner, and a series of stretched out half-melodies. The overall effect was deliberately unsettling.

Mike went over to the bar and nodded to the barman. Bald and muscular, he was an occasional roadie for Mike's band.

"What the hell's that, Bob?" He nodded towards the speakers.

"It's a Trenka composition. Late 20th century."

"Lovely. What do you listen to that old shite for?"

"No class, Mike." Bob shook his head. "It's genuine. Not like all the manufactured pap the proles listen to."

"I hope you aren't including me in that label."

He smiled without warmth "Not you, Mike. You're an original." He reached for the pump, a glass in the other hand. "The usual?"

"Might as well."

He paid for the drink and scanned the pub. Over in the corner a familiar figure was hunched over a pint of stout and a tobacco pouch. Black leather jacket, worn leather beret, tired eyes. Tom.

The old man had been in the music business a long time. He'd been a cult legend among other musicians and had almost broken through with his band 123God, but had dropped back into obscurity when he suddenly bailed during their world tour. The band fell apart after that and everyone went off and joined other bands, some of them quite successful. Tom, though, had shown up at the Albion and had been here ever since. He never spoke about his departure from the band, but every now and then he'd talk music.

Mike took his pint and walked over to the corner. He hesitated a moment, then put his pint down on the table and pulled over a stool.

"Hi, Tom."

The older man nodded. He didn't say much, but when he gave them, Mike had found his opinions worth having. He looked up at Mike from under the old black beret.

"What've you got?"

"Is it that obvious?"

"I can see the energy coming off you. Late night?"

"Early morning. Here. Give this a listen, will you?"

Tom popped in the offered earphones and swiped the play icon. He listened.

One eyebrow went up, about as much emotion as Tom ever showed.

"Complex time signature. Little bit fiddly but it works. I like that long repeating rhythm sequence you laid over the top. Original. How'd you come up with that?"

"You wouldn't believe me if I told you."

Tom pulled out the earphones and put them down on the table, then picked up his tobacco pouch and took out some rolling papers. He rolled a cigarette, focusing completely on the task. Mike sipped his pint and watched him.

Tom finished his work and put the cigarette in his mouth.

"Wouldn't take much to make it a big song."

Mike responded faster than he'd intended. "Would you work on it for me?"

Tom leant back in his chair as he lit the cigarette and peered at Mike through the smoke. There was a long pause. The delicate grey threads spiraled up to the pub ceiling.

"OK."

Mike went for broke. "Today?"

Tom's head tilted forward as though contemplating his pint, his eyes hidden beneath the beret. Mike became aware of a clicking noise and the sound of someone breathing heavily. The Trenka composition playing over the pub speakers was approaching its finale.

Tom's voice was quiet. "Pushing it a bit, Mike."

"I'm sorry, Tom. We have a show tonight. We're supporting Cash For Guitars. Live net feed. We may not get another shot like this."

Another long pause.

"All right. Meet me at my place at 1."

# *15*

# Something You Don't Know

Harry and Cassie walked into the office. Harry strode over to his desk and sat down while Cassie turned to face the door and stood there completely motionless.

He picked up the handset of the antique black phone and repeatedly stabbed his forefinger into the holes on the dial face, inputting a number with short, swift arcs of his finger. The distant purring of an ancient ringtone, a sound that most of London had long since forgotten, filled his ear.

The phone rang three times, and then there was a loud click and a voice at the other end.

"Jeremy Wells."

"There's a rat in the kitchen, Jem. I want to move the money."

There was a pause, as if Jem was considering his reply.

"What's got you spooked, Harry? This doesn't sound like you."

"Cassie showed up this morning. Not a scratch on her, but a big piece of her memory is missing. I've got to assume that someone got the passcode."

"We went over this last night, Harry. The money's solid. Even if someone got the passcode from the Judy, it's useless unless they have mine too. They couldn't use them anyway unless they dial in on the secure line in your office. It's serious, yeah, I get it – someone messed with your Judy – but it's not the end of the world."

"Easy for you to say, Jem; it's not your money."

"No it's not, but you hired me to look after it for you, Harry, and I'm advising you not to move it. You'll take a hit if you shift it now, a big hit. Look, the security is still top notch; all we have to do is reset your passcode. Come on down to the brokerage and we'll run the biometrics on you and get it done."

Harry stood up and walked over to the window, the spiral cord attached to the phone pulled taut behind him. He stared out through the blinds at the river, the high rises, the maze of brick, stone and concrete that was London.

"What's going on, Jem?"

"Eh?"

"What's happening? There's more to this than meets the eye. Wheels are turning out there. I can feel it."

"I…Harry, I don't know. I'm just the money guy."

"Never mind. I'm thinking out loud."

"So, you coming in to do the reset or not?"

Harry breathed out his tension onto the glass of the window. A circular patch of condensation appeared briefly then evaporated.

"Nah. It can wait. I've got a few things to take care of first. Look, I'll call you later."

"Fair enough."

"Bye."

Harry turned from the window, walked back to his desk and hung up the phone.

On the other side of the Thames in his suite atop the Shard, Wei swiped an icon on a screen and the audio feed from the Coronation Tower stopped.

On one wall was projected an image of Harry's office window in high res close up. Harry's stony face stared out through the slats of the blinds, a black phone handset pressed to his ear, his eyes focused on something other than the view.

Wei turned and looked down at a thin faced man bent over a screen on a desk. He was typing rapidly.

The man glanced up at him, then spoke in short clipped tones, typing all the while: "Jeremy Wells, goes by Jem. Financial Manager at Churchill's. Offshore specialist. No criminal record. Lives in the DeBeers ultra-high security estate. No family. From his social profile…" he paused, skimming the screen for information, "…he's a member of the Groucho Club, likes to eat at Buckingham's, a regular at the Eye & Pyramid."

"Tell me something I don't know."

The man looked startled.

Wei spoke: "Wells has been working with Harry for five years. He has the bulk of Harry's money locked up in high risk, high return investments in overseas markets. He's done very well for Harry. He's a hedonist who pursues alcohol and women to excess. And he has a voracious appetite for designer drugs that a friend of his sources for him from the underworld."

Wei gave a narrow smile. "Know thy enemy." The smile vanished. "So, what can you tell me that I don't already know?"

The thin-faced man had resumed skimming the screen while Wei was speaking. He tapped a couple of images and read rapidly through some reports.

He leaned back in his chair.

Wei raised an eyebrow.

"Wells purchased some military hardware about six months ago; a field grade powerscroll. It's the hot toy among a certain class of conspicuous consumers. Looks hard-core and fits in the pocket. Impresses the hell out of the other kids."

"So?"

"It's the military's most robust data storage, used to route large volumes of real time encrypted data coming from multiple sources under combat conditions. If you wanted to securely store a high value passcode, or maybe even move a lot of expensive data from A to B, that'd be the tool to do it."

Wei smiled. "You may go."

The man rolled up his screen and tucked it in his jacket pocket. He started towards the door.

"Oh," said Wei, "one more thing."

The man stopped, turned to face him.

"Where did he get it?"

"He picked it up off a street trader in Notting Hill. Name of Terry Carter. Goes by the street name of Scruff."

Wei spoke to the air, "He's leaving. Pay him."

He nodded at the thin-faced man who wasted no time in turning and leaving the room.

Wei spoke again to invisible ears. "Have the cuckoo visit the street trader. I want to know all about Mr. Wells' powerscroll."

He walked over to the enlarged image of Harry's face on the wall. He stared at the hard, craggy features for a moment, then with his middle finger he tapped the wall right in the middle of Harry's forehead. The screen went blank.

# *16*
## Down in the Dirt

Xander strolled down the narrow ravine of Swain's Lane and cut left on to the footpath through Highgate Cemetery. It lengthened his walk, but he took the detour so that he could go by Karl Marx's tomb and its great bronze sculpture. The death of Communism had been a staple of his grandparents' stories of their early years, and the weathered bronze head evoked a sense of nostalgia for him.

He wasn't a fan of the sculpture itself, a giant brooding head that reminded him of a Cro-Magnon wax figure that he'd seen in the British Museum. It had too much forehead and facial hair and was far too literal to evoke any artistic response, but Xander felt that at this remove from Marx's influence on the world, he was able to view it with just the right level of detachment.

Still, there was something in the simplistic bulk of the thing that he found intriguing; a relic of a less complicated time when workers of all lands might indeed have been inspired to unite. Not much chance of that now, and likely to be even less in the future. The digital chains by which they were bound were both powerful and invisible, and grew stronger every day.

Xander made his solitary way along the leafy grave-lined path and stopped in front of the tomb. He eyed Marx's bushy face and considered the events of the last 24 hours. Deep in thought he was surprised by rapid footsteps from behind. Two pairs of strong hands grabbed his upper arms and pulled him backwards while a familiar face appeared in front of him, one finger raised in front of the lips, eyes darting sideways to check the lane.

He was hauled through the undergrowth and dense stands of monuments into the depths of the cemetery. Branches hit the back of his head and his feet knocked against carved stone. When they stopped dragging him and dropped him to the ground, he looked around and could see that he was boxed in by a rectangular tomb on each side, and the men at front and back. Here at the heart of the oldest part of the cemetery, they were screened from the distant paths and the skies alike by the many headstones and the thick foliage.

Xander eyed his captors. The two heavies behind him could have been any of a dozen interchangeable thugs that he'd seen before, but the shorter stocky man in front of him was all too familiar.

"Alexander. You are such a creature of habit."

The man sat down on a monument shaped like a column broken off near the base. He tutted.

"A dangerous thing these days, when an algorithm can all but read your thoughts and can track you from the air." He waved a hand at the invisible skies above the green canopy.

"Of course, to find you some of us need merely to know the time of day." He nodded his head as he looked at Xander with sad, steady eyes.

Xander propped himself up on one elbow and brushed his hair away from his eyes.

"It wasn't my fault, Valentin."

Valentin pursed his lips and continued nodding as he looked off to left and right.

"I'd like to understand that, Alexander. Help me to understand that." His eyes, gazing directly into Xander's were melancholic, expectant.

Xander sat up.

"Well, there was a problem with the software. For some reason it did not work correctly and the *robota*, it malfunctioned. It was a very dangerous situation. I was not there, you know; there was nothing I could do."

"And how do you know that this is the way things happened? How do you know that the software did not work?"

"He – Nick – he told me. He called, very angry, and said the software had broken the *robota*, and that he had not been able to get the money. He said that the deal is off."

Valentin nodded slowly. "The deal is off," he echoed, his voice flat. He stood up and began walking around Xander. "And what did you say, Alexander?"

Xander turned his head to watch Valentin as he circled him. "I tried to reason with him. I told him that this was no good. I told him he had to get the money, and that there were obligations to meet, and that...that you would be angry..."

Valentin stopped walking. "You told him my name?"

"No, I didn't use your name. I said that my . . . friends would be angry. I told him that you were dangerous people and that he should be afraid. I tried, Valentin, but he would not listen."

Valentin continued his circumnavigation. "And where is he now, Alexander?"

Xander looked around, for all the world as though he were actually expecting to see Nick step out of the foliage. "I don't know. He's gone somewhere. He said that there were others chasing him."

Back in front of the broken column, Valentin stopped walking and watched Xander with his solemn steady eyes. There was the sound of birds fluttering among the trees overhead. One of the heavies coughed.

"What...what do we do now?" asked Xander.

Valentin looked down at his hands, then once again turned his lugubrious gaze on the prone artist. "Why, Alexander, we shall settle our accounts."

He nodded at the two men standing over Xander and turned his back.

In a flurry of wings, the birds fled the trees for the open skies.

# *17*
## Time to Go

In Covent Garden the pubs were already doing a brisk Friday lunchtime trade, and the Piazza was circled by business people looking for something to eat and tourists looking for something to do. High above in a blue sky dotted with clouds, the unseen drones tracked their peripatetic movements, looking for patterns.

Nick skirted the square, giving a wide berth to the usual motley collection of street entertainers. He scanned the faces in the crowd, wondering if any of them were synthetics. It was hard to know. They couldn't taste or smell – that was one thing you could use to identify them – but apart from that there was really no way to tell. Nick wondered if one day they'd be so similar to humans that there would be essentially no difference.

He walked along the north side of the Piazza and cut through to Langley Street by way of several narrow alleys. Half way along, he checked the street in both directions, then stepped through the glass doors of the Pamplemousse Dance Studio. Instantly incongruous amid the leotards and exercise gear, he walked up to the reception desk.

The receptionist glanced at him and raised her eyebrows in surprise.

"Nick," she smiled with sympathy, "how are you?"

"Been worse. Allie here?"

"Studio Two. She expecting you?"

"Don't know. She doesn't call me back."

"Good luck."

The receptionist watched Nick walk up the short flight of wooden stairs and turn down the hallway. He walked along it and opened a door into a large studio with wooden floors and mirrors on the walls.

There was a dark-haired woman in a leotard sitting in a yoga position in the middle of the room. Dust motes gleamed in the sunshine streaming down through a row of skylights. He stood and looked at her for a long time before speaking.

"How are you, Allie?"

She turned and saw him, then sighed.

"What are you doing here, Nick?"

"I wanted to talk."

"You're not usually much of a talker. Anyway, I didn't think there was much to say after our last chat."

"I've been busy since you kicked me out. Lots going on. I came here to tell you a couple of things."

She stood up.

"First, I'm going away for a long time."

"That sounds dramatic. Where? Prison? To visit your mates in Liverpool?" She laughed. "Same thing, really, isn't it?"

"Lot further than that. Chances are you might not see me again."

"That's hardly news, Nick. You told me you never wanted to see me again last Saturday night. I didn't expect anything else after what happened."

"Yeah, well, that brings me to the second thing I wanted to tell you."

She read something in his stance, the look in his eyes. She raised a hand to her mouth.

"Oh God, Nick..."

"I know there's someone else, and I know who it is."

Her face filled with emotion.

"Oh God, I'm sorry, I'm sorry."

She crossed the bare boards between them and reached out and wrapped her arms around him.

"I'm so sorry." She put her face down into his chest. He put his arms around her and they stood like that, while minutes passed in silence.

She looked up at him and tried to read his face. He looked miserable.

"I don't know what to say, Nick. I'm sorry and I feel awful, and I don't have an explanation."

"I'm not looking for one."

She stepped away, brushed her hair from her face, and dried her eyes with the back of her hand.

"What *are* you looking for?"

"Nothing. I told you – I'm leaving town."

"That's it?" Her eyes wide, she studied his face.

"That's it."

"When?"

"I'm already on my way. Be gone tomorrow. This is more of a stop than I can afford. I just wanted to say goodbye."

He turned to leave.

"Nick."

"What?"

"You aren't going to do anything silly are you?"

He turned back to face her.

"It's a bit late to hope for that, Allie."

She nodded.

"Try not to get yourself killed."

"Thanks. Do one last thing for me, would you?"

She raised her eyebrows.

"Just for the next few days, keep a low profile."

"OK."

"Bye."

"See you."

She watched him walk out of the studio. He didn't look back.

She walked across to the corner where her bag lay. She reached in and pulled out a phone, pressed a button, and held it to her ear. Leaning with her back against the wall, she slowly slumped down to sit on the floor.

Someone picked up the call at the other end and it made a clicking noise, a replica of the sound of an analog phone from a century ago.

"Hi."

She sat in silence.

"Alison? What's up?"

She looked at the ceiling. Tears ran down her cheeks. Finally the words came.

"Oh God, everything's such a mess, Harry."

# *18*
## Punch the Judy

Friday afternoons at the Crick & Watson were usually dead, and this particular Friday was no exception. The large lounge bar was populated by a few small tables of workers pushing off early and the odd cluster of tourists. Dave, Chopper, and Billy were at their usual table between the mural of the eponymous scientists and the flashing Lottery machine.

Billy's money card was slotted in, and he was tapping at bright sequences of images and numbers on the display. He hit the Start button and an addictive little jingle played as the colours swirled on the screen and formed into a pattern that brought a scowl to his face. An attractive but sad looking blonde appeared in a small window and said as though it were the end of the world: "Sorry Billy, you're not a winner." Then she broke into a stunning smile and said in a voice that was both enthusiastic and imploring, "Let's try again, Billy. I'm sure you'll get lucky next time," and she winked.

He tapped the green flashing Go For It icon, and a new set of images and numbers appeared as Dave arrived with the next round and put the full glasses on the table. He looked over Billy's shoulder as he sipped at his pint.

"Are you winning?" said Dave.

"I don't know yet."

"How many goes is this?"

"Haven't been counting."

"27," said Chopper, examining Billy's selections.

"Bloody hell. Why're you feeding all that cash into that stupid machine? You'll never win, you know."

"That's not the point, is it?"

Dave laughed." Really? What exactly is the point?"

"It's entertainment."

Dave nodded at the wall screen on the other side of the room where a repeat of Punch The Judy was showing. "What? Like that stupid quiz show? It's just about as intelligent, as far as entertainment goes." He mimicked the presenter: "'Ladies and gemmen, and now our contestant will try to pick the synthetic out of the crowd by punching one of them in the face!' Yeah, bloody hilarious."

Billy frowned as he hit Start. "You just don't get it, mate."

"Oh, I get it; I just think it's stupid. Real entertainment has a story, characters, action."

"Like what?"

Dave considered for a moment. "Like that remake of Gone With The Wind that just came out – Liz Taylor, Richard Burton, Sassy O'Neill, George Clooney. Brilliant cast."

"Well that sounds stupid to me. Apart from Sassy they're just simulations. You're just watching a computer program."

"You can't tell the difference."

"I'd rather watch real people," said Billy, eyes on the swirling patterns on the Lottery screen.

"Yeah, well, each to his own."

The jingle ended, the pattern formed, and this time it was a gorgeous redhead that popped up to express her regrets to Billy.

"Talking of real people, or rather the opposite," said Dave, "have you heard the news about the Long Man?"

"What about him?" said Billy, taking a break from the machine to address his pint.

"He went and got himself a synthetic."

"Seriously?" said Chopper "The Long Man; Danny Wilde. He went and spent some of his own money on something? Bloody hell. What kind?"

"One of those historicals. Bill Shakespeare."

Billy grinned and chipped in: "Surely thou art shitting me."

"Nah. Looks just like him. Slaphead. Big doily round his neck and everything. Speaks like they did back then, all this verily forsooth and that."

"What a plonker," said Billy as he put down his pint and turned his attention back to the Lottery.

"Shakespeare?"

"No, you div; Danny Wilde." Billy said over his shoulder. "He's got enough dosh to buy a nice looking Judy, and he goes and buys himself bloody Shakespeare. What's he going to do with that?"

"I dunno. It *is* a bit of a laugh when it starts spouting off."

"Like what?"

"Well, we were out at the offie a coupla three days ago, and Danny's trying to pick out some ales. The bloke behind the counter is splitting himself looking at Shakespeare, and the thing notices and goes over to him and says something like, 'What, thou varlet, mak'st thou mirth at my expense?'"

He paused to take a drink.

"This gets the bloke completely cracking up, and Shakey's getting all pissed off. Danny comes over, but Shakey's pointing his finger and launching in with a big long speech about how 'the basest villains do but laugh themselves to death when in mockery they jest' or something like that. Anyway, the bloke's just about on the floor by now, tears running down his cheeks, Danny and Shakey are both yelling their heads off, Shakey in rhyming verse, and now I'm losing it, it's so fucking funny."

Dave gave a loud laugh and paused for another drink from his pint.

"Long story short, Danny was seriously bent out of shape and I had to get both of them out of there before he piled in to the shopkeeper. So the next thing is, we're there in the middle of the high street, people walking past, Danny and Shakey still yelling their heads off and I'm pushing them down the road. What a bloody commotion: the tallest man in Deptford and Bill Shakespeare spouting off like a couple of nutters. They didn't shut up until we were halfway to the bus station."

All three of them laughed for a minute. Then Chopper frowned. "So how's this synthetic getting into an argument? I thought they weren't able to get into fights."

"Oh, they can't get into fights, unless, y'know, they're like Cassie, but it doesn't stop them having a row. Something to do with the programs you load them up with. I talked with Danny about it later. You can change the character settings so they behave in different ways. I told him he better make Shakey a bit calmer before he goes getting Danny into a fight. Imagine what'll happen if he takes him down the Bedford."

"Oh that would be a laugh," said Chopper. "That's priceless. We have to set that up. Let's get Danny down there for a beer on Sunday."

"Danny's promoting a show tonight. Three bands, I think, over at the New Clarendon. You should go along and ask him, Chopper. Maybe he'll bring the thing with him."

"Yeah, perhaps I will. The boss wants me to keep an eye on the Judy; take it out for a test drive. Might as well take it somewhere I can have a bit of a laugh."

Over on the screen, Punch The Judy had paused for advertising. The advert was promoting the products that had been the butt of the show's slapstick humour just moments before. From the other side of the room, where they stood, the audio was hard to make out, but the slogans that rolled across the screen told the story.

Live from the bleeding edge of technology!

More real than real!

Preferential financing terms available to qualified buyers!

Custom models by arrangement. Standard models available now for less than the cost of a Porsche!

Aren't you worth it?

# *19*
## Analog Dreams

It was closing time on Portobello Road and as the evening drew in the last shoppers were wandering the stalls. Scruff had started packing everything away at his record stall, Analog Dreams. He waved to another trader opposite.

"About 10 minutes, Charlie?"

"Righto, Scruff. I'll go and get the van in a few."

Scruff knelt down to get the boxes under his stall. He was moving records between them when he got a call from Nick. He tapped his lapel button and answered.

"'Sup Nick?"

He continued working and listened to the voice on the lapel speaker, bent over with his mane of hair hanging almost to the ground as he organized the records.

"Scruff, I need some gear."

He replied into the microphone built into the collar of his jacket. "I'm in a hurry, name it."

Nick's voice spoke rapidly as Scruff busied himself sorting albums among the plastic storage boxes, clicking shut the lids. While Nick detailed his requirements, Scruff continued to fuss around under the stall, commenting here and there with a clarifying question as to sizes, specifications and quantities. It took a few minutes, and then Nick was finished.

"Ah, yeah, that's quite an eclectic mix of hardware there, Nick. Very hard to come by and not cheap neither. When do you need it?"

Scruff took a box and swung it around, depositing it on the ground behind him as he listened to Nick's reply. He turned back under the stall. "Bloody hell. Well, it's a stretch but I think I can do that. Say half ten tomorrow?" He moved another box. "I can't wait too long for the dosh, though. Monday? Deal. See you then, Nick."

Scruff hung up the call with a tap of his lapel button, then stood up to grab the boxes on top of the stall. Through the mass of his hair he saw a young man in a well-cut suit and flamboyant tie looking at him. Scruff took in the build, the stance, the attitude.

"Help you?"

"I'm sure you can." The man adjusted his tie, displaying a large gold wristwatch.

"I don't follow."

"Never mind." The man glanced up and down the Road. "I'm looking for something."

Scruff started sorting out the remaining boxes. "I'm just closing up, so if you don't mind, I'd like to make it quick."

"This won't take long. I'm looking some information about a piece of equipment."

"Oh yeah?" Scruff lifted a box and placed it behind him.

"Military. Word is you might be able to help."

"Is that the word?" Scruff spread his arms wide. "Look at my stall. See any guns?"

"Do I see any guns?" The man nodded and raised his hands level with his breast pocket. He examined his fingernails, his left hand in his right, a short reach from the inside of his jacket.

Scruff caught the movement, tipped his head back. "Hey man, broad daylight, busy market. I got a lot of friends on the Road."

"I'm sure you have," said the man, his gaze still on his fingernails. He turned his left hand, the watch glinting in the late afternoon sun. "Look, we're both in a hurry, let's do a quick Q&A and you can get on your way."

Scruff raised a hand to scratch his head. The hand vanished in the mass of hair. He kept it there.

"Make it really fast."

"You sold a powerscroll to a City broker a while ago. Jeremy Wells. Remember him?"

"I sell a lot of stuff. I don't always get names."

"You may not get names, but I'm sure you remember assholes. Blond hair, loud mouth, money, full of shit. Ring a bell?"

Scruff glanced upwards and pursed his lips as if he were considering the description. "Sounds like a lot of City finance guys. What do you want?"

"Passcode for the 'scroll."

Scruff grinned. "Why?"

"Asshole didn't give it to me."

"I mean why do you think I'd have it?"

"Terry, Terry. It is Terry, isn't it? I thought we agreed we were both in a hurry. And here you are, wasting time asking stupid questions."

"It's Scruff, and I think it's time you left, mate." Scruff pulled his hand from his mane, cast his gaze to the left and right of the man's head, and said, "Hello Charlie, George. Thanks for dropping in."

The man's posture changed in an instant. He slowly lowered his hands and took a step backwards. "Sorry to have troubled you," he said, without feeling. "Scruff."

He turned his head in each direction and sized up the two hefty street traders who had appeared behind him.

"I'll be off then," he said, and he turned away and started walking towards the flyover. After a few steps he stopped and looked back. "Oh, one more thing. Tell Nick I'll be seeing him." Then he strode off down the Road.

Scruff nodded at his two friends. "Thanks."

"No worries, Scruff," said Charlie, and they both turned and went back to pack up their own stalls.

Scruff stared down the Road. The man was gone.

He tapped his lapel button.

"Nick? Just had a visit from a friend of yours."

Nick's voice was calm, dry. "Didn't know I had any of those left."

"Slick looking. Custom fit suit, snazzy tie, cufflinks, wristwatch. Bit of a wanker."

"Pete. No friend of mine. What'd he want?"

"Passcode to a powerscroll I sold to a broker named Jeremy Wells. Know him?"

"Heard of him. Why'd he need the passcode?"

"Didn't say, but judging by his attitude, it's very important. Also, he overheard me talking to you about the gear you wanted."

There was a silence at the other end of the line, then Nick's weary voice "Scruff."

"I know, mate. Sorry."

"How much did he hear?"

"Hard to tell. I don't think he heard anything important."

"Shit. Yeah, well. Can we bring the delivery forward?"

"I'll see what I can do. I'll ping you when it's ready."

"Bye."

In short order, Scruff finished packing the boxes and signaled to Charlie at the stall opposite that he was ready to go.

"Couple of minutes, Scruff."

"Thanks, Charlie."

Scruff watched the crowd as it dispersed, people heading for home or the pub, wishing he were one of them, wishing he was on his way to the Albion for a few pints. He walked round to the front of his stall and with a sigh folded up the sign that read Analog Dreams.

# 20

## Dead Loss

Xander regained consciousness with the smell of dirt and damp in his nostrils. He could taste blood in his mouth and his body hurt like hell.

He rolled over onto his back and groaned with the pain. His face was puffy and swollen, his body a mass of bruises. It seemed like there wasn't any part of him that didn't hurt, but the worst was in his hands. There was something very wrong with his hands.

He lay there with his eyes closed as he gathered his strength. It seemed to him as though it would take a superhuman effort merely to sit up. The sounds of the cemetery were muffled: the faint sound of birds chirping the evening chorus, some animal pushing through the undergrowth. He opened his eyes and peered through his swollen lids at the branches above, but in the fading light he couldn't make out much of anything.

Xander tried to sit up, but couldn't. It was as if all the energy had been drained from his body and replaced by pain. With great effort he rolled back onto his side. His vision was blurred, but he could see the lichen-spotted face of one of the tombs.

There was little he could remember of how things had ended with Valentin and his two thugs, but the evidence of how things had gone was all over his body, especially his hands. Oh God, his hands.

Fear rising from the pit of his stomach, Xander lifted his hands to his face. They throbbed with pain, although for some reason his fingers felt numb. When he managed to get his hands up where he could see them, he found out why.

They had taken his fingers.

His screams were barely audible hoarse moans coughed up through his battered mouth. Thrashing and writhing amid the dead leaves he mourned his mutilated hands, his broken future.

At length the shuddering and convulsions ceased and he lay still. Then the anger came. He felt the burning heat of it as it consumed him, and it gave him the strength to push himself up to his knees, and then to crawl over to the tomb and prop himself up with his back to it.

He forced himself to look again at his hands. They had not completely mutilated him, he saw now: they had cut off both the little and ring finger of each hand. The stumps were black with dried blood and dirt. He looked around the clearing, hoping to find them, perhaps take them to a surgeon and have them restored, but it was hopeless. The undergrowth was a wild tangle, it was growing dark, and he knew that Valentin would have made sure he would never find them. He would have hurled them far into the overgrown cemetery, or dropped them down a drain, or fed them to a dog.

Xander felt sick and weak, but knew he had to get out of the cemetery before the gates were locked for the night. Using his legs, he pushed himself up against the tomb, and was able to lever himself upright using his shoulders and then his elbows. He stood there for a few minutes, drawing breath, gathering his strength, and in a drunkard's walk he lurched from tombstone to monument, tree to crucifix, as he made his way back to the path.

There was no one about as he staggered to the cemetery gates, occasionally stopping to lean against a tomb or sit on one of the park benches for a few moments' rest. He reached the exit and stepped out onto the steep rise of Swain's Lane. Step by plodding step he walked up the hill, dragging himself along the wooden planking of the fence, and the red brick wall that came after that.

A few passersby gave him curious looks, but walked on. He had his arms crossed over his chest and his bloody hands tucked inside his jacket. With the cuts and bruises on his face, and the dirt that was ground into them, he didn't look any grimmer than the down and outs that occasionally hung around outside the off licenses or the tube station.

His only thought was to get back to his house, get off the streets and get some help. A visit to a hospital's emergency department would only bring many questions and deeper trouble.

It was dark when he made it back to his house. He'd taken back alleys and side streets wherever possible, and he'd had to stop to rest many times along the way. At last he staggered up the steps to his front door. His phone was gone, and with it his ID chip, but he punched in the code sequence using his right thumb. The door opened and he stumbled inside, kicking it shut behind him.

Xander made his way to the back of the house, to the kitchen, and he slumped into the leather armchair where he'd sat drinking coffee back when the world was normal. He spoke to the phone.

"Call Dr. Armitage."

There was a pause, then the purring of a ringtone, then a voice.

"Hello, Xander. Rather late. How are you?"

"Armitage. Not good. I need you urgently at my house."

"Xander, you sound awful. Do you need an ambulance?"

"No ambulance. No hospital. Need you to help me here."

"What's the problem?"

"I…I had a beating. I…am badly hurt. Please. Hurry."

"Oh, my God. All right. I can be there in 20 minutes. Hang on, I'm on the way."

The phone clicked off.

Xander lay with his head against the back of the chair, gathering his strength. Then he spoke again.

"Call Nick Turner."

As the phone made the connection there was the sound of the ringtone, then an answering service.

"Nick Turner is unavailable. Please leave a message."

"God damn it, Turner. They got me. I told you. I told you so. They're coming for you now. Run. Run as fast as you can, you son of a bitch."

# *21*

# The Eye & Pyramid

In a dimly lit booth at the back of the Anchor, Wrecked John was slumped over, head on his left arm, his right extended across the table as though he were holding an invisible drink. The sleeve of his denim jacket was dark with the beer it had soaked up from a pint he'd spilled earlier. His greasy mop of hair shrouded his face, the ends soaking in the pools of beer on the table.

A young man in a dark pin-striped suit sat down at his table. He glanced around the sparsely populated pub, but no one was paying any attention to the unlikely pair.

"John. Hey, John."

Nothing.

"John. John, it's Kevin. You in there?"

Kevin grimaced, reached out and grabbed him by the shoulder. He shook it vigorously.

"Eh?" John's head snapped up. "Wha'?"

He looked up at Kevin with wandering eyes.

"Hey, Kev. Hi, man."

"Hi John. How are you?"

"Oh, the usual."

"Great. Great. You look, uh, like you normally do."

He paused, looked around. "Anyway, enough chit-chat. You got my stuff?"

John was quiet. Since he didn't retain eye contact for more than a few seconds at a time before his gaze went drifting off somewhere else, it was hard to tell if he'd heard.

"John?"

"Yeah, yeah."

"You got my stuff?"

"Eh?" His eyes lined up on Kevin for a few seconds. "What?"

"My stuff. You know, the gear?"

"OK, OK." John stared at his wet sleeve.

"Now would be good, John."

"Yeah. Right. Here y'are."

John used his dry arm to reach inside his denim jacket and pull out a small white bag. He handed it over, then he put his head back down on his other arm.

Kevin opened the bag, glanced at the pills inside.

"Er, John? How much?" he prompted as he pocketed the bag.

"Um. Two hundred," John mumbled into the table.

"Yeah, right," Kevin tucked a hundred under John's dry sleeve and got up to go.

"See you, John."

There was no answer. Shaking his head, Kevin got up and left the pub.

Outside in the growing darkness, he cut through a cobbled alleyway that smelt of piss, and turned on to Cannon Street. He passed half a dozen packed pubs before turning down a side street and reaching his destination.

It was the usual Friday night in the Eye & Pyramid. The crowd of young drinkers spilled out into the street beneath the giant neon dollar bill that stained their faces an unearthly green.

Kevin pushed his way past the crowd at the entrance and through the giant sized reflective silver doorway shaped like the eye of a needle. He paused to pat the nose, worn smooth by countless palms, of the stuffed camel that stood just inside the door then headed for the bar.

The place was heaving with a vibrant mix of City money and local colour; brokers, dealers, wide boys, secretaries, and people whose method of earning a living didn't come with a job description. It was three deep at the giant horseshoe bar that arced across the middle of the pub, and each of the glass-topped tables that filled the room was surrounded by its own circle of sitting and standing drinkers. At the back end, by the toilets, the half-dozen booths were less full, but it was still early.

A rugged handsome blond man in a grey designer suit was holding court with a group of younger men in off-the-shelf gear. Kevin edged his way into the pub and went over to join them.

As he approached the group, the blond man held up a hand for silence, and turned away as with one finger he touched the gold and platinum stud-phone embedded in his right ear.

"Yes, Harry?" He tilted his head for a few minutes, listening.

"The biometric reset? Hour or so, I reckon." He listened again.

"Got it. 10 tomorrow. I'll be there."

He tapped the phone and turned back to his disciples who had been joined by Kevin.

"Big meeting, Jem?"

"Everything's big when I'm in the room, know what I mean, Kev?"

"You're full of it, Jem."

"Always packing a full load, Kev."

"Do you ever think about anything but your cock?"

"Yeah."

"Like what?"

"Shagging, girls, footie, beer, shagging…"

"You left out dosh."

"That's a given, mate." He picked up a tall glass of lager. "'Scuse me, lads, got some business to do." With a wink, Jem turned his back on the group, leaning in to Kevin.

"So," said Kevin, "Decent Friday, then?"

"Can't complain. Got something on tomorrow, too."

"On a Saturday?"

"Money never sleeps, my son." Jem raised his beer in a toast and drank half of it down. "And speaking of staying up all night, have you got it?"

"Would I let you down?"

"Why break the habit of a lifetime?"

"Funny."

With one hand Kevin reached into his jacket pocket and worked his fingers into the white bag. By touch he picked up three pills and brought them out. He held them close to his body at waist height and dropped them into Jem's waiting upturned palm which clenched into a fist and disappeared into his trouser pocket.

Jem turned to the group of hangers-on. "Here, Quentin, get a pint sorted out for Kev."

He turned back to Kevin. "Nice one, geezer. I'm going to get started." And with that he headed off towards the toilets.

"Got a story for you when you're finished," Kevin called to his back.

Jem nodded and worked his way through the crowd. He pushed open the toilet door and stepped into the relative quiet. He looked over at the stalls and didn't see any feet under the doors; he was the only one in the room. Quickly, one at a time, he swallowed the pills, washing each one down with a mouthful of water from the sink tap.

As he lifted his head from the sink after the final pill, he eyeballed himself in the mirror. A tuft of hair was sticking up at the back of his head.

He wet his hand in the sink and smoothed it down but it wouldn't quite sit flat. He wet his hand again, swiped the hair with more water and now it looked really obvious.

*Crap.*

He grabbed some paper towels and scrubbed at the wet hair. It helped a bit, but now the stray ones poked out in several different directions so he threw the towels in the bin and tried smoothing it down with his hand again. He tilted his head and examined himself in the mirror.

*Not too bad. Serviceable.*

Then he felt a hot surge in his chest. He checked the front of his shirt and half expected to see blood soaking through it. The sensation vanished, and he was starting to feel the buzz come on when in the next instant he felt like his bladder had given way and he'd pissed his pants. This was new. He looked down at his crotch. Nothing.

*Felt bloody real though. What the fuck has Kev given me?*

He opened the toilet door and went back into the pub. Right then the chemicals sent a surge of energy from his gut to his head and a wave of euphoria hit him.

*Oh yeah, that's better.*

It was the last coherent thought he ever had. A series of random sensations swept over him: the ghostly green light coming in through the windows, a tall, thin blonde staring at him, the smell of cheese and onion, a wall of dark suits. Then the drug kicked in with a really fast acceleration and as he crossed the pub, it pushed him through euphoria and right out the other side into dizziness and disorientation like a drunk stumbling through a revolving door.

He was halfway back to the bar when it turned physical on him. He gave a quick, twisted grin in response to Kevin's stare, and then his bowels and gut gave way with a sudden horrible lurch and he lost all motor control. The crash he made as he flailed his way to the ground through a table stacked with empties turned heads on the far side of the bar. He went down amid breaking glass, hitting the beer-soaked carpet with a thump. To raucous laughter someone yelled "Sack the juggler!"

The last thing his brain registered before he lost consciousness was a final wild-eyed scan of the faces looking down at him, some frowning, some concerned, most laughing. None of them looked human. Then he shut down.

# 22

# Who the Fuck are You?

The New Clarendon followed in a long tradition of London hotels that were neither new nor any longer a hotel. Instead, courtesy of the large disused ballroom, it had become one of the top city venues for live shows. On this Saturday night the crumbling finery of the lobby and ballroom were complemented by the post-apocalyptic chic of the crowd lined up around the block.

When Mike arrived, the punters were streaming in through the front doors. The black clad figure of Danny Wilde was unmistakable at the entrance, towering a good head above the hefty bouncers. As Mike walked up, he could hear Danny dealing with an aggrieved rocker and his female companion.

"No, son. No plus-ones tonight. Named guest list comps only. Sold out gig. You can come in, but she can't. Hello, Mike. This way, mate. How was the sound check this afternoon?"

"Hi, Danny, not bad. New song was a bit rough but I think it'll be all right."

Danny nodded and turned his attention back to the crowd. Mike walked past the bouncers and into the hotel lobby while behind him Danny continued yelling at the crowd filing through the entrance.

"Hey, you! No gang insignia. Lose it or you don't get in."

Inside the lobby were trade stands selling band recordings and merchandise. Mike scanned the faces, but didn't see Scruff, who usually had a stall at the big gigs. He made his way through the scrum at the bar and went into the ballroom.

He took in the crowd. Mostly hip young things, but also groups of rough looking locals, some City types trying a bit too hard to blend in, longhair techies in lab coats and flying helmets, and quite a few speed freaks. The latter were here for the first support act, Stash Pocket, and were already out of their heads and soaring on whatever was hot this week. They'd vanish into the night before Mike's band was on.

He walked over to the stage. Bob from the Albion was adjusting one of the amps.

"All right, Bob?"

"Hi, Mike."

"Seen Dr. Teknikal?"

"He was backstage earlier. Looked like he was off his head already."

Mike grinned. "He's the only one of us who doesn't do any drugs. Totally clean."

"Funny. Out of all you lot, he always looks the most wasted."

"Yeah, well, he's the decoy. Can you give him the set list for me?"

Bob held out his hand. Mike pulled a piece of paper from his inside pocket and unfolded it.

"Hang on a sec." He took out a black marker and made a change, crossing out one of the songs in the middle of the set and writing in 'Synthetic Dreams'. He handed the list up to Bob and put the marker away.

"Thanks, mate."

"No worries."

Mike looked across at the bar to see a familiar face making his way towards him. It was Zelley, dressed for the night in torn jeans, an artfully distressed brown leather jacket accessorized with small strips of steel grey duct tape, and a white T-shirt spray painted with the slogan: 'I Am Living Beyond Your Means'.

"Hi, Z."

"Mike. Good Lord, you're still alive. Feels like forever."

"Yeah, well, I've been busy."

"Apparently." Zelley made a point of staring at the instruments on the stage.

"Hey, I'm making a living. Look Z, you know I don't like to talk business on a night out, but I have to ask you some questions about an illegal synthetic when you have a bit of time."

"Thinking of coming back to work for me?"

"God, no."

"Charming."

"I do my best."

"You really shouldn't bother," said Zelley looking over Mike's shoulder. "Oh," he continued with faux nonchalance, "who's that behind you?"

Mike turned to find another Zelley standing behind him, arm round a girl. The Zelley was identically dressed, down to the rips in the jeans and the duct tape. The girl was a dark-haired waif in skintight leather trousers and a T-shirt that bore the slogan, 'Silver Spoon, Paper Plate' stitched in sequins.

The two Zelleys stood there, grinning at him. The girl looked from one to the other, her mouth open.

"Oh, for God's sake!" said Mike.

"Come on. Have a go. Who's the fake?" asked the recently arrived Zelley.

"Both of you, I reckon. Look, I'm not in the mood, Z. If it's all the same, I'd rather talk to the real you."

"Does it matter that much?"

"It does to some of us. And where's Samantha?" asked Mike

"I broke up with her," said the Zelley with his arm round the girl.

"Yes, you most certainly did, you heartless bastard," said the other.

"Look who's calling who heartless."

"Yes, well, in my case it's only metaphorically true," said the solo Zelley.

"And that makes you a better person?"

"It at least makes me a person, which is more than can be said for you."

The Zelley with the girl gave an exaggerated pout.

The first Zelley looked at Mike. "Where were we?"

"You were showing off."

"It is rather magnificent, isn't it? Come back and work for me, Mike. We're doing some fascinating work on next gen character programming."

"I'm out of the synthetics business, Z."

"The legal end of it, at least."

Mike gave him a look. "It's a damn shame we can't do character programming on people."

"Touché. My dear boy, where did this newfound wit come from?"

"Living on the edge."

"Edge of disaster, judging by your last recording."

"You listened to it?"

"Only with one ear."

Mike looked around and realized that the two Zelleys were the centre of attention. A number of people at the bar were recording the sight. Others were chatting and pointing, and a couple started taking snapshots.

"If one of you two doesn't bugger off soon, I'm going to ask this lot if they feel like a game of Punch the Judy," said Mike.

"Lost none of your subtlety, I see," said the first Zelley, "Fair enough." He looked at the other Zelley. The girl had shrugged off his arm and was staring at him from a short distance. The two Zelleys regarded each other.

Almost simultaneously they said, "One of us has got to go."

The first Zelley started laughing and reached out a hand to the girl. "Come here, my darling, I promise you'll have a much more entertaining evening if you stick with me." To the other Zelley he said: "As for you, my dear boy, I'll walk you to the door. Mike, drop by and see me when you get bored of this sex, drugs, and rock and roll thing."

Mike nodded. As Zelley and his lookalike turned away, he pulled the marker from his pocket and gently made a small black X on the right shoulder of the doppelganger's jacket. The arm gave an odd little twitch as he wrote, but it kept on walking with Zelley towards the exit.

While they'd been chatting, Stash Pocket had been getting set up on stage. A ragtag group of longhairs, they were loud and unsubtle which was just what their audience was looking for. There was a whine of feedback and a couple of thumps on a bass drum and they launched into their first number. The area in front of the stage broke into a melee of frantic stumbling activity, the leather-clad fans colliding with each other in a crazed Brownian motion. Every now and then someone would go crashing to the floor, only to be pulled up by the scruff of the neck to hurtle gleefully back into the roiling mass.

Mike rolled his eyes and headed backstage.

# *23*
# Nothing Doing

Inspector Hodges rubbed his eyes and wished he were somewhere, anywhere, else on this tedious Friday night. The Fenchurch Street Situation Room was quiet at the moment, but he knew it wouldn't last. As the clock counted up the minutes and hours, the trickle of crime on the city streets would rise, and by midnight it'd be a river flowing through the incident rooms in the basements below.

It was crime, yes, but it was almost all routine Friday night crime. Hodges was there in case anything major came in, but it was nearly always the same. Drunken bankers getting into fights, smashed shop windows, car accidents, stolen street signs. Perhaps there'd be a stick up at a corner shop or a hit and run, but really not much chance of anything worthwhile.

In his twenty years on the Force and his ten working the City, he'd handled perhaps a dozen murders and a handful of significant crimes. Most of the real crime these days was online, and that was out of his jurisdiction.

It was true that things flared up now and again between the various gangs that organized so much of the crime on the streets, but they tended to handle things among themselves. When accounts were settled, the bodies rarely showed up and no one ever reported anyone missing. It was only when things spilled over into public view that the police became involved, as they had last year in Limehouse.

Hodges grinned. That had been quite a night. Harry standing in the middle of Butcher Row his arms spread wide, asking with genuine concern how the Inspector's family was doing, and wondering if he could set him up with a box for an international at Wembley. Meanwhile, a few streets away suspected members of the Bratva Mafia were being loaded into ambulances. They couldn't pin anything on either gang – Harry's men had vanished, and the Russians wouldn't talk – but everyone knew that a score had been settled.

*Well*, thought Hodges, *You can always hope.*

He looked from screen to screen as though that might make something happen, but it was all routine aerial and street surveillance video, traffic patterns, and infrared drone tracking of population flows.

He thought about his previous day's conversation with Larry. The gangster was a nervy sort, but someone Hodges had found that he could do business with. It paid to stay in with someone from each of the gangs, and Larry had been a reliable source of information over the years. He'd have to figure out somewhere else to talk him in future, though, since Larry was getting wobbly about the disused Tube station.

*Pity really, there are so few places these days where you can talk without being observed.*

He looked again at the screens. It was the usual: a few punch ups around the pubs; some stupid-arse stockbroker with a suspected drug overdose on his way in an ambulance to the King Billy; a smash and grab at one of the high end clothes shops. There were half a dozen drunk and disorderly arrests, including a naked Chelsea fan screaming at the river from Tower Bridge. The usual.

A bright red icon flared on his desktop screen and Hodges tapped it. The screen filled with stats and the face of the duty sergeant.

"Think you should take a look at this one, Inspector."

"All right, Jim." Hodges swiped the video icon. The time-compressed video was auto edited for key words and phrases, so he didn't have to watch the whole conversation; he took in the main facts from the digest.

Dr. Armitage – Highgate – confidential – patient mutilated – suspected gang involvement – amputated fingers – cult artist – Alexander Gorchakov – Russia.

As he absorbed the digest, the list of probabilities from the predictive analytics algorithm popped up around the photo of the doctor. Probability of lying 6%, probability of a crime having been committed 81%, probability of known offender 39%. To one side were the crime stats on Gorchakov and Armitage: parking tickets, speeding, nothing serious. On the other side, extracts from their social media presence scrolled by in coloured word frequency clusters. Art, blood, society, Highgate, sculpture. Surgeon, Royal Free, charity, rugby, scandal.

Hodges stopped the flow on the last word and brought up a summary window while he continued to watch the digest and listen to the essentials. When it stopped a minute later he turned his attention to the summary. Armitage had been involved in an experimental surgical programme that combined transplants and DNA modification. Ethical questions had been raised, and he had come close to being struck off. In the end he had kept his license to practice medicine, but had difficulty finding a hospital or clinic that would hire him. After the Board review was finished, he had gone independent.

Hodges called up the sergeant. "Why was this call routed to us, Jim?"

"Armitage has a small clinic in the City. Makes his living treating financial types, mostly."

"Why's he working on some arty character up in Highgate?"

"Don't know the connection, sir. They do both live in the area."

"OK. Which gang?"

"Armitage doesn't name it. I don't think he knows. If you see the full video, he says that the artist didn't want to talk about it, but he said enough to worry the doc. My read of it, sir, is that Armitage was doing him a favour, but when he found out what he was dealing with, he got worried about losing his license."

"When will we get something from Gorchakov?"

"No reply from his house. Car should be there in about 15 minutes."

"Get me the interview as soon as it comes in, would you?"

"Yes, sir."

Hodges ended the call. He looked at the information on the screen again. The mix of data and analytics gave the clinical picture of the matter, but it was his instincts and experience that made something of it. This was an odd one. Something from his many years on the streets was speaking to him: nothing intelligible, but a persistent voice all the same. There was a long period of silence as he sat and stared at the screen. Then it practically yelled at him: Bratva!

He grabbed his phone, tapped the Secure icon, and picked a name. Somewhere in the East End, Larry's phone began to ring.

# 24
# Bad Dreams

Stash Pocket had finished their set and the speed freaks were dispersing. A few sweat-soaked fans lingered in front of the New Clarendon stage, but most of them were headed for the exit, pushing their way through the hipper audience arriving to take their place.

Mike had finished his backstage preparations and was out in the bar chatting with the singer from Cash For Guitars. He took a drink, and looked over the crowd.

There's a certain vibe that goes on at any club, and when people aren't in tune with it they stand out, usually in a bad way. Samantha was standing out. Mike saw her as she made her way through the crowd on the far side of the room. She was stumbling and her head was swiveling randomly from side to side like a confused animal.

"'Scuse me," he sighed, as he put down his drink and headed over to intercept her before she reached the ladies' toilets.

He crossed the dance floor quickly, but didn't reach her in time. She pushed open the toilet door and stumbled in. Mike followed her; the place was empty and Samantha had gone into one of the stalls.

"Hey, Sam!"

She turned slowly to look at him. She was dressed in a pair of stretch jeans that looked as though they'd been sprayed on, and a white top. Most days Samantha looked good in anything, but not tonight. He took in the lowered plastic toilet lid with the long parallel grooves cut into it, a fixture of the New Clarendon toilets, and the baggie of white powder she'd placed next to them.

"Oh God." She picked up the baggie and made to walk past him.

"Hey, hey, Samantha."

She stared at him. Big pupils.

"What?" She kept turning her head this way and that.

"Samantha, it's Mike."

She lurched back a step. "So?"

"You don't seem right."

The look on her face was probably supposed to be anger, but it looked more like confusion.

"Sam, are you on something?"

"What if I am?"

"Show me. Please?"

She held out the baggie for him to see. It looked like an ounce or more, and there was a round yellow sticker on the side featuring a blissed-out smiley face with X's instead of eyes.

Mike winced. "Sam." He paused. "Why don't you let me keep it for you? If you need it you can come and find me. OK?"

She looked at him for a few seconds, her head wavering, then she handed it over. Mike made it vanish into an inside jacket pocket.

"You don't think I can handle it do you? I can, you know. He doesn't. He doesn't think I can do anything. He doesn't care. He's not even real anymore."

"Who? Oh god, yeah, Z. Look, I'm sorry Sam."

"He's not real so he doesn't care. I've got to find the real one."

"Samantha, I don't think that's a good idea at the moment. Anyway, he's not here."

She looked at him. "How do you know?"

Mike fumbled for a moment. "He's, well, he was here. Before. But he left."

"I've got to find him. Let me go!" She brushed away the hand he'd raised to take her arm and walked past him, head turning side to side once more.

Mike followed and took her arm as they both left the toilets. As she continued to protest, he steered her towards the entrance.

Danny Wilde was standing nearby talking with one of the bouncers.

"Danny, need a favour," said Mike. "We're on in a few, and my friend here's not doing very well. Can you ask one of the girls to keep an eye on her?"

Danny took a look at Samantha, who was now standing quietly with a dazed look on her face.

"She's a bit stoned, but I stopped her before she did any more. I think she's all right, just a bit out of it. She's had a rough night; broke up with her boyfriend earlier."

Danny nodded and signaled to one of the women staffing the merchandise booths.

"Thanks, mate." Mike said. He turned to Sam. "They're going to look after you for a bit, OK, Sam?"

She nodded once.

Mike turned and made his way as fast as he could through the bar to the stage door where a few punters had begun to gather. He showed his tag to the bouncer who opened the door and let him through. He walked down the narrow hall, the walls covered in old band posters and graffiti, to the dressing room behind the stage.

The three other band members looked up as he walked in.

"Nice of you to show up, Mike," said Dr. Teknikal, a tall gangly figure in a Victorian frock coat and a large pair of wraparound shades.

"Yeah, well, I had a spot of bother to deal with. We ready?"

"We ready."

The stage manager looked in at the doorway.

"Any time, boys."

Dr. Teknikal led the way; Mike followed with the two guitarists close behind him. They rounded a corner and trotted up the few steps to the stage.

A ragged cheer greeted Dr. Teknikal as he strode up to the microphone stand while Mike settled in behind the drum kit/synth combo, and the guitarists plugged in on either side of the stage.

"Good evening, reprobates," began Dr. Teknikal. "For those benighted few of you who don't already know, we are The Vibing Concept, and you are about to have the time of your sorry little lives!"

With a flourish he raised one hand high into the air, and Mike counted in the first song. The band joined in, and they were off with the opening number, an eerie blend of fast tempo drumming and high wailing guitar and synthesizer. Stumbling across the stage, Dr. Teknikal panted out the lyrics in his deep, breathy voice. Their performance was like a drunk dancing along the edge of a cliff: always one step from disaster, yet blissfully unconcerned about the possibility of falling through space and crashing to the rocks below.

By the time they finished the first four numbers, the crowd was having as much fun as the band. Mike felt great, and his nervousness about the new number he'd composed with the rhythm sequence from the Judy had evaporated. They ploughed through the set list and the time came for the debut of the new song.

"This next piece of genius is a new one that Mike put together," announced Dr. Teknikal, "with a little divine help from 123God. These are Synthetic Dreams!"

He bowed low to the stage as Mike tapped his monitor screen with a drumstick, and the staccato rhythm sequence he'd programmed with Tom earlier that day thumped out from the speakers. The guitars came in raw and distorted, and Dr. Teknikal began wailing over the top of everything.

Mike pounded away at his kit with a genuine feeling of release, of joy, and as the stage lights dropped for a few moments he took a look out into the crowd to see how it was going down. He saw excited faces, bobbing heads, and then he looked right into the cold, still eyes of the Judy.

It was standing to one side of the hall with a small group of men who didn't look anything like the rest of the crowd there tonight. He felt a cold chill of fear and immediately lost his concentration, going off the beat. His bassist looked across at him. Mike turned his thoughts back to his hands, what he was doing.

*Shit.*

He tried to keep his mind on the playing, but thoughts were crowding into his head.

*Why is it here? Did I miss something in the memory wipe? Did I really see it?*

He forced himself to settle back into the beat, then he took another look. It was still there, staring up at him. One of the men who were with it had a finger in one ear and was talking urgently into a phone held to the other. He looked like a nasty piece of work, and whoever he was phoning, it didn't look like a social call.

Mike looked back to the kit and worked his way through the song. The joy he'd felt when they'd begun was gone, replaced by tension and fear. The band finished the number, a little shambolic even by their standards, but when it ended there was a general roar of approval.

Dr. Teknikal came over to Mike in the interlude before the next song.

"What the fuck, Mike? I know it's a new tune, but you fucking wrote it. You were all over the show."

"Sorry, mate, got put off a bit. Lost my concentration."

"Well fucking find it, will you? We've got four more numbers to do and this shit's going out live."

"Yeah, yeah, I've got it."

Dr. Teknikal nodded and went back to the microphone stand to talk to the crowd.

Mike looked back over to where he'd seen the Judy. It was gone.

# 25
## What Shadows Walk Below?

The night was softened by a fine drizzle. It filled the air and it stuck to every crumbling brick and weathered stone in the city. It clung also to the worn face of Wrecked John as he walked along the silent Embankment. He liked it here. There was a comfort in the slow strong flow of the river after high tide and the solid stone banks that hemmed it in. It felt as though it were simultaneously going somewhere and standing still. Wrecked John could empathize. He often felt the same way.

He wandered past Temple tube station and headed east along Victoria Embankment, back into old London. The City boundary marker, a silver dragon holding a coat of arms loomed over him as he passed by. John paid it no attention. Long experience had taught him to ignore the strange things that surrounded him, unless they moved.

As he was walking alongside the Inner Temple Gardens he saw something that was both strange and in motion. Three figures, solid shadows, detached themselves from the darkness beneath the trees and flowed across the road towards a tall man in a long grey coat who was walking about a hundred yards in front of him.

John stopped and instinctively faded back into the shelter of a granite pillar that supported one of the hundreds of tall black iron lamps that lined the Embankment. He looked into the wide monstrous face of the bug-eyed dolphin that wrapped itself around the lampstand, then looked away. It was safe. It wasn't moving.

Up ahead of him the silent shadows had crossed the road and were almost upon the tall grey man. As John watched, the man whirled to face them and there was a loud bang. One of the shadows folded in half and slumped to the ground, but the other two leapt towards the man, arms raised.

What followed was a frantic blur and over in seconds.

An hour later, staring at a pint of stout in the Anchor, Wrecked John tried to make sense of the jumble in his head. He was able to remember each moment, he just wasn't able to distinguish the order in which they had happened, or if they had even happened at all. To John everything felt like the present, and the present was coloured by his vivid chemically-enhanced imagination.

As he watched the bubbles rise to join the white foam floating on top his pint, the moments came back to him like a deck of cards that had been thoroughly shuffled and then laid out at random face up on a table, one after the other, snap, snap, snap.

Snap – Two dark gargoyles flew towards a slender grey dragon that flexed and curled as they descended upon it. There were flashes of silver amid the blur of movement that followed, and the three fell in a tangle of limbs.

Snap – Three figures were running towards him, in front was a man in a grey coat clutching one of his arms. The man had steel hair. The two shadows pursuing him had green glowing eyes, and long articulated limbs that ended in silver blades.

Snap – His eyes were blinded by a neon flash, and a high pitched whine filled his ears. Three shapes rolled on the concrete and separated. Two of them lay twitching for a moment while the third, a grey dragon, rose to its feet.

Snap – Two shadows lifted a third from the ground and carried it to a waiting car. A door opened and the three of them vanished. The car sped off into the night.

Snap – A grey dragon, its wings flowing behind it, ran towards him. There were two dark shadows in its wake. The dragon leapt onto the wall that bordered the river, and stumbled.

Snap – There were dark stains on the pavement. He walked around them, avoiding contact. There was an acidic smell, and one of the stains shimmered in the lamplight.

Snap – He looked into the eyes of the dragon. Its mouth was wide and perhaps it was screaming. It looked down at him from atop the wall as a flash of silver flickered from behind it and tore one of its wings.

Snap – Two dark shapes were crouched on the wall looking towards the river. They had long arms that pointed at the blackness, and at the end of them there were rapid flashes of blue light. There was a repeated plop-plop-plop sound as something hit the water.

Snap – A car screeched to a halt on the road. It was so black it seemed to absorb the street lights. It was there, but it seemed as ill-defined as a shadow in the night.

Snap – The grey dragon flew into the river.

Wrecked John picked up his pint and took a sip. He looked around the public bar of The Anchor. There was something about this place that was important. He remembered that a dark man in a suit had been here before, or maybe it was a man in a dark suit. John reached into an inside pocket and took out some money. He stared at it for a few minutes, then put it back in his pocket. Then he remembered what it was that was important. He'd done what he was supposed to and passed on the package to the man from the Eye & Pyramid. All in all, it had been a busy night and John felt tired. Closing his eyes, he stretched out his arm on the table and laid down his head.

# 26
## Dead End

The Vibing Concept finished their set and the audience gave a final roar then headed for the bar or the toilets as the need drove them. Some of the house lights came up and Mike looked across the crowd. There was no sign of the Judy or the thugs that had been with it. He stepped down from his kit and headed backstage with the rest of the band.

Dr. Teknikal was still brimming with energy and he wandered round the dressing room, a drink in one hand, dissecting the performance.

"We were all right. We were all right tonight, except you, Mike, you were a fuck up." He flashed Mike the smile that said he was taking the piss. "I mean, what was that business on the new song? You just went off into your own world there for a minute."

Mike nodded, grabbed a beer, opened it, and downed half of it in one go.

Dr. Teknikal kept on rambling. "And what about that technochick in the front row? She was grooving. Did anyone see what happened to her bra? Probably still on the stage. That is what I call audience participation. Yes, a good night, my lusty gentlemen, and now we must party."

Mike downed the rest of his beer. "I've got to run and take care of a few things lads. Can you ask Bob if he'd mind taking care of my kit by himself tonight? I've got a friend who's in a bit of bother."

The other band members drank and nodded. Dr. Teknikal made an elaborate bow and waved one hand in the direction of the door. "Do as you must, Sir Michael, and we shall see you on the morrow."

"Say hi to the technochick for me," Mike smiled, and he left the dressing room. In the corridor he squeezed past a member of Cash For Guitars who was drinking with some hangers-on, and made his way to the backstage exit. He pushed the door open, stepped past the bouncer, and worked his way through the liggers that were clustered there hoping to get backstage.

He moved as fast as he could to the bar where he could see Danny Wilde, a good head taller than everyone around him, relaxing with a few friends.

"Hi, Danny."

"Mike. Nice show. Except for that bit where you were shite."

"Thanks, thanks Danny. Where's Sam?"

"She faded pretty fast. Seemed more wiped than stoned. Tania took her home."

"OK. All right, thanks. Let Tania know I owe her one, would you?"

"We're family, Mike. You'd do the same."

"Yeah, well, it's still above and beyond, Danny. Did you see a tall blonde here earlier on, attractive, skinny, artificial looking?"

Danny waved a hand at the crowd. "Take your pick."

"This one had a small group of gangster types with her."

"Can't say I remember her, but I wasn't on the door the whole time. I can ask around for you."

"Nah, it's OK. It looks like she left anyway."

"Someone you'd like to meet?"

"Some*thing* I'd like to avoid."

Danny nodded, scanned the crowd. "You coming in to watch CFG?"

"Nah, I've got to run. Follow up on a few things."

Danny picked up his drink and headed for the ballroom. "Laters."

Mike looked the crowd over then returned to the backstage door. As he worked his way through the hangers-on a few of them called out to him as he passed "Hey Mike!" "Mike." "Mikey." "Get us in, Mike." "Ask Len to come to the door, would you, Mike?"

Mike reached the door, squeezed past the bouncer and went backstage again. The corridor was busier; some groupies and friends of the bands had been allowed in while Mike was talking with Danny. There was a loud cheer from the ballroom where Cash For Guitars were taking the stage. They started their opening number; from backstage it sounded like an angry giant thumping on the side of the building.

He slid down the corridor, past the dressing rooms, and reached the hotel stage door exit. The bouncer sitting on a stool by the door gave Mike a mirthless grin. "Just a mo," he said.

He opened the door a crack. "One coming out."

There was an answer that Mike couldn't hear, then the door opened. Mike stepped out into the back alleyway, past a couple more bouncers, and a second group of punters trying to blag their way backstage from the other direction. The door closed behind him, and the thump-thump of the band, although still loud, was muffled.

It was raining, and Mike pulled the hood of his jacket over his head as he headed off down the alley. The cobblestones glistened in the rain where the light from an occasional streetlamp touched them. He passed a couple of garage entranceways sealed with metal shutters, and turned the corner that led back to the main road, the walls of the alley black with shadows.

One of the shadows moved. Mike froze. Then it spoke in a voice that was slow and gruff, but almost friendly, like a concerned uncle.

"Hello, mate. How are you?"

Mike knew that tone. He'd heard it before in the playgrounds at school, in back streets in his neighbourhood, in pubs in Liverpool and Manchester. His mouth went dry. This was not going to end well. He glanced over his shoulder and saw three dark figures standing behind him.

"I'm all right."

"Good for you."

A man in a thick black coat stepped from the shadows. He was bulky but light on his feet, like a boxer. The little light that came from the corner streetlamp behind Mike glinted off the man's glasses and shone on the rain that ran off his bald skull.

He stood there and looked at Mike for a long time with his head tipped to one side as though trying to figure something out.

"I hope it's no bother," he said with genial menace, "but I'd like a bit of a chat. Oh, I'm Harry, by the way."

Mike stepped to one side of the alley, so he could see along it in both directions. "Hello, Harry. What do you want to talk about?"

"You know, Mike, you're an interesting bloke. Done some acting I hear; not a bad musician by all accounts; bit of a wiz with software. They say you're a smart fella, worked on synthetics. Can you guess which one of your many interests I'd like to chat about?"

"The Judy?"

Harry was on him. He screamed into Mike's face. "Yes, the fucking Judy!"

Mike felt a bit better now that Harry had dropped the mask, but not much.

Harry continued to yell at him, their faces inches apart. Mike waited for the punch line, but it was a long time coming. Finally Harry reached the end of his torrent of abuse and leaned back. His eyes, framed by the thick black old-fashioned rims of his glasses, stared at Mike through the spots of rain on the lenses. He spat out the question he'd been building up to. "What did you do with the code?"

Now Mike knew he was in real trouble.

"I don't know anything about any code."

Harry didn't move; he didn't even blink. "Get out here," he said.

To one side of Harry's meaty skull, Mike saw the Judy step gracefully into the scant light cast by the corner streetlamp.

"Anything coming back to you?" asked Harry. "No? How about this?" and he gestured to the Judy.

It opened its mouth to speak. Mike had a brief moment of confusion as he listened. The sound that came out wasn't speech. It was a recording of the track Android Dreams from the performance not an hour ago. As Mike listened, the layers of sound were stripped away, leaving only the repeating rhythmic loop, the staccato drumming, that Mike had recorded from the Judy's tapping fingers. It seemed like a very long time ago.

"Recognize that?" said Harry. "Tell him what it is, Dave."

"It's an audio translation of a numeric code sequence."

"A code sequence." Harry nodded. "Would have gone unnoticed if Chopper here hadn't brought Cassie down to the club for a test run. Unlucky for you. You see, Mike, there's only one place that code sequence could have come from, and you're looking at it."

Harry leaned forward. "Now, tell me Mike, how does that unique code sequence, that very secret code sequence that was locked away in her memory, end up being broadcast on stage in your fucking song?"

Mike didn't answer. He knew it was hopeless, but he ducked to one side and sprinted as quickly as he could past the Judy. It shot out a hand faster than he could see and gripped him by the arm. He waited for what he knew was coming next.

Harry stepped up behind him and spoke directly into his ear.

"You're going to tell me, Mike. You're going to tell me what you know."

"And then what?" Mike gasped, not wanting to know the answer.

"And then we'll see."

# 27

# Pattern Master

In the dark comfort of his suite atop the Shard, Wei played the recordings from his synthetics, projecting the three different points of view onto his wall screen.

There was the rapid smooth approach from across the road as they closed in on an unwary Nick Turner. When they were almost on him, he caught sight of them; a weapon was fired, and one of the points of view scanned the ground before falling sideways on the pavement and then blanking out.

The remaining two featured a choppy sequence of hand-to-hand fighting, blades glinting in the melee. There was a bright flash and a whining noise, and both of the projections on Wei's wall went blank for a few seconds.

When the visuals returned, he saw the night sky and a blur as the synthetics got to their feet. Then they were chasing Turner, closing on him as he ran, his grey coat spread like wings. As they gained on him, he leapt for the top of the Embankment wall and almost fell.

One of the synthetics lashed out with a blade, and he saw it catch Turner high on the shoulder. Wei stopped the recording and replayed the moment in slow motion. He watched the blade slice through Turner's coat, producing a quick vivid slash of red.

The recording resumed at normal speed, and he saw Turner take a flying dive at full tilt into the Thames. There were a few seconds of visual chaos while the synthetics jumped on to the wall, and then the view of the dark river, the faint trace of where Turner had hit the water.

The view flicked briefly to infrared and there was nothing to see but the cold, dark water. It went back to normal, and he watched as the synthetics fired a coordinated pattern of bullets into the river, the blue muzzle flashes lighting the splashes that they raised on the surface.

The firing ceased and he scanned the Thames through their eyes. Nothing. Then there was the pinging alert of an approaching police drone, and the two synthetics whirled, ran back to pick up the third, and tumbled into the waiting car. The recording ended.

Wei closed his eyes and let his mind run over the sequence of events that he had just watched. The first time he had seen it, through live transmission from the synthetics, it had been a blur of action. Now he meditated on what he had seen; something near the end of the recording nagged at him.

He opened his eyes and re-ran it, slowing it down at the point when the drone proximity alarm had sounded. In ultra-slow high res he watched the second or two of recording as the synthetics turned their heads. There. Behind the pillar and the lamppost: a witness. He tried multiple combinations of enhancement to the recording, but couldn't make out more than a blurred dark blue figure in the shadows. Nothing he could do about that, and in any case the chances were the police surveillance cams would have caught the action. He moved on.

Next he reviewed the last moments before Turner dove into the river. It was hard to tell for sure but the wound to his shoulder looked significant. Not lethal by any means, but it was going to slow him down.

Finally he watched the river gunfire sequence but learned nothing new. If the bullets had hit him, he supposed, the body would have surfaced. He concluded that Turner had probably struck for the bottom to avoid being shot; the river was six or seven metres deep at high tide. He could have gone downriver or swam across to the South Bank; there was no way to know.

Wei shut off the projection and walked over to the window. The rain that had begun as a faint drizzle earlier in the evening was heavy now, screening from view all but the lights of the city. He tried to see if the light was on over in Harry's office suite, but with the poor visibility he couldn't make it out.

"Come in," he said.

The door to the suite opened, and as if he had been waiting for his cue, a man entered.

"Damage report."

"Significant trauma to mid thorax skin and underlying structure. Blast damage to cortex. Unit is likely not repairable and suitable only for cannibalization for parts."

Wei nodded, but kept his eyes on the city outside and the blurred navigation lights of the Coronation Tower, as though he could penetrate the veil of rain by sheer force of will.

"Where is Jeremy Wells?"

"He was admitted to the King William V Hospital earlier this evening. His condition is critical, and he is under surveillance in the Intensive Care Unit."

"The drug was only supposed to make him malleable so that we could get the access codes. What happened?"

"Either the dosage was too large, or the effects on his physiology were greater than expected. He collapsed in the middle of the bar and the ambulance was called before our agent could intervene. In any case, the situation made intervention extraordinarily difficult."

"Is he expected to regain consciousness?"

"Unknown."

"Get access to his room and his belongings. I want his powerscroll."

"We requested access but the ICU is secured overnight and they will not allow visitors before tomorrow morning."

Wei moved fractionally, a tilt of the head and a drop of the shoulders. His voice was acid.

"Then send someone in the morning. Send the cuckoo."

"Yes, Mr. Wei."

"Leave."

The man stepped back into the doorway and the door closed behind him.

Wei remained where he was. He turned his gaze from the distorted view of the City to the rivulets running down the outside of the window. They twisted and curved across the glass, a complex chain of interactions driving their paths. Together they combined to create a pattern that shifted and changed unpredictably, a pattern that was unreadable. A pattern of chaos.

# 28
## Castlehaven

Nick reached up and grabbed the bronze mooring ring hanging from the lion's mouth. Its pale green face stared out over his head, looking forever at something on the opposite bank, the bank where a short time ago he had almost been killed. His feet scrabbled against the Embankment wall and found enough of a foothold for him to haul himself up out of the river. He stood there in the rain and looked at the stern face surrounded by its wreath-like mane.

*When the lions drink, London will sink,* he thought, then, *Bloody hell, get a grip, Turner.*

He scanned the other side of the river. The synthetics were gone. So was his gun, at the bottom of the Thames along with his coat and his phone. He checked his trouser pockets. He still had his keys, his money card, and the storage drive that Mike had given him.

Nick moved his injured arm. The pain had subsided, but it still hurt and he couldn't see how deep the cut was. He looked up above the lion's head to the lamppost. It wasn't far, but he'd have to do it all with his left hand and he was weakened from the fight and the swim across the river.

*Better sooner than later.*

Using the mooring ring like a stirrup, he planted his foot in it and pushed up hard. He grabbed the base of the granite pedestal supporting the lamppost and pulled himself on to the top of the Embankment wall.

The rain was heavier than before, and the few people walking along the South Bank had their umbrellas tilted into it. Focused on staying dry, they weren't likely to pay him much attention, and the rain would also help to screen him from surveillance cameras. The traffic above on Waterloo Bridge was moderate but moving rapidly, and he figured the drivers wouldn't have noticed a soaking wet man climbing out of the river. Londoners were used to seeing stranger things on a Friday night, in any case.

He took a look at the wound in the lamplight. It was a five or six inch slash down the back of his arm. Clean but bleeding; it would need suturing. Nick used his left hand to pull his knife from his boot. He cut a strip from the bottom of his shirt and tied it over the wound using his good hand and his teeth. He was shivering from the cold and the post-combat shock, and it took him a few minutes to complete the task. Afterwards he put the knife back in his boot, then walked up the steps to Waterloo Bridge to look for a cab.

Licensed cabs were plentiful, headed for the West End, but they only took electronic payment and that would leave a trail. It took about ten minutes, but at last an illegal cab appeared out of the rain, skimming the edge of the pavement, the driver aware of him in his peripheral vision. Nick signaled to the cabbie and the taxi pulled over to the kerb. He opened the back door and almost fell inside.

From the other side of the bulletproof plexiglass, the driver eyeballed his soaking clothes in the dashboard video screen as Nick closed the door. His voice came over the roof speaker.

"You're a bit wet, mate."

"Yeah, well, fell in the river, you know?"

The cabbie laughed. "Right. Where to, then?"

"Camden. Castlehaven."

"Got it." The cab pulled away from the kerb and joined the traffic, a mass of bright cells streaming through the city arteries.

The adrenalin flowing through his body was making it hard to think clearly, and he was still shivering. He focused on steadying his breathing while he ran through a calming mantra in his head. By the time they were on Kingsway, his autonomous systems had begun to normalize and he was able to start working out his next steps.

He had to get off the streets and patch his wounds. His field medical kit was at the flat he'd shared with Allie, along with a lot of his stuff that he hadn't had time to move yet, including his other gun. Allie wouldn't be happy to see him, but there was nowhere else he could go. That was just how it was. They'd both have to deal with it.

What else? He needed a phone to connect with Scruff about the gear he'd ordered. He needed a phone now, he realized. He looked out of the window as the cab entered Russell Square.

"Pull in by the hotel," he said "I need to get something."

The cab pulled over and stopped. Nick loosened his belt and pulled some cash from a concealed pocket in the back. He counted out some bills and put them in the drawer in front of him. The driver pulled it forward to his side of the plexiglass and took the money.

"Deposit," said Nick. "Hang on, I'll be right back."

The driver nodded and turned his attention to his GPS police scanner and the traffic flowing around the cab. Nick got out and went to the autovendor in the hotel wall. He tapped the screen and worked his way through the menu choices. Electronics – Communication – Phones – Basic Models. He needed voice and text, nothing else. He found a model that would do and slotted in a money card. It would leave a digital footprint, he knew, but there was no other way to do this.

A glass panel slid open in the front of the autovendor. He reached in, grabbed the flat, black plastic box, and dashed back to the cab.

The cabbie drove off as soon as he was inside. Nick opened the package and prepped the phone, linking in his various numbers from his online cloud safe.

They crossed the neon strip of Euston Road and sped north past the railway station. Nick thought for a moment of leaving the cab here and jumping on a train, any train. Just head north and lie low for a while. Then he remembered what Wei had said to him about getting out of town, and he felt the anger rising.

*Bastard.*

Nick wasn't 100% sure that the synthetics were Wei's, but he knew they weren't Harry's, and he didn't think the Russians had the cash to keep three of them in the field.

The pubs and bars in Camden were very busy and between the drunks crossing the road and the traffic crawling along it in the rain, it was slow going all the way up the High Street. As they crossed the canal, Nick said, "By the Hawley is fine."

The cab turned right and pulled in just past the Hawley Arms. Nick paid and got out. He watched the cab drive off and waited for the lights to vanish round a corner before he set off up Chalk Farm Road. The flat was a few minutes' walk further on. He stayed close to the shop fronts as he went, periodically checking behind him.

He reached the Reject Ironmongers and stopped outside the metal grilled door that was sandwiched between it and the café. Nick put his key in the battered lock and turned it. There was a click. Allie hadn't changed the lock.

He stepped into the short corridor, closed and locked the door behind him, and flipped on the light switch. He waited. No sound either from upstairs or outside the door he had just closed. He went up the steep flight of stairs to the flat, the thick moldy carpet muting his steps. At the top he listened at the door to satisfy himself that Allie wasn't home, then let himself in.

He turned on the lights and went straight to the bedroom. Lying down on the floor, he reached back under the bed until his fingers met the handle of the small canvas bag he'd put there many months ago. He pulled it out, the dust from beneath the bed sticking to his wet arm, and went to the bathroom.

First he pulled the shoulder holster and his gun from the bag, loaded the weapon, and re-holstered it. The bloody shirt went in the bath, along with the strip of cloth he'd used as a bandage. Then he pulled out the medical kit, numbed his arm with the anesthetic auto-injector, and cleansed his hands and the cut with antiseptic foam. The bleeding was slow, and the wound looked clean – no fabric or other contaminants that he could see. He ripped the packaging on the surgical stapler and, staple by staple, he closed the wound. After that it was a matter of gauze, bandages, and some painkillers and antibiotics.

Nick cleared up the mess, picked up the gun, and went back to the bedroom where Allie had piled his clothes on the floor in the corner. He rummaged through them, changed out of his wet things, and put on the holstered gun. Back in the living room, he looked around. The framed photographs were gone; the evidence of his life in this space had been removed.

He sighed and went to the kitchen. At least the Scotch was still where he'd left it. He took the bottle and a glass back to the living room, plugged the phone in to charge, sat down in the armchair and started pouring the Scotch. Three glasses later, Nick Turner was sound asleep.

# 29
## Water of Life

Hodges finished pouring the Scotch and handed a glass to Larry. He watched as Larry all but finished the drink in one big swallow.

"Thanks for coming in, Larry."

"Yeah, well, 'Odge, I wouldn't like to make an 'abit of it." Larry scanned the four walls and the door of the interview room in which they sat, deep in the bowels of Fenchurch Street.

"You did say that you wanted to meet somewhere else," said Hodges.

"This wasn't exactly what I 'ad in mind, 'Odge. Less dogs, more coppers. Not really an improvement from my point of view."

Hodges smiled.

"It's one of the few private places left, Larry. There's underground – the tunnels, the sewers, the old bomb shelters – there's moving vehicles, and there's the river. Not much else. The old cop shop, however, has no one but us old coppers."

Hodges took a drink.

"It's an odd thing, Larry, but you're safer talking to me here than just about anywhere out there on the street."

"Yeah, says you. 'Ow do I know everything's private in 'ere?" Larry looked at the walls, the ceiling.

Hodges tilted the glass in his hand, examined the gold oval of Scotch.

"A question I ask myself every day." He looked at Larry over the top of the glass. "I tap the icons that are supposed to shut off all the monitors when I'm talking to privileged sources. But I don't know if that really means that no one's recording it. Nothing has happened in 20 years to make me believe otherwise, but who's to say? You can't move out there," Hodges nodded upwards, "without leaving a trace. Why should you expect to move in anonymity down here?"

Hodges drank down his Scotch and refilled his glass.

"You know me, Larry. I've been in this game a long time. Learned everything I know about this city out on the streets. I mean, don't get me wrong, I know how to use the tools I've been given. I know how to interpret the predictive analytics, scan the time-condensed interviews, assimilate the data sets, all that bull. But there's no substitute for just knowing people. We're born into a world where everything is tracked, everything is analyzed, but the one thing you can't predict, even now, is what two men will do when they sit down together and talk."

Larry held up his empty glass, wiggled it slowly.

"Well, apart from the obvious," Hodges laughed and refilled Larry's glass.

"What's going on then, 'Odge?"

"That Russian data squirt from the Corrie Tower that I told you about."

"Yeh. Been scratching my 'ead about that one."

"Russians popped up on the radar again tonight. Do you know Alexander Gorchakov?"

Larry shook his head.

"Something of a cult artist. Specializes in interpretations of the body. Anyway, he had a bit of a run in with some rough people earlier this evening. Someone interpreted his body; they cut off four of his fingers."

Larry shrugged. "So? That's a Russian gang punishment, innit? He probably pissed off someone high up in the Russky mafia."

"Yes, but it's a punishment dealt out to members of the Bratva, not civilians. Which means Mr. Gorchakov is part of the mob. Now we have two incidents in two days signaling that the Bratva is active. They've been quiet for a good few weeks. I've been wrong before, Larry, but my gut tells me there's a link. I can't tell you what yet, but something connects your boss's problems and our newly mutilated artist. Anything else you can share about your operation that might help me here?"

Larry shook his head. "Can't think of anything. The Judy's back. Turned up with a bit of memory missing but otherwise fine. The boss is out and about with it and some of the lads. It's taking up all 'is time, figuring out who done it. Obsessed, 'e is."

"Well, Larry, keep your ear to the ground will you? It feels to me like something's going to blow up."

"Will do, 'Odge."

There was a knock at the door. Hodges got up and opened it. The duty sergeant stood in the corridor.

"I know you didn't want to be disturbed, Sir, but there's a surveillance video you should take a look at right away. Shooting incident."

Hodges smiled. "It's turning into quite a busy night. Catch you later, Larry"

"I'll just finish my drink if you don't mind, 'Odge."

Hodges nodded and left the room. Larry turned his attention to his Scotch.

Sixty seconds later the door burst open and Hodges was back.

"Larry? Where's Nick Turner?"

# *30*
# His Master's Voice

Valentin picked at the remaining food on his plate as he watched the tracing software do its job. He'd hacked Xander's phone earlier and despite the encryption programs, had extracted Nick Turner's number. The tracing software was working its way through the phone networks and now it was just a matter of time. Valentin was nothing if not patient.

After he'd left Xander at the cemetery, he'd come back here to the Bratva headquarters not far from the derelict Stratford Olympic Stadium. The urban wasteland that surrounded the ruin, circled by one of the few remaining Thames tributaries to flow above ground, was the undisputed turf of Valentin's mob. The flat above a corner grocery shop from which he directed operations was as anonymous and secure a location as could be found in London.

There was the ping of an incoming call. Valentin tapped an icon on the screen. A window opened showing a dark haired man looking up. Behind him was the immobile shape of a thin angular quadruped with long curved running blades where there would have been the legs and feet of a living thing. It had a sinuous spine, like a greyhound, but with sensors and combat blades deployed along its length. Made entirely of black composite materials, it was designed to move with speed and stealth.

"Yes?" asked Valentin.

The dark haired man gestured to the mechanical hound. "The *Borzáya sobáka* is ready."

"Good. You can release it as soon as the trace is complete." He looked at the tracing program to check progress. "Not long, I think." He tapped the button again and the window closed.

Valentin picked up a frayed and battered paperback book from the desk. The cover was tired and beaten, its corners worn to a fine furred softness, and it was held to the book itself by yellowed tape. On the cover a faint drawing of a vicious looking black cat was barely visible, its claws like talons, one paw holding an antiquated gun. The title and the name of the author had long since been eroded. It was a testament to its value to Valentin that the frail and worn collection of pages existed at all.

He looked at it without expression. He put it back down on the desk, and said to himself in a soft voice, "Who are you then?" Valentin drew a deep breath and pushed it out.

He rubbed his eyes and looked around the room at the tired carpet, the peeling wallpaper, the plaster ceiling rose that had been overpainted so many times its shape was a blur. He looked at the window, a rectangle built of smaller ones stuck together with grime and dirt, then at the sharp bright screen on the desk and the small, matt black piece of machinery that drove it.

Valentin got up from his chair and walked around the room looking at the walls with his slow, sad eyes. He'd been in this room a thousand times and he knew the lines in the wallpaper, the cracks in the paint, the cobweb in the corner.

Next to the door, on the wall, was a round black bulge housing an old Bakelite switch. The switch itself was a thin black lever topped by a metal ball. He reached out and put his thumb on it. He knew that it connected to nothing in the room that worked, but he pressed down on it anyway. The resistance of the switch against his thumb was satisfying in a way he couldn't describe and it dropped with an audible click. He stood with the ball of his thumb against the ball of the switch and looked at it as though it were something new.

There was a low chime from behind him. He turned and walked back to the desk, reached out and activated an icon with a smooth swipe of his finger.

London appeared on the screen, the long dark winding path of the river separating the bright sprawl of the city to the north and south of it, mapped out in the interconnecting patterns of the people who lived there and the data that defined them. At this moment, Valentin cared only about one piece of data among the billions that were at his fingertips.

He tapped an icon at the corner of the screen and a video window opened. The dark haired man was picking his nose. The dog-thing stood like a statue.

"Send the Borzoi."

The dark haired man wiped his hand on his overalls and leaned towards the hound-shaped machinery. "*Okhota*," he said. The composite beast leapt forward, gone from the screen in a flash. The dark haired man gave a thumbs-up and Valentin shut off the video link.

He watched the Borzoi's projected route flicker and shift across London as it incorporated live information updates. It was a jagged and convoluted line that would adapt to avoid visual or camera sightings. The journey would take more time, but it gave a lower chance of being intercepted than a direct path. The route optimized then blanked out. The Borzoi was running dark. There would be no further communication until the kill.

Valentin was nothing if not patient. On his screen a red dot was blinking slowly over Castlehaven.

# *31*

# Idle Hands

Xander regained consciousness for the second time in 24 hours, on this occasion in his bed at the top of his house in Highgate. Armitage had treated his injuries and left him with several kinds of heavy duty painkillers. He'd swallowed a handful and lain down in his bed, then passed out almost immediately. As the drugs had worn off, the throbbing of his injuries had brought him back to a state of semi-paralysis, afraid to move and get more drugs in case the pain worsened, but anxious to do something about it.

He looked at his bandaged hands in numb despair. The punishment that Valentin had meted out was both surreal and harsh. He found it hard to believe that it had happened, and yet from the shape of his hands it was clear that it had.

He forced himself to sit up. The room was illuminated indirectly by the orange glow of London through his rain spattered window. Xander reached out and took some pain meds from the selection on his nightstand and as they saturated his bloodstream the pain subsided to a dull ache.

He walked over to the window and looked out at the city. The rain blurred the view, screening out even the aircraft warning lights that blinked at the top of the Coronation Tower. He envisaged the man in his suite near the top of that tower, and his money, and how close he had come to taking it. Then he looked around his studio and felt anew the beating and the humiliation and the fear of what might happen if the trail led Harry to him.

He had no good options.

Nick had brought him into this, but he was being pursued by Valentin, and Harry too, for all Xander knew. In any case, Nick had already made it clear that Xander was on his own.

Zelley had been a generous patron, but he wouldn't get mixed up in this. Perhaps if Xander could navigate his way out of the mess Zelley would help him get biomechanical prosthetics to replace his missing fingers, but he had to stay clear of further trouble first.

And Valentin? The Bratva was a closed door to him. He was fortunate that Valentin hadn't had him killed there in the cemetery.

Xander's biggest worry was that Harry would somehow find out his involvement in the attempted theft. Valentin's punishment was one thing, but Xander had no illusions about what would happen if Harry knew that he had been the conduit for the software that had messed up his synthetic. As far as he knew, though, the trail would only come back to him if Nick revealed his identity, and Nick probably wasn't going to last the weekend.

He still needed protection until things were settled. There was only one place left to go: the one who had connected him with Nick, the architect of the whole fucked up situation, the one person in London who might stand between him and Harry. Might.

Xander looked at the phone for a long time. *If you lie down with the devil, you wake up in hell,* he thought. Then he leaned forward and said, "Call Wei."

The phone was silent as it made the connection, through a series of anonymizers and encryption sites, then he heard it ring. It rang for a long time before the call was picked up. A smooth voice, not Wei's, came over the speaker.

"Yes?"

"I need to talk to him."

"Why?"

"I will tell him, not you." said Xander

"He is not taking calls. You can leave a message. What is...?"

A voice cut in, cool, level, precise. "Leave us."

"Yes, Mr. Wei."

Xander stared out the window, trying to pick out the lights of the Shard through the night and the rain. He pictured Wei in his suite across the river, on the other side of the city.

"Why are you still living?" Wei said.

"What? I...what do you mean?"

"I assumed that by now your comrades would have deposited you at the bottom of a canal."

Xander stammered. "I, they, it was not my fault. The product did not work."

"So I heard. Nonetheless, they have a long history of blaming the messenger."

"I was punished. The Bratva punishment."

"Ah." There was a pause. "A harsh thing for an artist to endure. You have my condolences. Why are you calling me?"

Xander coughed. He stared hard through the window into the night.

"I need help. Protection."

"But it is unnecessary now. You have already been punished."

"Not from Valentin, from...Harry."

There was a much longer pause.

"Why would Harry have any reason to seek you out?"

"Well, none, as far as I know. But there is Nick. If he talks to Harry then he could make the connection to me. And there is Valentin. He could implicate me in your plan."

"My plan." Wei's voice was a dry echo on the line. "What does Valentin know about me?"

"Well, nothing, I think."

"Did you talk to him about me?"

"I, no, I don't think so. I don't remember saying anything."

"Did Valentin have you beaten?"

Xander felt tears come to his eyes. He nodded silently for a few seconds before he gasped out "Yes. Yes he did."

"Do you remember what you told him?"

The tears were running down Xander's cheeks. "They beat me until I passed out. I don't know what I said."

"Then you are in danger, Alexander. Stay where you are. I will send someone to your house."

Xander nodded again. "Thank you," he said in a hoarse whisper.

Wei ended the call. Xander stood looking at the rain outside. It splashed against the window as the wind blew in fits and starts. Each new burst of rain wiped out the trails of drops from the previous one, scattering them from the glass before creating new winding rivulets that twisted and combined in unpredictable patterns. Xander nodded as he watched them descend.

"Down. Always down," he said.

# 32

## The Judy Bricked Me

When the phone rings between midnight and sunrise, it's usually nothing good. The call that Nick received that night was an exception.

He picked up the phone to hear a voice tell him "Get your arse out of bed; you've got work to do."

Nick was groggy from the anesthetic and the Scotch. "What the fuck?" He looked around the flat, got his bearings.

There was a dry laugh at the other end of the line. "Gotcha. It's Mike. Remember me?"

Nick scrunched up his eyes. "Yeah. How did you get this number?"

"Scruff. Owed me a favour. Funny how that works. He told me to let you know your gear's ready."

"That all you called for? Cheers. Love to chat, but I've got a lot going on at the moment."

"So I hear."

"What do you mean?"

"I had a run in with your boss tonight."

Nick got out of the chair, drew his gun and walked into the bedroom. "Oh yeah?"

"Yeah. Charming bloke."

Nick parted the curtains and looked out the bedroom window at the street outside. The lights illuminated the pouring rain, but it was hard to see anything moving out there except for the few passing cars.

"How'd he find you?"

"Incredible. You wouldn't fucking believe me if I told you. Another time, maybe. Anyway, he knew I'd worked on the Judy. He had it kick the shit out of me, and I told him about your visit. Sorry."

Nick finished his review of the street, then went to the back of the flat.

"Not your fault, mate. You wouldn't be talking to me now if you hadn't told him. He was on to me, anyway"

"Yeah, actually that's why I'm calling you. He let me live on condition I turn you in. Told him I could track you down."

Nick looked out the back window of the kitchen. Pitch black. Rain against the glass.

"Thanks for the warning," Nick continued. "You'd better find somewhere to lie low until this blows over."

"Actually, that's not what I had in mind," said Mike. "I want back at him. Figure you might be able to help me do that."

"I don't think you want to go there, Mike, he's a bad person to mess with."

"Surprisingly enough, I know that, Nick. Too late now. Look, you know what I can do. How do I hurt him?"

"In the wallet, where else?" Nick stared into the darkness outside. "All right, we'd better do this fast. Here's what you don't know. I was after Harry's money Thursday night. The code you extracted from the Judy is an access code. You put the code into a unit at his desk and you get to his bank accounts. I was going to extract the code, move his money, split it with my… partners, and leave town."

"What did you want to do that for? You work for the bloke."

"Worked. It's a long story and it can wait. Anyway, you know how that all turned out." Nick trailed off.

There was silence at the other end of the line.

"You still there?"

"Yeah," Mike said. "This code, though. You know it's only half of what you need, don't you?"

"What?"

"There are two halves to the code."

"How the fuck do you know that?" said Nick.

"Your old boss did a lot of yelling at me a few hours ago. He's good at that. One of the things he yelled quite a few times as the Judy was twisting my arm was, 'Does he have the other code? Does he have Jem's code?' Naturally, I didn't have a bloody clue what he was on about so I said no, and because I didn't have a bloody clue what I was on about, I was very convincing. They stopped kicking me around after that."

While Mike was talking, Nick walked back through the living room into the bedroom. He looked out the front window again.

"The old bastard," said Nick. "All right. Can you trace someone?"

"You've seen my workroom."

"Right. I need you to find Jeremy Wells. He's a stockbroker, finance guy, that sort of thing."

"Give us a minute."

"You can call me back."

"Literally. Give us a minute."

"Right." Nick pulled one of his jackets from the pile in the bedroom. It was a black bomber jacket with multiple pockets on the inside. He put it on and started filling the pockets with items from his canvas bag: ammunition, anesthetic injectors, useful odds and ends.

"Found him."

"Where is he?"

"Hospital, apparently."

"What happened?"

"From what I can skim, he's in the intensive care unit at the King Billy. Some sort of drug problem. Comatose. Access restricted."

"All right. We need to get to him. I'm going to go there and see if I can get in to see him."

"Why? He's not going to be able to tell you anything."

"Can you hack a powerscroll remotely?"

"Course. You have the access code?"

"No."

Mike sighed.

"Does that mean you can't?" said Nick.

"Just once, can you bring me something to do that's only moderately fucking difficult?" Mike sighed again. "Yes, I can do it, but I'll need time."

"How long?"

"As much as you can get me."

"I'll see what I can do."

"We'll need some gear, though. You'll need to be wired. A body polymer with short range transmission."

"Text it to Scruff. Tell him you have something to add to the shopping list."

"Lovely. Meantime, I'll see if I can smooth your way at the hospital. Get you privileged visitor status."

"Thanks. I'll be in touch."

"You know, you're easier to work with at a distance. Less property damage."

"I only break things when I have to."

Nick ended the call. He sat down and started writing a note to Allie. He was halfway done when he heard the familiar clang of the street door closing at the bottom of the stairs.

He put the unfinished note under the bottle of Scotch, and went to the flat door and listened. He knew who it was climbing the stairs. For a moment he considered going out the back window, then he went and sat down in the armchair.

The door opened. It was Allie.

"Nick? What are you doing here?"

"You're out late."

"That's none of your business anymore."

She looked him over, taking in the bomber jacket, the gun in the holster, and the half empty bottle of Scotch.

"I think you should leave."

"I get that a lot these days."

"What do you mean?"

"That fucker Wei. Told me to get out of London."

"You told me you were getting out of town when you came by the studio. I didn't expect to see you again after that."

"Yeah, plans change. It's only temporary. I'm going to have to go; I just don't want that bastard thinking he can order me around. Anyway, I can't stay here and wait for one of them to get me."

"One of who?"

"Wei, the Russkies, the cops, Harry."

Allie stared at him.

"You know," he said with a humourless grin, "seems like everyone wants me these days but you."

"Jeez, Nick. Can you leave it alone? We've been over it."

"Yeah, and it feels like it's been all over me."

She turned away. "Always making jokes."

"There's always something funny."

Her shoulders lifted slightly and he felt a cold pit open up in his stomach. She turned around and walked up to him, yelling, "No there bloody isn't! There bloody isn't, Nick! There's nothing funny about this, nothing at all!"

He took a step back.

"You never say what you're feeling. You never talk about anything. You're just locked up in your own little world. Some of these bloody robots are more emotional than you are."

Nick looked past her. His mouth was a thin line.

"I've tried, I've bloody tried, but I'm tired, Nick. I can't try anymore, don't you see that? When you asked me to marry you, it was too little, too late."

Nick looked at her, grimaced.

"This is all I am, he said. "You've known me long enough. You want a poet, go find a poet."

"I don't need a bloody poet, Nick, just someone who'll talk to me."

He looked around the flat as though he was about to make a quick exit.

She stepped to one side. "Like I said, it's time you left."

Nick nodded. He zipped up the bomber jacket and walked past her to the door.

"Be careful, Nick. Just because we're finished doesn't mean I don't care about what happens to you."

He paused, his hand on the doorknob. "Yeah. You too, Allie."

Nick went through the doorway and closed the door behind him. He went down the dark stairs to the street door in a rapid and near silent trot. At the bottom, he listened. It was as quiet outside as it ever was in London.

"Well," he said to himself, "whatever's out there can't be much worse than what's in here." He pulled the door open and in one swift movement, he stepped outside.

# 33

# Black Dog

London is crisscrossed with streets and alleyways, roads and paths, all tracked and monitored by video cameras, synthetic remotes, and drones. As complex as the city's geography is, the product of millennia of expansion, nothing can move in the main thoroughfares without being recorded, logged, and reported to the authorities.

But London is also riddled with tunnels and underpasses, patterned with parks and woodland. Not every space can be monitored. Bipeds have a hard time passing unseen, but a fast low-slung quadruped with a well-written avoidance program can be almost invisible.

The Borzoi leapt from the Bratva office in Stratford, skimming the ground on its thin curved running blades. Wherever possible it drifted through darkness, but it was always as far as it could put itself from watching eyes, whether they were at street level or in the skies above.

Onboard sensors monitored for active police drones and sentinels, mapping out a continually changing course that minimized any chance of detection. Moving with stealth meant also that it sent no signals back to Valentin at the Bratva office. The Borzoi was programmed to communicate only if the target was not at the expected location, or upon a successful kill.

A short distance from the office, the Borzoi slowed and slunk its way into a narrow sewer entrance under a railway embankment. Travel below ground was slower but brought with it the best chance of avoiding detection, and the Borzoi was designed to move through confined spaces that a human could never reach.

It was soon creeping through Victorian sewers and long-forgotten wartime tunnels as it journeyed westward. In the sewer network it pushed with its curved composite blades on the damp old bricks lining the floor and sides. When the sewers did not go in the right direction, it crossed into used service tunnels, telecommunications conduits, ventilation shafts, any underground or shielded route that it could find.

At one point it moved through an abandoned underground mail station, passing a long-forgotten office in which a bottle of Scotch and two glasses lay in a dusty drawer, and where not 48 hours earlier a police inspector and a criminal had been having a private chat.

The route west took it below Bethnal Green to the Regent's Canal where it slipped into the rain-patterned water without a sound and swam, using its curved blades as fins to weave its way forward like a serpent. When it reached City Road Lock it surfaced and clambered up the steps, along the lock and down the other side into the water again, a grey blur.

As it travelled, the Borzoi's onboard predictive analytics took in the real time environmental input coming through its sensors – police presence, likely traffic patterns, weather conditions – and combined it with stealth mapping software to optimize its route. At this point, though, the presence of the canal made things easy. The canal would take it on a winding northwestern pathway that curved to a point that was only hundreds of feet from Castlehaven.

The canal narrowed as the hound swam beneath the eastern portal of the Islington Canal Tunnel. The canal was nowhere deeper than couple of yards, but here in the tunnel it was shallower. The Borzoi moved more slowly through the dark water, hemmed in on all sides by the quarter millennia-old structure.

The half mile of tunnel ran northwest beneath Upper Street and the residential neighbourhoods surrounding it. Above it at surface level, Londoners were almost all indoors, sleeping, turning restlessly, or rising for an early shift, while the few outside on the streets at this hour staggered home, or kept watch, or went about business best conducted under cover of night.

At the other end of the tunnel, the Borzoi emerged into the waning darkness, still swimming, invisible below the surface. It continued on along the canal, passing the silent narrowboats, the occupants sleeping peacefully mere feet away from the agent of death passing them by.

It moved ever westward, under the wide bridge that carried the railway lines that headed north from St. Pancras Station. It was now little more than a mile from Castlehaven and its planned rendezvous with Nick Turner, but still it maintained communications silence, using only passive sensors to measure the surrounding activity.

Another 20 minutes of slow steady underwater progress took it to Kentish Town Lock, and here it left the canal for the final time. The Borzoi surfaced under the Kentish Town Road bridge and waited motionless in the dark and the rain while its sensors read the world, its angular snout pointed up into the sky.

Nothing was moving and it resumed its journey, trotting through a low arch under the railway to Castlehaven Open Space, a small park surrounded by trees. Here, crouched by a set of swings in a playground, it plotted out its final route to the kill zone.

Mere seconds passed and then it was off again, hurtling with precision under whatever cover was available, through back gardens, hugging the sides of buildings, until it had no choice but to come out onto Chalk Farm Road, not far from the parade of shops that featured the Reject Ironmongers and the battered metal grilled door that Nick Turner had entered not six hours earlier.

The Borzoi switched from stealth to combat mode, and all onboard sensors swept the area for its target. It was ready to complete its mission. It was ready to kill Nick Turner.

# 34
## Code Alpha

Hodges pulled the police car over to the side of the road. The rain was finally easing off, but he kept the wipers going after he shut down the engine. He looked at Larry, a picture of discomfort in the passenger seat next to him.

"This the place?" said Hodges.

"Yeah." Larry looked up and down Chalk Farm Road as though he were terrified that despite the rain and the darkness, someone would recognize him. "That metal door by the ironmongers."

Hodges watched him with amusement as his head swiveled this way and that. "The car windows are one-way, Larry. No one's going to see you."

"Yeah, well, 'Odge, that doesn't mean they won't know I'm 'ere. I'll just keep an eye out, if it's all the same to you."

"Whatever you like, Larry. You coming with us, or you going to stay here?"

Larry looked back at the two armed officers in the rear seats and watched for a few seconds as they prepped their weapons.

"I'm coming with you 'Odge. Nick's a mate. I don't want anything stupid to 'appen."

"Fair enough." said Hodges. "You armed?"

"What if I am?"

"I'd just like to know who's got a gun in case there's any shooting."

141

Larry glanced up and down the road again, as though something out on the street would tell him how to answer the question.

"Yeah, I've got a gun."

Hodges nodded. "Try not to use it, alright Larry? I'd rather not have to arrest you and explain who you are."

Larry grinned. "We're on the same page, then, 'Odge."

"All right," Hodges looked back at the two officers. "For the record, lads, it's Detention Protocol. Deadly force response only if imminent threat to life." Hodges looked out of the front windscreen. "You can stun the bugger if you like, though."

"Carlisle, you take the back garden. Thompson, cover me while I get the front door. And bring the net; we might need to bag him. Larry, you're with me. Let's see if you can talk him into coming along without any trouble."

Carlisle's body armour rustled as he turned to open his door. The rain pattered on the back seat as he left the car and pushed the door closed behind him with hardly a sound. In the rear view mirror, Hodges watched him vanish into the night.

Time passed, marked by the sweep of the wipers clearing the rain from the windscreen. An icon lit up on the dashboard monitor. Carlisle was in position.

Hodges turned off the wipers. He was about to order Thompson out of the car when events began to move very fast.

The grilled metal door, faintly reflective in the low street lights, vanished to be replaced by a dark rectangle, out of which stepped a tall lean figure in a black bomber jacket. Nick Turner.

Later that morning, in the crappy grey light coming through the station window, Hodges would think over the next five minutes again and again and wish that things had gone very differently.

Now, though, he felt the adrenalin squirting into his bloodstream. He spoke quickly into the collar mike. "Carlisle. Target on the street. Southbound. Assist."

Turner was walking south on Chalk Farm Road, down towards Camden Town. He had his back to the police car.

"Let's go," said Hodges.

"Fuck!" said Larry, and the three men exited the police car. Hodges had his gun drawn. Thompson was carrying a long black metal tube with a trigger grip.

They followed Turner from the opposite side of the road. He was moving at a rapid pace. As they hurried to catch up with him he angled across to their side and carried on walking southward, hugging the long high brick wall on their right that bounded the Stables Market and continued all the way down to the railway bridge just before the canal.

Carlisle emerged from a side street opposite and joined the pursuit. Hodges and the other two were thirty paces behind Turner, and he was about to tell Larry to call to him when things went out of control.

A proximity alert buzzed in Carlisle's body armour, and he whirled to look behind him. Something swept towards him, low, angular and fast. He gave a startled cry, raised his gun and fired, but the thing kept coming. It leapt, flying past him at head height. There was a flash of silver in the streetlight and Carlisle fell to the pavement, both of his hands wrapped round his neck, blood pouring down his chest.

The thing landed, crouched low on splayed blades. Hodges and Thompson, their suit alerts also buzzing, turned to face the threat. Larry had stepped back against the brick wall. He called out, "Nick!"

Nick Turner had turned when he heard the gunshot and he watched as the hound sprang toward the three men who stood between it and its quarry.Larry, the rearmost of the three, was the closest to the thing. He pulled out his gun and shot at it. The gunfire flashed blue in the night, and the reports echoed down Chalk Farm Road. It was futile. The bullets bounced off the composite armour and it closed in.

"'Odge!" Larry cried, and it was on him.

The Borzoi leapt upwards, slicing off his gun hand at the wrist with one blade, while another slashed across his belly. Larry gave a stifled cry, fell to the pavement and was still. The Borzoi rolled past him and up against the brick wall where it sprang into a low crouch, ready to pounce again.

Thompson was in motion. He pointed the long black tube at the hound, and as it paused before its next leap he pulled the trigger. A high tensile mesh net flew from the end of the tube, expanding as it went, and wrapped itself around the Borzoi. The thing went into convulsions, its blades working at the net, trying to cut loose.

Nick looked from Larry lying motionless on the ground, to the Borzoi thrashing at its bonds, to Hodges staring at him with cold despair on his face and a gun in his hand.

"Don't move, Turner, you're under arrest!"

Turner laughed. "You stupid fucking copper, we'll all be dead in a minute. Look." He pointed at the Borzoi.

Hodges glanced at the thing. It had already cut away part of the net and continued to saw away with its killing blades. When Hodges looked back at Turner, he found himself looking into the barrel of a gun.

"Hold it!" Turner gave a warning tilt of his head. "We're even now, sonny Jim. Well, not exactly. You and your mate are next in line before it gets to me." Turner nodded at the Borzoi.

The proximity alerts had triggered calls from Police Control. Thompson was in conversation with a dispatcher through his collar mike: "Officer down, UGV engaged, suspect on the scene." He looked from the Borzoi to Turner, and back again. "Code Alpha!" he yelled, and then he took aim and fired at the Borzoi.

"You're coming in, Turner!" Hodges shouted over the pounding of Thompson's gun. "Drop your weapon!"

Turner backed away, yelling at Hodges. "I'm out of time, matey. You might make it to your car if you're quick, but I can't wait. That thing's coming for me!" He looked at the writhing Borzoi, unharmed by Thompson's bullets, at Larry bleeding out into the cold rain, and finally he stared Hodges in the eye, holstered his gun, turned his back, and ran.

Hodges watched him run, the dark shape shrinking in his sights, becoming one more shadow on the London streets. Behind him the gunfire stopped. Hodges whirled around to see the Borzoi shrugging off the torn net and Thompson turning towards him, his mouth open wide in a soundless scream.

# 35
# Thieves in the Night

It was quiet in Harry's office at the top of the Coronation Tower; only the clock on his desk made a sound as it ticked away the seconds. He sat at his desk staring at the screen while over on the sofa, the Judy sat motionless, its systems idling. Harry himself was a statue, moving nothing but his eyes; they flickered over information as it popped up or scrolled across his screen.

He'd been sitting here since his return from the New Clarendon, while his gang spread out across London looking for Nick. So far, nothing.

He swiped a couple of icons on the screen and tried to connect with Pete. The icon blinked steadily for a few moments then it cut to his messaging service. "If you know who this is, you know what to do."

"Bollocks," Harry said to the recorder, and glared into the darkness, as he cut off the call. He rang Colin.

"Yes, boss?"

"What's going on, Col?"

"Sorry, boss?"

"It's all falling apart. Cassie goes missing; comes back with a chunk of her memory gone. Pete's out there somewhere but I can't get hold of him. Nick's gone – we know that, but still, after all these years? And where's Larry? No one's seen him since yesterday. He's a useless bastard, but he's usually more reliable than this. It's not how we operate.

We've been top dog on our turf for years and now we're like a load of amateurs. Like I said, what's going on?"

There was a long silence at the other end, then, "Look, boss, this isn't easy to just talk about over the phone. Things have been a bit tense with the lads since, you know…"

"Since when?"

"Since you got the Judy."

It was Harry's turn to be silent. He looked over at the unnaturally still form of the Judy on the sofa.

"You still there, boss?"

"Yes I'm still bloody here. What's the Judy got to do with anything?"

"Well, you know. It's competition, isn't it?"

"What are you on about, Col?"

"Look, boss, I told you this wasn't going to be a simple chat. Some of the lads, they're thinking the Judy's a replacement. They reckon sooner or later you're going to decide you don't need 'em any more. They're thinking this might be the end of the run, time to find something else before you decide they're finished. These machines are popping up all over now, who's to say…"

"Stop. I get it."

"…and it got worse after that business earlier on with the muzo in the alley. I mean, why even bother to have us there…?"

"I said I get it, Colin. Bloody hell. I should've called Martin, day one. I knew something was up, something rotten, I could smell it. So, then, you reckon Larry's done a bunk too? Reckon he's in on it with Nick?"

Colin sighed. "I don't know, boss. I'm as confused as everyone else. I didn't think Nick would do something like this, so I just don't know any more. We were tight, you know? We've been in lots of scrapes and always come out on top together, and now this. I s'pose people change. Or things happen to change them. Anyway, here we are."

Harry nodded. "Yeah. Here we are. Keep on it for me, Colin. Can we get someone over to Larry's place?"

"I'll have Chopper take a look."

"Right." Harry reached out to end the call, paused. "Thanks, Col."

"No problem, boss."

Harry tapped the icon, sat back in his chair. He looked over at the Judy. It might as well have been a sculpture, a piece of art dropped off from the Tate Modern. Woman on a Sofa.

He got up and walked over to it, to Cassie. Its sightless gaze stared straight ahead into the room as Harry crouched down and looked it right in the eyes. Cold glass. Cassie looked out unblinking, through him into the middle distance. He put one hand on its neck. Cool, almost cold. The skin felt real, but not quite. He took his hand away and stood up.

The old fashioned phone on his desk rang, a jangling twentieth-century reaction to a call from one of a handful of people who had the number.

Harry walked over, picked up the handset. "Yes?"

It was Allie. "Harry, things are getting worse."

"Yeah, tell me about it."

"I'm serious Harry. There was a battle on my street just now."

"You what?"

"A battle. Guns, an explosion."

Harry glanced at his screen. There at the top a news story was scrolling. Unconfirmed Report: Gunfire in Camden.

"Are you all right?"

"Yeah, yeah, I'm fine. It's just…Nick was here. He left about five minutes before the shooting and I'm worried…"

"Nick? Right, right. Listen, Allie, where did he go?"

"What? Oh, he didn't tell me. We had a sort of a row and he ran off down the stairs. I heard the security door bang shut, and then there was nothing until the shooting. I was in the kitchen washing a glass and the next thing I know, there's guns going off and then a couple of loud bangs."

Harry was typing rapidly on his keypad. Messages flew out to Colin and the rest of the gang as he continued talking to Allie. He hit another key and the Judy blinked twice as its systems came back online.

"Do you suppose he's OK, Harry?"

"Sorry?"

"Nick. Do you suppose he's all right? Is there some way you can check? I've tried calling him but he doesn't answer me."

"I... no. He doesn't answer me either, Allie. We've had a falling out."

"Oh, God. He told me he was leaving town. Is it over me?"

"No, course not...I mean, yes it could be. He hasn't said. Have you told him about us?" Harry continued to send messages to the gang while he spoke, dispatching Colin and Billy to Camden, Dave to the scanners to see what he could pick up on the police chatter.

"No, not a thing," said Allie. "I thought it was bad enough when I turned him down last week. I couldn't make it worse for him."

"I know, I know. Look, love, I've got the lads out looking for him. If he comes back to the flat call me straight away, all right? He's in some sort of bother and he's going to need our help whether he wants it or not."

"Yes, he mentioned Wei. Said that he'd told him to get out of London. Nick was very pissed off about it"

"Wei? What's he done to Wei?"

"Didn't say. He did say something about some Russians who were after him too."

"Bloody hell. Is there anyone in London he hasn't pissed off?"

"What do you mean?"

"Never mind. Look, just call me if you see him."

"I will. Let me know when you find him, Harry. I can't help but worry about him."

"Yeah, I understand. This whole thing is a bit of a mess, isn't it? It'll look different in the morning, I promise. You stay at the flat and we'll get things sorted out. I'll send someone over to keep an eye on things outside. All right?"

"All right, Harry. Night."

"Night, love."

Harry tapped an icon, ended the call. He tapped another and the Judy stood up.

"Get to the flat. Check the area."

Without a word it turned and left the office.

Harry ran his fingers over his scalp and pushed himself away from his desk with his feet. He got up and walked to the window where he watched the diminishing rain as it pattered against the glass, the drops running down in crooked paths that were chopped into sections by the slats of the blinds.

He stared out into the night. Although the lights of London and the rain made it hard to see, he knew that the night sky above the clouds would be lightening fraction by fraction as the dawn crept westwards. On the other side of the river, he could see the lights of the Shard, and one floor below the roofline the dark strip that was Wei's suite.

Harry spoke to the darkness, his voice almost a whisper.

"You old bastard. What have you done?"

# 36
## Still Life

Xander was watching the skies over London. The rain had ended and the last few drops were hanging in blurry bulges near the bottom of his window. It was still too early for the first planes to show their lights as they ran down their glide paths to the tarmac of Heathrow. Overhead other eyes were circling in the sky and watching them as they slid in over France and Germany, still a half hour away from landing.

Xander turned away and looked back into his studio at the glass version of himself, the last few centimetres of the trepanned skull waiting to be filled.

He stared at his hands, then he went into the bathroom. The electric razor lay where he had left it two days ago and he reached out with his crippled right hand and picked it up. It felt heavy, unwieldy, between his thumb and two remaining fingers. Xander walked over to the statue and stepped up on to the pedestal in front of it.

Leaning forward, his head over the top of the glass skull, he used the razor to shave his long curling hair with short trembling strokes. It fell in clumps, adding to the mass of human debris already piled up in the glass shell. By the time he had finished shaving off all of his hair, the pile rose up above the crown of the statue's head. He stepped back down and gave it a critical look then he got up again, leaned over, and applied the razor to his eyebrows. With a smile he turned off the razor and hopped down from the pedestal. He threw the razor to one side.

Then with both hands he picked up a glass saucer that lay on a shelf next to the statue. He inverted it and placed it on top of the skull, like a bishop crowning a king. Xander stepped down from the pedestal and looked at it with a grim smile.

He was finished. Now all he had to do was come up with a name for it. Eighteen years of labour, and he hadn't settled on what to call his latest child.

*There's time enough for that*, he thought; *the important thing is that it's complete.*

In the next moment he knew, as does anyone who lives alone, that there was someone else in the room behind him. There had been no sound, no change in the light, but something told him that another body was in the room. He was about to turn around, when the interloper spoke.

"Nice gaff."

Xander looked back over his shoulder. There in the half-light was a shadow in a suit. It stood angled to one side, the head tilted as though sizing up the room.

"Too many stairs, though."

Xander turned to face the intruder. "How the hell did you get in?"

"The usual way. Through a door."

"I hope you didn't break anything."

"Nothing that can't be fixed." The man stared at the sculpture against the wall. "Well not yet, anyway."

"What the hell do you want?"

"Mr. Wei asked me to come over and take care of you."

"Why couldn't you have just rung the bell?"

"There's a police car out front."

Xander sighed. "Do you have a name?"

"Pete."

"Fine."

"What's that?" said Pete, pointing at the sculpture.

"It's my latest work. I just completed it."

"You an artist, then?"

Xander sighed again, gestured around the room with one of his broken hands.

"Oh, right. What's it called?"

"Still Life."

Pete nodded. "Sounds heavy; what's it mean?"

"It's a statement – a reflection on existence and mortality. I think it's probably my best piece yet.

Pete gave it a sideways look. "Don't get me wrong or nothing, but it doesn't look like it was that hard to do. I mean, filling a glass sculpture with hair and stuff. Where's the art in that?"

Xander walked over to the window and looked out at the city. "Have you ever thought about the fact that not one cell that was used to build your body in your first years of life is still alive?"

He turned around and looked at Pete.

"Everything that you think you are is really just a pile of cells in a constant cycle of genesis and apoptosis. The body that you live in has been completely recycled. Not one cell remains from those you started with. So, are you today the same person you were when you were born? It's a paradox. You're a ship of Theseus."

"I'm a ship of what?" Pete snapped. "Cut the arty crap. What's your point?"

"You're a squatter in your body. The cells you're made of – they're not really you."

Pete shrugged.

"So, then. What are you? Who are you?" asked Xander.

"Bit obvious." Pete looked from side to side as if inviting other opinions. "I'm me."

Xander glanced at the ceiling. "It's hard to explain to people like…" He stopped himself.

"Look, there's the artistic vision and the sheer time involved. It's taken me eighteen years to build it out of the dead cells cast off by my body. I don't mean to sound rude, but I wouldn't expect you to understand."

"Ah." Pete took a step back, nodded as he reached inside his jacket.

"Eighteen years to build a copy of yourself out of dead body parts, eh? I could have saved you a lot of time, mate."

"What do you mean?"

Pete pulled out a gun and shot him in the chest. Xander fell back, shock blanking his face. He dropped to the ground in an untidy pile, writhing on the studio floor. Pete stepped forward and stood over him.

Xander's ruined hands pressed against his bloody chest. With wide eyes he looked up at Pete.

"One more for luck, eh?" Pete said, and he shot him in the face. Xander stopped moving.

"See? How long did that take? Eighteen seconds?"

Pete holstered his gun and looked around the studio. He took a last look at the sculpture, tipped his head sideways again and squinted at it.

"Nah, not my cup of tea."

He turned and walked out of the studio.

Through the window behind him the distant warning lights of the Coronation Tower blinked endlessly on and off as the first anemic light of dawn bled through Xander's window.

# 37
# Digital Dreams

Inspector Hodges rubbed the palms of his hands across his eyes. He gave the thin light coming through the windows of Fenchurch Street station a weary glance, then picked up his mug of tea and took a long swallow.

"Inspector?" said the face on his desk screen. "I'm waiting."

Hodges looked at his mug as though it were an old friend that he didn't want to say goodbye to, and put it down on the desk. He peered at the screen with itchy eyes and spoke in a voice thick and cracked from lack of sleep.

"You've seen the recordings. It was a bloody mess. I've got two men dead and another in intensive care. Three of the gangs on my patch are suddenly acting a bit lively and one of them's deploying some serious firepower. I've been up all night, my bastard hand hurts," Hodges waved his bandaged left hand at the screen "and you're wasting my fucking time. What else am I supposed to tell you?"

The face on the screen raised an eyebrow. "I'm aware of the obvious, Inspector Hodges. You're paid to uncover the obscure, so I'll ask you again, is the civilian just a bystander or part of this mess?"

"You can read as well as I can. He's Larry Summers, a consultant of some sort, according to the few records we have. Got some petty theft convictions, and did a little time for them. He was carrying a weapon, fired it at the dog. If you'd let me get on with it I might be able to give you some answers, though I don't know why I should."

"Yes you do, Inspector. The moment our interdiction drone responded to the Code Alpha from Thompson and engaged the Unmanned Ground Vehicle, this became a cross-jurisdiction affair. Incidentally, a little thanks and humility wouldn't go amiss here, since you'd have a lot more than that hand wound to worry about if we hadn't stepped in. You were seriously outgunned; the UGV is clearly a combat model. Let's take another look, shall we?"

A second window opened on the screen and a recording started playing. It was an aerial view of a nighttime London street: Chalk Farm Road. There was no sound, but the night camera visuals were sharp despite the rain. Metrics played around the edges of the recording: height, speed, range. Centre frame, the Borzoi wriggled in the net; to the right Larry was prone and immobile on the pavement. Thompson and Hodges stood to the left but Turner was out of frame. As the recording played, Hodges watched himself pointing his gun at Turner, still out of view under the Camden Lock railway bridge. Then, as the hound began to cut loose from the net, the scene changed.

Hodges saw himself turn to look at Thompson. He saw the Borzoi appear to widen as it shed the bonds of the net and its combat blades moved into an attack posture. It seemed to Hodges now as it did then, that they all moved in slow motion compared to the Borzoi. Thompson fired repeatedly at the thing, emptying his gun, the flashes bright blue in the night vision of the drone's camera.

Then it was loose. It took Thompson by the leg and got to work on him with the blades. Hodges could hardly bear to look at the screen; he knew what came next. He fired his own gun, uselessly, at the Borzoi as it finished off Thompson, neatly and efficiently dissecting him then crouching on its running blades, ready to spring. Hodges felt again the thrill of fear that had flashed through him at that moment, remembering how he'd wanted to run but couldn't. How sure he had been that he was about to die.

On the screen, missiles streaked from either side of the camera's point of view down at the Borzoi. It rolled to one side, its sensors picking up the new threat a fraction too late. The rockets hit it square on, blasting chunks of brick out of the wall in a bright searing flash that momentarily blanked out the drone's camera view.

When the scene was once again clear, the Borzoi was a tangled wreck in the rubble. Hodges looked at himself on the screen, flat on his back a dozen metres away.

He had no memory of what had happened during the few minutes after the explosion, and he watched the recording fill in the blanks: the lights coming on in neighbouring flats; the police cars and ambulance pulling into the frame; a small crowd gathering; the flurry of activity as the medical staff worked on the fallen men; Hodges himself being helped into an ambulance. The recording ended.

"So. There we are, Inspector. Your fat being pulled out of the fire. Now, between your casualties and my assets, we ran up the taxpayer's bill a little last night, so I think you'll agree that we're going to need to see some results out of this fiasco. Since there is no evidence of military or paramilitary involvement for the time being, the murder investigation remains a civilian matter. As your liaison, I will expect you to keep me fully informed of developments. I look forward to hearing from you about the status of Mr. Summers and the ownership of the UGV. Take care, Inspector."

The face on the screen disappeared and the frame shrank and vanished.

Hodges reached again for his tea and took a sip. With his other hand he tapped an icon.

"Jim?"

"Yes, sir?"

"What came of the Highgate incident last night, the artist with the missing fingers? I haven't seen anything about an interview. Weren't we able to find the bloke?"

"Alexander Gorchakov? No. There was no reply from the house, no sign of anyone inside. I parked an unmarked car on his doorstep to watch for him. Nothing yet, sir."

"I think we've waited long enough. Get a warrant to search the house. I reckon we can draw enough of a line to connect him as a person of interest in the Turner business."

"Right-o, sir."

A call alert popped up on the screen. Forensics.

"Thanks, Jim, got to run." Hodges dropped the duty sergeant's call and picked up Forensics.

"What've we got?"

"Onboard systems self-destructed so we can't retrieve much from those, not without a lot more time, anyway. What we do know is it's mostly Russian with some cannibalized parts from other sources. High end composites, probably military. Not much else in the carcass."

"You're not making my day," said Hodges.

"Not my primary objective. However, your car's monitors did pick up that it sent an encrypted data squirt right before the drone wrecked it."

"Better. Destination?"

"Unknown. It bounced off a public tower and vanished down a series of rabbit holes. We'll keep working on the UGV, but our best bet is to crack the transmission that your car grabbed."

Hodges nodded. "How long?"

"Hours. Maybe this afternoon."

Hodges finished his tea and put down the cup.

"All right. Listen, I'm playing this one really close and trying to keep outside influences at bay. How, um, *firm* is the identification of the dog as military?"

There was a knowing laugh from his screen.

"Hardly at all. In fact I don't know why I even mentioned it. It won't be in the preliminary report."

"Thanks," said Hodges. "Owe you one"

"You mean one *more*."

"Yeah, that. Don't ask me to settle up all at once, all right? Cheers."

"Later."

Hodges got up from his desk and walked over to the window. Outside, the rest of London was waking up. The light was thickening to a sickly grey as the streets filled with the everyday people on their way to work. Hodges watched them go by, wishing he were one of them.

# *38*

# Death in the Morning

Valentin slipped his backpack over his shoulders and left through the back door of the corner shop. He headed out along the Greenway, across the River Lea and past the crumbling shell of the Olympic Stadium. After the disaster in Camden early that morning, he'd evacuated everyone from the Bratva offices. The final data feed from the Borzoi had included some low res video recorded during its attack; it was grainy but clear enough that he could make out at least one dead policeman.

The morning was grey and overcast but the rain had stopped. He kept up a steady pace along the path until he arrived at the corner of East London Cemetery where he turned into the greenery alongside the path and clambered over the pointed iron railings. He walked more slowly now, following the zig-zag line of the railings so as to remain in the cover of the trees that grew alongside. His route took him down the less frequented western side of the cemetery, past the older graves.

He stopped for a few minutes when he drew near the grave of Elizabeth Stride, murdered almost two centuries ago by London's most famous killer. The white headstone was overgrown and the rectangular cement border of the grave was spotted with lichen and almost invisible in the tall grass.

Valentin had an affinity for London's many burial places, and he knew this spot as well as anywhere in the city. He was aware that he should keep moving, and that the police could even now be breaking down the door of the Bratva offices, but he couldn't help himself. He walked over to the grave and looked down at it.

The grave border and headstone were of relatively modern origin, but his thoughts were on the bones ten feet below the surface. Already, in the few centuries that had passed since her death, the city had buried her deeper.

London was a series of layers going back thousands of years. Every Londoner thought that the period in which they lived was somehow special, somehow different from all the others but in the end their time was just another layer in the accumulating sediment of the city's history. The dust, the rubble, and the dirt piled up and obscured the past, pushing it further from living memory until some day it might not be remembered at all.

*One day,* thought Valentin, *this marker will be gone, this cemetery will be covered over or built on, and no one will remember who lies here.*

He stood for a few minutes thinking about the places he had known growing up, the shops that were already closed or demolished, and the buildings put up to replace them, buildings that were already crumbling and adding to the detritus that was the foundation of the city. The wandering trail of his thoughts was broken as from overhead came the sound of a plane taking off.

He looked up at the grey cloud layer, wondering if somewhere above it a police drone was already stalking him. He shrugged his pack into a more comfortable position and began walking again, his route taking him back under the tree line and down to Grange Road. At the corner of the cemetery he hopped over into the Memorial Recreation Ground, and strolled along the backs of the houses until he came to the exit.

From here he took a curving diagonal route southeast, along footpaths through public parks whenever they presented themselves, and any available tree cover. It took him about an hour of steady walking, but about breakfast time he arrived at Royal Albert Way bordering the old dock. On the other side of the water was London City Airport.

The morning flights were scooting in and out on their steep paths over the city, fewer in number than on weekdays, but a brisk traffic nonetheless.

Valentin walked over to the Connaught Bridge and crossed the old lock on the pedestrian footpath. From there he walked to the terminal building beneath the snaking shadow cast by the Docklands Light Railway viaduct. He went inside, wandered over to the coffee shop, bought a drink and sat down to wait.

He didn't have to wait for long. The flight from Dresden arrived fifteen minutes early and he watched as the passengers streamed through the terminal. When a gaunt man in a black coat entered the hall, Valentin got up and followed him to the front entrance. A taxi pulled up as the man stepped to the kerb and he opened the door and climbed into the back. Valentin got in after him.

The driver looked at them in the rear view monitor. "Good morning, sir," he said, "It's good to see you back in London." The gaunt man nodded and the cab pulled away.

"How was your flight, Mikhail?" said Valentin.

The man turned down the corners of his mouth and made a non-committal gesture.

"Better now it's over."

Valentin nodded. They sat in silence and watched London go by as the taxi drove through Poplar, Limehouse, Shadwell. The double helix of the Coronation Tower popped into view every now and then as sight lines opened up at random through gaps in the rows of buildings lining Commercial Road.

"You really fucked things up, Valentin," said Mikhail quietly as they rounded Aldgate and drove along London Wall. "This was supposed to be a surgical strike. Hit him where it hurts – in his pocket – and disappear with the money. Instead you have woken him and the London police."

A flash of annoyance crossed Valentin's face. "I ran the operation by the book. We have been plagued with problems. The hack did not work as it was supposed to and the Borzoi ran into a police patrol and was destroyed. We have had a run of bad luck."

"Bad luck?" Mikhail turned his head to stare at him. "This is a little more than bad luck, Valentin." He looked out of the window again.

"Where is Turner?"

"We don't know, we lost him after the Borzoi went offline. He's running. I expect he's out of London by now."

"When this is done with, we will all be out of London, Valentin. We will finish the job tonight and then there will be a long stay somewhere far from here."

Valentin cast his sad eyes on the familiar landmarks passing by. "And our London operations?"

"There will be no London operations for a long while. If things are put right tonight, then perhaps you will be able to come back one day. We shall see."

Valentin pursed his lips and nodded. As they drove into the West End, he stared at the early risers threading the streets and wondered for a moment what it would be like to walk this town without a care in the world. He knew that it was going to be a difficult night. A very difficult night.

# *39*
## King Billy

It was still quiet on the streets as Nick Turner pulled up in the car park outside the self-storage unit on the edge of Ladbroke Grove. He killed the engine and got out. The car was an old piece of crap, but it had been easier to rip out the manufacturer telematics than it would have been on a new car. This didn't mean that the police wouldn't find it eventually, but in this day and age the problem wasn't detecting crime as much as it was having the resources and the inclination to deal with it. The police probably wouldn't get around to it for a couple of days.

The storage unit, like most such places, was located in an unflattering corner of the city, in this case between the Latimer Road tube viaduct and the Westway. Above him, cars whizzed by on their way out of the city, while away to his left dilapidated rolling stock carrying a cargo of Saturday morning shoppers rattled along the train tracks.

The roll-up door was already open on one of the units and he walked straight in. The lights were off, but he could make out shelves filled with cardboard boxes, and plastic crates lining both walls and what looked like the pieces of a market stall propped up in the far corners. A sign leaning against the wall read 'Analog Dreams'.

There was the sound of a box being dragged along the floor at the back of the unit, and then a voice.

"Nick."

"Scruff."

Nick walked further back into the unit. Scruff was busy moving records between boxes. From under the mass of hair he flashed a grin.

"Running late. Usually got the stall up for the early punters by now. You've cost me some sales, today, Nick, me boy."

"What? People actually buy this crap, then?"

Scruff stopped and gave him a look.

"Bloody philistine. These are collector's pieces, mate. Vintage. Look at this."

He held up a seven inch square of paper wrapped in a thick mylar bag. Nick squinted his eyes in the dim light to make out the writing on the white circle cut out of the middle.

"'The Sex Pistols. God Save The Queen'? What the fuck is this?"

"Vinyl single. Very limited edition on A&M, never released. Worth a mint."

"I meant why 'God Save The Queen'? Bit old fashioned. That's two monarchs ago."

Scruff put the record away. "Never mind," he sighed. "Let me show you something a bit more up-to-date."

He moved a couple of cardboard boxes aside and pulled out a large black duffel bag. After wriggling the zip open he shone a small torch inside.

Nick scanned the contents.

"Well thank god for that." He nodded, and Scruff zipped the bag up and handed it over.

"Something a bit easier to get hold of next time please, Nick. And make it a while before there is a next time, if you don't mind. I'd like my involvement in this to be over now, thanks very much."

"Yeah. I hear you. Thanks, Scruff." Nick headed for the entrance.

Scruff picked up a large box of records and followed him. At the entrance Nick headed off to his car while Scruff went over to a small van, calling back over his shoulder.

"Be careful with that lot, mate. Don't use it all in one place."

Nick waved as he put the duffle bag in the boot of his car. He partially unzipped it, took out a thin oval of translucent polymer, and zipped it back up again. He shut the boot and went round to the driver's door.

"Hope you manage to flog some of your old plastic."

"Vinyl," said Scruff.

"Yeah, that. See ya."

Nick got into his car and drove off towards Holland Park Avenue. At the Avenue he headed east through the south edge of Notting Hill and then past the groomed wilderness of Hyde Park and its long-buried river. The traffic flashed by: cars, buses, courier bikes, taxis. One of the cars held two Bratva members who would have been very interested to know that Nick Turner was passing by them in the opposite direction.

He went east along the same ancient route that Valentin and Mikhail had taken coming west, then angled down to Ludgate and past the great white bulk of St. Paul's Cathedral. There was a brief moment of open sky and greenery around the cathedral and then he was swallowed by the maw of the City.

He drove deeper into the belly of the beast, taking a winding route through some of the lesser byways. It would have been easier to cross the river at London Bridge, but that would have taken him past the Shard. Although crossing at Tower Bridge would bring him close to the Coronation Tower, he felt that, just barely, it was the lesser of two evils.

On the south bank of the river he continued east. A hundred years ago this had been an urban desert. Then it had been redeveloped post-collapse into a boom des res area of high end apartments and housing. Although it wasn't generally recognized, the crest of the decades-long boom had recently passed and the first signs that this part of London was on its way back down had begun to appear.

Some areas weren't able to command the prices they had in the past and lower income residents had moved in. Crime had increased and as a result security had been ramped up around the pricier properties. The buildings themselves had begun to show signs of age: cracks in the facades that weren't repaired as fast as they might have been; lights that went out and stayed out for weeks; business signs that were weathered or painted over. The public parks and waterfront walks were attracting both dealers and druggies, and well-heeled runners out on their early morning jogs saw syringes and bottles lying in the grass alongside the running paths. Nick didn't pay attention to any of it; south of the river was a different world as far as he was concerned.

In another ten minutes he was at the King William V Hospital, built a decade before on the site of an old print works at Surrey Keys.

He parked as close to the car park exit as possible and checked that the coast was clear. From the passenger seat he picked up the translucent polymer oval and peeled away a sheet of backing paper. Then he lifted his shirt, applied it to his stomach, and smoothed it flat. Within seconds the polymer had changed colour to match his skin. It was tapered at the edges so that once he had finished and pulled his shirt back down, it appeared only that he had put on a few pounds round the middle.

Nick punched a contact on his phone. Mike's bruised face popped into view on the small screen.

"I'm at the King Billy. How's it looking?"

"Hang on a sec, Nick. Yep, looking good. Ready to roll. Remember, I'll need as much time as you can get, so take a bowl of grapes or something."

"Why the bloody hell would I do that?"

"You're visiting a sick mate, right?"

"He's in a fucking coma."

"Just thought it would be a good diversion, you know? An excuse to keep you in the room a bit longer."

"I'll handle the tactical stuff, all right?"

"I'm just saying."

"Yeah, well that's enough of that. I'd better not hang about; don't know who else might be interested in Mr. Wells. I'm on my way. I'll call as soon as I get out."

"Good luck." Mike cut the line.

Nick put his gun in the glove compartment, his phone in his pocket, and got out of the car. One of a small number of visitors at this hour, he walked to the front entrance of the hospital and up to the reception desk.

"Hi, I'm here to see my friend Jeremy Wells."

The receptionist gave him a professional smile. "Which ward?"

"He's in Intensive Care."

"Oh yes, here he is. I'm so sorry. I'll need some identification."

"Of course." Nick held up his phone and tapped the ID icon.

The receptionist watched as his information came up on the screen. Nick made a show of looking at the news feed on the wall behind her, hoping that Mike was as good at hacking phones as he was at rebuilding synthetics.

The receptionist's eyebrows flickered up for a second, and then she turned and gave him a sad look.

"Your admission credentials are loaded onto your phone. The ICU is on the second floor; the lifts are just over there." She pointed down the hallway.

"Thank you very much," said Nick.

As he turned to go she added "I'm really sorry about your fiancé, Mr. Lyer."

Nick gave a loud spluttering cough and nodded his head as he went over to the lift. He stood in front of the doors trying not to laugh. It took forever to arrive, the doors took ages to open and close, and the ride up was achingly slow.

He stepped out into a corridor on the second floor. The security door opposite was a piece of opaque glass covered with notices and logos: King William V Intensive Care; Admission for authorized visitors only, please see Reception; CZB Synthetics. A small sign to the right of the door read 'Please present credentials for admission' and there was a silver phone icon next to it.

Nick walked over and held his phone near the sign. There was a chime and the frosted door opened.

He stepped in to be met by the comforting face and smile of the ward nurse. She was dark haired with warm rounded features that he found attractive and comforting at the same time. She was also completely synthetic.

"Hello, Mr. Lyer. I'm so sorry about your fiancé, Mr. Wells. Please, follow me." She turned and walked down a long corridor lined with doors.

Nick followed the synthetic, troubled by the emotional response she'd created in him. He knew that they were designed for that purpose, given features that had been statistically analyzed and created to provoke a sense of security and reassurance. He knew also that they were high performance machines with capabilities beyond any human nurse.

They could work 24 hours a day, and the newer models had built-in patient monitoring tools as well as medical interpretation software. The patient's medical records could all be accessed instantly and treatment administered faster than by a human.

Diagnostic software took care of ongoing patient maintenance once the doctor had made the initial diagnosis and treatment recommendations, and the doctor could be alerted instantly if there was a change in the patient's condition. They could take control of the synthetic to carry out interventional care if required, but it was capable of carrying out many procedures by itself. Within its torso was a collection of complex medical machinery that could be deployed in seconds to perform surgery.

Patients weren't always happy about the increasing trend towards automated care, but in certain areas such as intensive care or emergency treatment, it was becoming the norm.

In any case, Jeremy Wells wasn't in a position to complain about who was caring for him. Comatose since he'd collapsed at the Eye & Pyramid, he lay in a private room, his vital signs stable but his encephalographic activity minimal.

The synthetic led Nick to the room then stood to one side to let him pass. Nick looked around: advanced biometrics on the lock, sealed windows, no sharp objects, and the white semi-circles of recording cameras hanging discreetly from the ceiling at the corners. Not that it mattered anyway with the synthetic in the room.

Nick looked at the motionless shape of the broker on the bed. There was nothing to distinguish him from the synthetic that now stood behind Nick, silent and perfectly still. For a minute the three looked like an artist's installation, a set of sculptures meant to represent a moment or an idea.

Then the only sentient living thing in the room broke the silence.

"What's the prognosis?" murmured Nick.

"I am authorized to tell you that his condition is serious but stable. Significant organ damage was incurred and transplants will be necessary. Replacement kidneys are being bioprinted and will be ready tomorrow."

"When will he regain consciousness?"

"I'm so sorry, that is hard to say."

"I see." Nick looked around the room. "May I see his things?"

The synthetic moved fluidly over to one of the cupboards lining a wall and touched a button. There was a whirr and a click and a small door opened. Inside was a pair of shoes, a grey suit, shirt, tie, all neatly folded, and a sealed transparent plastic bag lying on top of them.

Nick reached in, picked up the things and put them on the bed. He took the plastic bag from the pile and examined it from several angles. It contained a designer powerscroll – one of the latest models – a pen, some pieces of paper, a stud phone, and a packet of contraceptives. He peeled open the bag, and took out the powerscroll. The battery light was green.

He pulled the flexible OLED screen out from the side of the metal tube; it clicked into the open position. The display illuminated and showed a password prompt. He put it under his left armpit and held it there as he reached into the bag with his right hand and went through the pieces of paper. Nothing meaningful: a ticket stub for a dry cleaners, a shopping list, and a scribbled phone number and the name Angela.

Nick put the bag to one side and slowly, still using only his right hand, went through each of the pockets in the pants and jacket. He found nothing. He brought the powerscroll out from under his armpit, and then clicked the button to withdraw the screen. It rolled back up into the tube and he put it back in the bag with the other things and resealed the bag. Then he peeled it open again, took out the packet of contraceptives and opened it; there was one left in the multi-pack. Nothing else. He put it back, and sealed the bag.

He leaned over the comatose broker and stared into his face for a moment. Then he straightened up, turned around, and left the room. Behind him, the synthetic quickly refolded the clothes, put everything back into the cupboard and closed the door. Stealthy and swift, it left the room and was walking alongside Nick in an alarmingly short space of time.

Nick glanced sideways at it as it appeared at the edge of his field of vision, startled by the unexpected speed at which it had appeared, but he did not otherwise acknowledge its presence. It accompanied him to the lift doors and stood as Nick pressed the call button. The lift took a long time to arrive. The synthetic waited next to him, smiling its warm sympathetic smile.

The lift arrived.

"We'll call you as soon as your fiancé's condition changes," the synthetic said. "I'm so sorry about everything."

Nick nodded. "Thank you," he said, and then he stepped into the lift, turned around and pressed the button for the ground floor. He saw the synthetic turn back to the ward as the doors closed.

Nick left the hospital and walked to his car. Once inside, he undid a couple of buttons on his shirt, peeled off the flat oval of contour polymer from his stomach and spread it out on the passenger seat. He swiped an icon on his phone and the screen lit up. Mike's face filled the window.

"How'd we do?" said Nick.

"The powerscroll was tight. Almost didn't make it. Where were you holding it?"

"Under my armpit."

Mike sighed. "I told you to get it as close as possible to your gut. The polymer has a very short range on purpose. Harder to detect."

"Yeah, well I'm not sure that would have looked very natural. Get to the point."

"I got his home access codes, personal bank accounts, bunch of contact information, lots of crappy games software, and a load of porn."

"And?"

Mike's face broke into a broad grin. "And a very interesting encrypted key."

"How long?"

"Running it now. Probably an hour or two."

"All right. I'm not planning on using it until tonight anyway. The only thing now is figuring out how to move the money."

"I think I've got that covered, too."

"How d'you mean?"

"I have a former employer who's trying to get me back into the fold. It's a long story, but I think if I agree to come back, then he might be willing to help move the dosh."

"Can we trust him?"

"Oh, no problem with that. He's not exactly straight as an arrow himself."

"Well, I'm out of options, so do your best. Check in this affie if you get anywhere. Oh, Mike. One last thing. Fiancé? Mr. Lyer?"

"Thought you'd like that. Probably should have told you to take flowers."

"Just play it straight next time, would you Mike?"

Nick cut the call on Mike's laughing face.

# *40*
## Good Morning

In a bedroom in a flat in West Hampstead that she didn't recognize, Sam woke up. She felt cold and tacky lying beneath the sheets in her clothes from yesterday. Her final memory of the previous night was of someone helping her into a taxi. She was fairly sure that she'd had another shitty conversation with Zelley, and she remembered Mike talking to her a lot, but she didn't remember anything they'd said. She rolled over and squinted at the window. It might have been mid-afternoon for all she could tell through the dirty glass.

She sat up in the bed and looked around. A cheap chest of drawers, a packed bookshelf, old wallpaper, posters of bands on the wall, a slight smell of damp; student flat, she decided. A long veteran of waking up in places she didn't recognize, Sam got up and went over to look in the mirror on the chest of drawers. No surprises there; she looked like hell.

Sam ran her hands back through her hair, and smoothed down her white top to try to make it look less creased than it was. It didn't help.

She looked around the room to see if she could find any clues as to whose place she was in, but there was nothing that she recognized.

Long practice had made her almost immune to shame. She went over to the door and opened it to find a hall with a front door to the street on the left and a couple of side doors on the right. Beyond that, the hall opened out into what looked like a kitchen area at the back.

*Ground floor flat, then.*

Sam turned right and headed back to the kitchen. A bright-eyed young woman sat at the kitchen table reading a magazine. She looked up with a grin as Sam entered.

"Hi."

"Hi," said Sam. "Any tea?"

"I'll put the kettle on."

Sam sat down in the other chair at the table while the young woman got up and went over to the sink.

"I'm Samantha."

"Yes, you certainly are. I'm Louise."

"How bad was I?"

Louise looked back at her as she filled the kettle. "I've seen worse. Not much, mind." She smiled again. "Are you hungry?"

"Not yet."

"Good thing. There's nothing much in the flat to eat."

Louise put the kettle on and sat back down.

"There's a spare toothbrush and that in the toilet if you like."

"I'm fine, really. Thanks."

"OK." Louise flipped a page in her magazine, stared at it.

Sam looked around the kitchen: glass jars containing lentils and pasta; a few wine glasses; a bread bin; a packet of biscuits; unwashed mugs. Through the window over the sink she could see the brick wall and kitchen window of the next door house. They sat in silence for a while.

Sam looked at Louise again. "Thank you," she said.

Louise looked up at her, nodded.

"I mean, I must have been a real pain in the arse. Sorry about that. I've got... I've got so much going on at the moment." Her eyes began to tear up.

Louise smiled. "It's all right. I thought as much. Let's get that tea sorted out, eh?" She got up and went over to the kettle. Sam watched her while she dropped tea bags into two mugs and poured the boiling water on top, then stood waiting for the tea to brew.

"I've just been binned by this wanker who I've been going out with for a long time. He's such a bastard. I tried so hard, I really did. I tried so hard to be the person he wanted. I went everywhere with him, talked to his friends. Some of it was really fun but most of the time I was just wondering if he thought I was good enough for him."

Louise dug out the tea bags with a spoon and poured in milk, then reached for the sugar.

"I don't take any…" Sam began.

Louise added sugar to both cups and stirred. She brought them over to the table, handed one to Sam, and sat down.

"Thanks," said Sam.

They sat in silence and drank tea for a little while.

"I can't hate Zelley, even though he binned me using a fucking robot. Part of me hates him for doing that and part of me knows why he did it. He's odd. He's gorgeous, I mean like a film star. Classic good looks, but a bit sad too. And he can be so charming, so witty. Ha. I could just imagine if I'd run into him with that robot and I'd dumped him because he'd been deceiving me with it. You know what he'd say? He'd say something like 'I'm beside myself.'" Samantha laughed. "He's like that."

Louise looked at her as if she was mad.

"Oh, I know. It sounds stupid. You must know what I mean though. Is that weird, to still love a man even when he's been a bastard to you?"

"I don't know."

"You've never been in love?"

"Not with a bloke." Louise looked over her teacup and grinned. "I'm queer."

"Oh. Right." Sam looked down at her tea as she drank.

"I know what you mean, though. There was this singer. Redhead. Wore tight dresses. Fucking cute, you know? We had a thing for a little while, but in the end she was married to the band. Last time I fall for a muzo. Do you go for musicians, then?"

"Never really thought about it."

"Mike was very worried about you last night. Nice bloke, Mike."

"Yeah? You trying to set me up?" They both laughed.

"We're mates. Have been for years." Sam smiled. "Me going out with Mike'd piss off Zelley in a big way."

"Why?"

"Mike used to work for him. He's really clever. Zelley owns this company that makes synthetics and Mike used to design the software for the personality profiles."

"And he gave that up to play in a band? Doesn't sound that clever to me."

"Yeah. There was some sort of falling out. Neither of them talks about it."

Louise finished her tea and got up to put the cup in the sink.

"So. What now?" said Sam looking up at her, then out the window at the grey sky.

"It's Saturday isn't it? Seems like a good day for a fresh start."

# *41*

## An Offer You Can Refuse

The lunch crowd at the Eye & Pyramid was normal for a Saturday. In other words, it was almost empty.

Quentin sat at a table by the window. He cast worried glances around the pub and watched Kevin as he walked over from the bar with a pint in each hand and sat down opposite him. Kevin handed him one of the glasses and took a sip from the other.

"How're you holding up, Q?"

"Bit shaky still, you know? Can't believe it, really. The hospital's not saying much but apparently he hasn't come round yet. Sounds really serious. I wonder what happened to him. One minute he was right as rain, next thing he's passed out on the floor. What do you reckon, Kev?"

Kevin looked out the window.

"No idea, mate."

"So, what you want to know then, Kev?"

"Got a few questions for you about Jem and some of his business dealings. S'alright, I'm not looking for anything proprietary. It's just – something funny happened this morning and I need to check on it."

Quentin shrugged, nodded his head.

"Alright, so this bloke calls me up, yeah? And he says he's got a once-in-a-lifetime opportunity, right? Offer-you-can't-refuse type deal. So I'm thinking Nigerian oil funds, or North Korean leadership stash, or one of those other online scams, but I keep listening 'cause I'm thinking it might be a good story later.

"Anyway he gets right to the point. Says if I'm very discreet and want to make some major money in a hurry, he knows someone who's got a proposition for me. Turns out he's the middleman for someone who was one of Jem's clients."

Quentin's eyebrows shot up and he spluttered into his beer.

"Shit."

"Yeah, I know, I know. Anyway, he was not a happy bunny; he was practically spitting the words out."

"So I say, 'all right, what if I did want to take the job? What's involved?'

"So he says he's going to have his boss meet me at this secure site, gives me the address and a password to login, then hangs up.

"I thought about it really hard. Could have been a sting operation, you know? A set-up. Then I thought, well, I hadn't done or said anything illegal, and it wouldn't hurt to find out a bit more. I mean, Jem's done some major deals.

"So I log in and I'm online looking at some stocky bloke I've never seen before, bald, getting on a bit, decent dresser, but a bit of a tough. Been in the wars a bit, know what I'm saying? Hard eyes.

"He looks at me and starts firing off questions – How well do I know Jem? Am I connected at Interbank? What's my background in Forex? Bloody hell. If I'd known it was going to turn into a bloody job interview, I would've said no in the first place.

"Anyway, this goes on for a bit and eventually he stops asking questions and tells me what he wants me to do. He wants me to get into Jem's accounts and find the password key to move some money for him but without anyone knowing.

"Then he asks if I have any questions and to make it quick.

"'What's in it for me, then?' I ask, and he says 'five percent.'

"'Five percent of what?' I ask. Wanna guess, Quentin? Eh? Go on. Have a go."

"I don't know. A hundred million quid."

"Not even close." Kevin leaned forward. "Seven hundred and fifty million nicker, mate. That's three and a quarter million my share, just in case you can't do the maths. So I think, well if he's willing to offer that much up front, and he's got to go back door and quickly, then I'll push him a bit, so I ask for ten percent. Nice round number, you know?"

Quentin raised his eyebrows. "What happened?"

"He just stares at me for a long time. Face like a stone. Then very slowly he asks me if I'm fucking serious. Just like that. Deadpan. 'Are you fucking serious?'

"So I say, 'Well? Are you?'

"He says, 'Look at me. What do you think?'

"I tell you, Quentin, I've never seen anyone look more serious in my whole life.

"So I say, 'yeah, alright, you look like you mean it, but so do I. That's a lot of money to move around, and I'll be sticking my neck way out.'

"He stares for a bit longer. Then he says, 'five and that's it,' sort of snarls the words out.

"For a second, only a second like, I thought about haggling a bit more, and then I thought, nah, best not. There was something about the whole thing that was starting to give me the willies, so I thought I'd better bail.

"So I say, 'look mate, I'm having second thoughts here, I'm not sure this is a good idea. '

"He jumps in: 'Don't you fucking play hardball with me, sonny, it's on at five or nothing.'

"I wasn't even trying to haggle but now I can see it starting to go pear-shaped, so I bail. 'Listen mate,' I say, 'You'll have to find someone else,' and I pulled the plug."

Quentin was wide eyed. "That was it?"

"Straight up."

"You've got some nerve Kev, turning down over three million quid."

"Yeah, well, you haven't heard the whole of it."

"What's that?"

177

Kevin paused for effect, leaned forward.

"Just before I can shut down the link, the bloke leans into the screen and says, 'You tell a fucking soul about this and you're fucking dead.'"

He emptied his glass with a series of long swallows, and put it down on the table.

Quentin looked around the pub. "Fuuuck-ing hell."

There was silence while Quentin took a drink, then he scratched his head and said, "Hang on, though. Without wishing to appear the master of the bleeding obvious here, you just did, mate – tell someone, that is."

Kevin looked out the window. "Yeah, well, you don't count."

"Let's hope that bloke thinks so too. What do you reckon it was?"

"Dunno. Didn't look like the financial embezzlement type. Some sort of gangster, I reckon. Any of this ring any bells with you?"

"No. I mean, Jem has a private customer portfolio that I'm not privy to. Could be something in there, I suppose, but one of the partners went through it and contacted all his customers to let them know that Jem's in the hospital. There's no reason why anyone would go outside the firm."

Quentin took another drink, then added. "Well, on second thoughts, they might if it was a bit dodgy like you just described. Sounds like this bloke could be some serious trouble. Hope he isn't too pissed off at you."

Kevin shrugged. "I'm not bothered. He looked like he had a lot of other things on his mind."

Quentin finished his pint. "Didn't think Jem would be mixed up with gangster types, especially a nasty piece of work like that. Hey, that's not him over there, is it?" Quentin nodded at someone over Kevin's right shoulder.

Kevin tilted his head a fraction, almost turned to look, then grinned.

"Nice try, mate. Trying to get out of buying your round? Come on, you're slacking."

# 42
## Absent Friends

It was another miserable gathering in Harry's lounge at the top of the Coronation Tower. Harry sat in his favourite chair staring at his glass of Scotch. Cassie stood over by the bar. The members of the gang, with the exception of Nick and Larry, were scattered around the room. It was an almost exact copy of the gathering that had taken place in this room two days ago.

"I can't believe it," growled Harry. "How much can go wrong in a couple of days?" He looked around the room.

"It's not like we haven't had a bad patch before, but Nick going off like that, Wei sticking his oar in, and then poor, useless Larry. Any word, by the way, Col?"

"Can't get anything out of Fenchurch Street. All they'll say is he arrived at the Royal Free in critical condition. Intensive care, armed guard, no visitors."

"Yeah? We might have to see about that. Anyway, the question is what the bloody hell was Larry doing over at Nick's? I sent Cassie over there last night to sniff around a bit. What's the story, Dave?"

Dave looked over at Cassie standing motionless at the bar. "We went over everything she sent back. Nothing on the ground to speak of, but she was able to rip some recordings from local monitoring stations although they're not very good. There was a firefight. Looks like military as well as police action; at least one drone involved."

Harry nodded. "You reckon there's a joint mil/pol operation going on? Maybe Hodges has some pals over at West Drayton?"

"Bit early to say, boss, but you know Hodges; he's never liked the military. Why would he bring them in unless he had to?"

Harry got up and walked over to the window, looking down at London spread out below.

"Fair enough. Maybe this is bigger than usual. We know Wei's involved so maybe there's an international angle. National security and that. There could be some big shit coming down. Terrorists, maybe, paramilitary types, government stuff."

Several members of the gang exchanged glances but no one wanted to speak. It fell to Colin.

"Seems a bit of a stretch, boss."

Harry turned and speared him with his gaze.

"Really, Colin? Why don't you help us out with that? Give us the benefit of your fucking education."

"Look, boss, I just think, we all think…"

Harry exploded. "We *all* think? We *all* fucking think? When did we *all* start to think? *I* think. I run this show. I have always run this show. I still run this show. *You* don't need to think. *You* need to answer questions and do what I tell you, all right, Colin?" Harry extended his right arm, his forefinger pointed at Colin's face.

Colin rubbed his chin as though Harry's finger had bruised him, then he turned away.

"That's fucking right," Harry continued. He looked at each member of the gang in turn. "Anyone else got an opinion?"

No one met his gaze. Everyone in the room stood like a statue in a gallery, with one exception. Without anyone having noticed, Cassie had moved from her station at the bar and now stood behind and to one side of Harry. Her eyes moved in a staccato pattern, taking in each of them as though they were a target.

"Right, then," said Harry. "Here's the plan. Dave, cut into the local military transmissions. Yes, I know, just get on with it. Peter, I'm still fucking waiting for you to find Nick." He gave Pete a particular look.

"Chopper, Billy, get out on the ground and figure out what's going on with the Russkies, the Poles, the Chinks, the whole fucking lot.

"Colin," Harry paused. "I don't know what to tell you. Use your fucking education and do something useful."

No one moved. Harry leaned forward. "Bugger off. Now."

Colin turned and headed for the door. The rest of the gang followed. They filed through the door of the lounge into the reception area and the lounge door closed behind them. Once they were in the lift Colin hit the button for the parking garage and it descended.

The green lights on the panel started blinking out one by one and it was quiet for a few seconds. Then Chopper spoke. "Col. What's going on, mate?"

Colin, like the rest of the gang, was looking up at the ceiling. He spoke without lowering his eyes.

"I…I'm not sure the boss has a handle on things, Chop."

"No shit. No fucking shit, Col. Nick buggers off, Larry gets hurt, and suddenly we're a bunch of useless fuckers? It's been coming ever since he got that bloody Judy. We've been on the scrapheap the last two months; it's just chickens coming home to roost."

"Chopper, I don't…"

"Come on, Col. It's obvious." Dave launched in. "He's had one eye on getting rid of us ever since the Judy walked in here. That shit about calling Martin the other night was just about the last straw. The boss was going to put him in to find it? Like he couldn't trust us to do the job?"

"Look, lads, I don't feel any better about this than you, but the boss is the boss and we've still got work to do. He's not sending Martin to do it, he's not sending the Judy to do it, he's sending us to do it. All right? Think about it for a minute. Jesus."

It went quiet in the lift. On the panel the spiral of green dots continued to blink out. They were a few floors from the parking garage when Pete spoke up.

"Chopper's right, though, isn't he lads?"

No one answered. The lift stopped and the doors slid open. Chopper and Billy stepped out, followed by Dave. Pete had just started to go after them when Colin's hand shot out, grabbed him by his tie and shoved him against the wall of the lift. With his other hand, Colin grabbed Pete's right wrist and pinned it to his chest.

Colin spoke quickly and directly into Pete's ear. "I said you were a flash git, Pete, but you're a mouthy one as well. You've been giving it some since you arrived, and it's really getting on my tits. Now, pay attention, 'cause it's the only time I'm going to say this. There's a lot of history in this mob, history you're not a part of. If you want to be a part of the future, and I'm not sure you do, you need to shut the fuck up and do what you're told. I'm not going to ask you if you understand me, or if you get it, or any of that bullshit. I'm going to take it as read. Just know that you're one snide comment away from being gone."

Colin stepped back, releasing his hold on Pete's tie and wrist.

Pete made a performance out of adjusting his tie, then walked past him. He stared Colin in the eye the whole time as he got out of the lift, but he didn't say a word.

Colin joined the rest of the gang in the parking garage. They'd looked dejected in the boss's office a couple of nights ago but today they looked defeated.

"All right. Let's get busy, shall we? Get out there, see what you can find out, and call it in if you have anything at all. Then five o'clock, everyone to the Crick."

"What for, Col?" said Billy.

"'Cause I think we're all going to need a drink before this night's out."

# 43
# Friends Close

Mike looked around Zelley's apartment, taking in the expensive furnishings and the view of London through the vast picture window. "So this is how the other one per cent live."

Zelley smiled. "I know. It's a bit shabby. What can one say? It's a weekday pied-à-terre. A different story in the country, but in London one has to make do."

Mike grinned. "If you want to slum it, you should come round my flat."

Zelley gave a mock shudder. "Now, my dear boy, I hate to race through the delicious foreplay but I'm dying to know. Have you seen the light? Are you coming back to work for me?"

"Something like that," said Mike.

Zelley looked genuinely surprised. "I was being rhetorical. I assumed after seeing what you were doing for a living last night and looking at the state of your face this afternoon, that perhaps you were looking to borrow some money. You do rather look as though you've been through the wars."

"That's actually why I'm here, Z. I've been dropped into the middle of something. Last night after leaving the club I was smacked around by a gang looking for information."

"Can't possibly imagine what you would know that would make it worth someone's while to beat you up."

"I worked on a damaged synthetic. Someone had tried to hack it to retrieve a password from the core and while I was digging around trying to fix it, I ran into something rather funny. Any guesses, Z?"

"None whatsoever, but I'm all ears, especially if it's as humorous as you seem to think."

"Funny peculiar, not funny ha ha, Z. This synthetic, it didn't have a governor." Mike stood and looked Zelley in the eye. "Now, you and I know that's impossible because it's not legal and there's only a handful of people on the planet who could get away with it, and two of them are looking at each other right now."

Zelley looked away through the window at the view of London then walked over to a drinks table set out in one corner. He picked up a decanter and poured brandy into a glass. Turning, he said "Fancy one, Mike?"

"You know I don't drink the hard stuff these days."

Zelley reached back to the table, poured another brandy. He picked up both glasses and walked over to Mike.

"You look like you might need one today." He held out the glass.

Mike gave the drink a long look and then he took it.

"Thanks."

Zelley raised his glass. "The King."

Mike raised his in response. "Fuck him."

They both drank.

"And with the awkward social conventions behind us, tell me; what do you want Mike?"

Mike took another swallow from the glass.

"I'm proposing a new arrangement. I'll come to work for you again, but we have to sort out an understanding about what we are and aren't going to do. Mostly it's about keeping things kosher."

Mike raised his eyebrows. Zelley raised his glass and drank.

"And I'm only working part-time, and I need you to help me with some money."

Zelley nodded. "Mike, years ago you and I used to lend each other tenners to buy drinks. The sums might be larger now, but I think we can still reach an arrangement about whatever you need to borrow."

"Actually, Z, what I need is your help with moving some money. A lot of money."

"Aha. Mike, I suspect that you and I have very different ideas of what constitutes a lot of money. Perhaps you could clarify as to the amount that we're talking about."

Mike sighed. "Several hundred million pounds." He took another drink from his glass. "Actually seven hundred and fifty million pounds."

Zelley examined the brandy in his glass, his eyebrows raised. "Please don't make a habit of surprising me, Mike. Well, let's see. That's not a trivial sum, so it's clearly not your money. I presume that quite a lot of discretion will be required in moving it."

Mike nodded. "And it's going to be a bit tricky getting access, and there will be a very narrow window for moving it."

"I see. Anything else you can add to perhaps make it a bit more challenging?"

"Funny," said Mike, "These days I'm usually the one asking that question. No, that's about it. It just needs to disappear completely and without trace."

Zelley poured himself another drink. "What are you planning to do with all this cash? Good Lord, you're not thinking of going into business yourself are you?"

"Actually, I don't want it. I want you to move it for a friend. Well, not really a friend, more a sort of acquaintance…no, more a partner in crime, that I've gotten to know over the last couple of days."

Zelley's eyebrows went up. "I'm not sure I want to be associated with someone who hangs around with criminal types."

"Must be hard to look in the mirror in the morning, then," Mike grinned.

"Touché. Well then, we seem to have an arrangement. I'll take care of moving your cash and you start work, let's say…Monday?"

Mike nodded.

"Oh, and I'm afraid I'll have to dock your first week's wages."

"And why is that?"

"You ruined a perfectly good and rather expensive leather jacket last night. I don't know why you're so keen to be able to tell me apart from my synthetic. That marker isn't going to come out very easily, you know."

"The bloody thing's all worn and covered in duct tape."

"As I said, a perfectly good and rather expensive leather jacket."

A half smile formed on Mike's lips. "How about instead I fix that odd little twitch in the synthetic's arm?"

"I suppose that would be acceptable. What do you think is causing it?"

"You're still right handed?"

"Of course, what does that have to do with anything?"

"Probably wanker's cramp, then."

Zelley sighed. "Ah, sweet vulgarity! I can't believe how much I've missed you, Mike. This is really rather fun, but we'd better crack on. When does this money have to be moved?"

Mike looked out the picture window, toward the towers that dominated London's East End. "What time do the rooftop gardens on the Corrie Tower close down for the night?"

# 44
# Missing Link

"Thanks, Jim," said Hodges, reaching up to take the mug of tea. "On a day like this a good cuppa's about all there is worth living for."

"You ask me, sir, you aren't going to be living much longer if you don't get some rest. We've all grabbed five or six hours kip since last night and it's probably time you did, too. I can cover it, wake you if anything comes in."

Hodges nodded and let his gaze wander across his desk. "Fair enough, Jim. I get the feeling it's going to be another busy night. Let's take one more run through the gen and then I'll grab 40 winks, fair enough?"

"Where do you want to start?"

"All right. Let's back all the way up to when Larry told me about the Judy. So, someone makes off with a piece of Harry's property from the tower. Our transmission monitoring tells us that there's involvement from both the Russians, and Wei. Next thing we know, there's a Russian artist in Highgate with his fingers cut off. No obvious link, but it's a trademark Bratva punishment, so he's involved in something illegal. We just don't know what."

Hodges swallowed some tea.

"Then Nick Turner, longtime general of Harry's mob, is shot at on the Embankment, assailants unknown. From the recordings we know there was at least one synthetic involved. That's the first bit of expensive hardware we see on the streets. After that, Larry tells us that Harry's got his synthetic back and that he's tooling around London trying to find who's responsible."

Jim chipped in, "So far it's looking like a low level inter-gang bust up."

"Right. A bit nasty but nothing that might endanger civilians. Then we go to Turner's place and walk into a firefight. The second bit of expensive hardware, Exhibit A downstairs in the labs, arrives and cuts us up trying to get to Turner."

"How do you know it was going after Turner, sir?"

"He told me when we were pointing guns at each other. Me, Thompson, Carlisle and Larry were just in between him and the Borzoi. Anyway, even without that, we haven't had a UGV on the streets in four or five years. Seems a big coincidence that we'd run into one out of the blue.

"So, the thing kills two officers, puts Larry in intensive care, and damn near gets me too. Next thing the drone from the wankers at West Drayton almost takes me out, but manages to nail the UGV and now we've got the military involved. What do you reckon so far, Jim?"

The duty sergeant rubbed at his chin. "Someone's putting out a lot of expense and effort to kill Nick Turner. What's going on that would make him worth that? We know Wei and the Russians are both up to something so maybe they're launching a pre-emptive strike on Harry. Take out the synthetic and the top man in his gang as a starter before giving him a kicking. There's no love lost there."

"That's not bad, Jim. Harry's patch is prime turf, and both Wei and the Russians have history with him and good reasons to want him gone. It'd be an easier fight for them if he were short Turner and the Judy. Also, it turns out the UGV is mostly Russian tech, and Forensics has just told us that the data squirt it sent before the military wrecked it went to Bratva HQ in Stratford. Hang on to that thought.

"So then we have this morning's developments. We find the artist dead in his house and it looks like an execution. Clearly he's done more than just piss off the Bratva because it's not their style of hit."

"How so, sir?"

"Bratva is back of the head." Hodges tapped his skull. "Gorchakov was shot in the face. So, we work the house and find some interesting data sets. We run his home database through the analytics, and one contact listed as a Mr. Falcon turns out to actually be none other than Valentin Sokolov, so there's the Bratva connection.

"We also find the name of the seemingly ubiquitous Nick Turner, as well as an unidentified contact at the Shard. I think we can safely draw a dotted line from that to someone we know up there.

"Now, our artist friend is turning out to be a criminal Piccadilly Circus. I'd be hard pressed to find someone else with connections in all three of the big East London gangs. Interesting company for a sculptor, don't you think?"

"Maybe they're patrons?"

Hodges laughed. "Love your sense of humour, Jim, although that's not a completely crazy idea; Wei is an eclectic art buyer and Harry likes the odd painting, although he's pretty old school in his taste. In any case it turns out Gorchakov already had all the backing he needed. His most recent exhibition is sponsored by CZB Synthetics.

"Ah, the empire of the Robot King."

"The very same. Interesting name to pop up, given all the synthetics we've had wandering around, but we ran Zelley's profile and there's nothing dodgy in there. Yes, his company makes operating and personality software, but it's installed in half the synthetics walking the streets. Seems like just a coincidence that he happens to be funding Gorchakov's art. We're monitoring him, but I think we can put that to one side for now.

"Next thing, it looks like Turner's left town. We interview his girlfriend; she says she last saw him right before he stepped out into that bloody mess last night. He told her he was leaving town for good and so far, her story is holding up. We have her under surveillance, and there's been no contact with him since last night."

"So, we get the warrant to search the Bratva HQ in Stratford, get over there about lunchtime, and the cupboard is bare. Valentin and his mates are gone and there's nothing much to show that they were ever in residence. A small basement workshop, a few rooms furnished in old tat and badly in need of some new wallpaper, and that's it. We have local recordings of a van leaving the premises just before daylight, no plates, no ID tag. It might show up in the routine aerial surveillance, but nothing as yet.

"Valentin is seen leaving early morning. He heads down the Greenway and we lose him somewhere near East London Cemetery. That's the end of the trail so far.

"Next we get a flag telling us that Mikhail Volkov came into London on an early flight. In itself a worthy bit of news, but especially interesting when combined with the Bratva activity and the fact that he arrives at City Airport, a brisk walk from East London Cemetery."

The duty sergeant shrugged. "Maybe he's here to take over the show?"

"That would lend credence to the idea that Valentin has messed up. Volkov doesn't make social calls. So, funny thing: after he arrives at the airport, we have him on security cameras getting into a cab with Valentin. We look up the cab and it's unlicensed, unregistered. The numbers on the plates don't exist. They've disappeared. The incredible vanishing Russians."

Hodges finished off his mug of tea.

"Russians, Russians, Russians. Everything points to Russians. How does that fit then, Jim?"

"Like I said, the Russians have a grudge against Harry after Limehouse. They grab his synthetic, try to take it out, but something goes wrong. They also go after Turner, again trying to take him out, but miss him twice. Gorchakov was involved somehow – maybe he was something to do with getting the Judy, a connection to Zelley, who knows? Gorchakov screws up and loses some fingers. Valentin's buggered things up, so Volkov comes over to sort it out. Looks to me like it's all a Russian vendetta against Harry."

Hodges tapped his screen and it faded to black. "Yeah," he said. "So tell me, Jim, if it's all down to the Russians, and it certainly looks that way, why do I keep wondering what Wei is up to?"

# 45
## Alea Iacta Est

Pete adjusted his tie in the full length mirror of the lift. The subdued lighting made it difficult to judge the crease in the knot, but he stopped fussing with it just before he arrived on Wei's private floor. The doors opened and he stepped out into a corridor painted in simple warm contrasting greys and featuring the same low lighting as the lift. There was nothing on the walls other than two doors on each side of the corridor and a single door at the far end.

A man stood in front of the far door. Pete walked down the corridor, aware for the first time of how he looked to others in his fashionable suit, his bright tie, his cufflinks and gold watch. He felt disoriented by the simplicity of the space, clear and uncluttered with nothing to distract the eye.

He reached the far end and stood in front of the man at the door. The man held out his hand and Pete unbuttoned his jacket and held the left side open. The man reached in and took his gun from the holster. Pete buttoned his jacket up again.

The man turned and opened the door to reveal an unlit room. Pete stepped forward, but the man reached out with his free hand, palm towards Pete's chest, and halted him. Pete looked into the darkness, trying to make out the room beyond the doorway.

At last a voice spoke. "You may enter."

Wei.

Pete stepped inside and waited for his eyes to adjust. The door closed behind him. He could make out very little; some shapes that might have been chairs, perhaps a table off to one side, a statue in the corner. There was a click and light began to leak into the room as the picture window transitioned from black to completely transparent. Within seconds, the room was sketched out by the thin late afternoon light of the eastern sky.

Pete looked around. The furnishings were few and simple; a table, some low-backed chairs, a screen on the wall. The figure in the corner that he had taken for a statue was a motionless black-clad synthetic. Wei stood to one side of the picture window, looking out at the city. He said nothing.

Pete sized up the synthetic. It was lean with ordinary features designed to be hard to remember on a second meeting or to pick out in a crowd. It appeared to be unarmed, but you could never tell what they were concealing. His gaze wandered around the room, then back to Wei. He coughed.

"I am aware of your presence, Peter."

"I was just wondering if this was going to take very long."

Wei turned and looked at Pete. His face was as expressionless as the synthetic in the corner. He looked at Pete's suit, his tie, scrutinized his face. Pete shuffled his feet, adjusted the cuffs of his jacket.

"No longer than it needs to." said Wei. "Show me."

Pete reached into his right jacket pocket and brought out a silver cylinder: Jeremy Wells' powerscroll. He held it out to Wei. "Here."

"Bring it to me," said Wei.

Pete hesitated, then walked across the room and handed it over.

"Went through some major hassle to get that," said Pete, looking pleased with himself. "Had to bluff my way in without any tech support. Bloody synthetic nurse almost got me after the alarms went off. Hope it was worth the effort."

Wei nodded, gave it a glance, and threw it on the table. It rolled across the surface and dropped to the floor.

Pete cocked his head. "Well that's nice. I stuck my neck out to get that. Aren't you going to have someone analyze it? I thought you wanted the information."

Wei turned and looked out of the window. "It is irrelevant. The only important thing about it is that it has been denied to anyone else. A piece has been removed from the board. That is your function in this game: removing pieces from the board."

"I prefer to think of myself as a problem solver," said Pete as he moved to one side to keep both Wei and the synthetic in his field of vision.

"Perhaps you are, in a very simplistic sense of the word."

"I can leave if you like. I'm not very interested in standing around to be insulted. I can get as much of that as I want over at the Corrie Tower." Pete took a couple of steps towards the door.

"It was not meant as an insult, merely a description. The term 'simple' is not a pejorative except to those who perceive it as such."

"Trust me. I perceive it as such."

Wei smiled. "Then perhaps we should get to our remaining business before you are offended again."

"Fine by me," snapped Pete.

"I play the metagame, Peter. Sometimes I get what I want directly. Sometimes I get it in a circuitous manner. Because I play the game differently from my opponents, I increase my number of opportunities to win. There are no guarantees, of course; there is chance in every encounter. By managing the number of pieces on the board and their location, I try to weight the odds in my favour so that when the dice are rolled, my chances of success are greater."

Pete shrugged. "That sounds lovely, but I'd be happier if you'd cut to the chase."

"Very well. Tonight I believe that all the pieces will gather on the same corner of the board."

Wei pointed through the window at the Coronation Tower, steel grey in the gathering twilight.

"And?"

"I want you to contact the rest of the gang. Let them know that I will be coming on to their turf tonight. Warn them."

"Why the hell do you want me to do that?"

"It is what they want to hear. A call to action. A call they have been expecting and secretly hoping for because they are men of action, and they have been idle for too long. Because you bring the news they want to hear, they will trust you. And then there will be an opportunity for you to earn your final payment."

"What do you want me to do next?"

Wei stood in silence for a few moments, his eyes tracking from the lights at the top of the Coronation Tower to the streets far below.

"It is time for you to push the other birds from the nest."

# 46

# Banquo's Ghosts

The Crick & Watson was busy. Saturdays pulled a mixed crowd of drinkers kicking off pub crawls and tourists finishing up their day, and it was a lively place until early evening when everyone leaked out the door and stripped it of character.

The gang, minus Pete, had gathered around their usual table between the mural and the lottery machine. They were starting into a fresh round, and the table was already filling up with empties.

"I don't know if it's all gloom and doom," said Billy, "There's some upsides to these Judys."

"Really?" said Chopper. "Like perhaps they can do your job and you can make your money playing the lottery. Don't be soft."

"Yeah, but listen, right? One day in the future, like, we'll be able to put our brains in these things. I mean it's amazing what we'll be able to do."

Chopper laughed. "You'd put your brain in a synthetic? You?"

"Yeah. Well, if it didn't hurt and it meant I could live forever."

"But your brain'll eventually wear out, won't it?"

"Bit late for him to worry about that," said Dave to general laughter.

"Well, not my brain exactly. My personality. You know, all the stuff that makes me *me*. They could put it into an artificial brain."

Chopper took a serious drink from his pint. "Aside from the obvious about anyone even wanting to preserve your brain, there are a few problems with that. F'rinstance would you still be you?"

"What do you mean?"

"If they shift your personality and memories and everything over to a synthetic, then is it still you? All the bits of you are gone – your body and that. What part is still you?"

"Well…" Billy creased his brow. "My soul, I suppose."

Everyone looked at him; the surprise was general.

"I don't know. Sense of humour? What do you reckon, Dave? You're the techie."

"You should stick to playing the lottery, Billy."

The barman leaned in over the table. "Clear a few of these for you, lads?"

"Yeah, thanks, Jon."

Jon reached into the middle of the table with both hands and grabbed the empties. He was gone and forgotten in seconds.

"My round," Colin muttered into his pint as he went to the bar.

"What'd you reckon on the New Clarendon last night, Chopper?" said Dave.

"You mean apart from the whole kicking the shit out of the drummer thing? Poor unlucky bastard. Yeah, it was all right as nights out go. I just don't get the whole rebel rocker pose. What's the story with a bunch of lads playing music? What's so rebellious and hard about that? Bunch of nancy boys prancing around and singing. 'Oh, look, I'm so hard, I can play the guitar.' I tell you, they wouldn't last five minutes down the Bedford. Talking of which, everyone up for lunchtime beers there tomorrow?"

"The Long Man and Shakespeare going?" asked Dave.

"Yeah, I told him Jerry the barman wanted to meet him," said Chopper.

"Then bloody right we're up for it. Fucking excellent," said Dave.

"Between the Judy and Martin and the way things have been going, it might be our farewell drink," whined Billy.

"Don't be so fucking gloomy," said Colin, back from the bar. He had three pints in a triangular double-handed grip, and he parked them on the table before returning to the bar for his own.

The lads emptied their glasses and swapped them out for the fresh pints that Colin had brought. They sat and drank in silence for a few minutes. Billy was eyeing the lottery machine which had detected his money card and was working hard to get him to plug it in. The blonde hostess was on the screen making a seductive pitch, calling his name over and over and shedding her clothes at an interesting rate.

Colin returned and sat down. Billy dragged his eyes away from the blonde. "What are we going to tell the boss, then Col?"

Colin shrugged. "I'm open to suggestions. I don't see many of the pieces fitting together."

Chopper put down his pint, "It's simple. Someone, probably Nick, hacked the Judy and stole a chunk of its memory. The Russkies have shut down their Stratford office and disappeared from the map. Wei's up to something, but no one's talking about it and he hasn't been visible for a couple of days, which is in itself suspicious. We can't get anything from the cops 'cause Larry's still shut away in the Royal Free, and we don't even know if he's alive or dead. There was a gunfight outside Nick's place involving a couple of military drones – officially denied, so we know that's a fact – and Nick's vanished. Oh, and the boss thinks we're a bunch of clowns and we're probably all going to be signing on the dole come Monday."

"Very eloquent, Chop," said Colin. "But none of it makes any bloody sense. Someone set all this off for a reason, but I'm buggered if I know what."

"I do." said Nick as he appeared out of the crowd and slid into a seat next to Colin. "Hello, lads."

Billy almost choked on his pint. "Fuck me."

"No thanks, Billy." said Nick as with a quick look he read each of the gang. "No guns, lads. I'm here to talk." He cleared a space amid the empty and half full pint glasses on the table and put his hands there, palms down.

"Bit of a nerve, Nick," said Colin. "Boss finds out you're here, he'll probably have the lot of us killed."

"Yeah, he might at that. We'd better get right to business, then."

"All right," said Chopper. "Where the fuck have you been?"

Nick grinned. "I missed you too, Chop. I've been on the run. Things went belly up Thursday night."

"Did you fuck with the Judy?" said Colin.

"Yeah, I did."

"You'd have needed some help with that," said Dave. "Who?"

"Some people who were happy to help me mess with Harry."

"Just tell me you're not involved with Wei," said Colin.

Nick gave a wry smile. "I was, but I'm not now. Matter of fact, he's after my head. He almost got it, too, over on the Embankment last night. Between him, the Bratva, the law, and Harry, it's made for an interesting couple of days." He laughed. "About the only one who hasn't had a go at me is the Judy."

Billy grinned. "I can't say I was entirely unhappy that someone had fucked it up a bit."

"Yeah, maybe," said Colin, "but things are a real fucking mess now."

"Look, I know it's a shitheap, but it's not my fault, all right? Harry's the one who kicked all this off."

"What's going on?" said Colin.

"I can't tell you – it's personal between me and Harry."

"Well that's bloody helpful. We're standing around looking like a bunch of prats while you and Harry have a bust up. It's getting nasty out there, Nick, there's some serious hardware on the streets. Someone's going to get hurt before long and we'd rather it wasn't us, thanks very much."

"There's no reason for you lot to get in the middle."

Colin sighed. "Why are you here, Nick?"

"I just wanted to warn you to stay out of the way for a bit. Just 'til tomorrow."

"What does that mean?"

"Stay away from the tower."

"Nick, let's not get into it. I don't want to have to make any choices."

"There's a few scores to be settled, Col. I don't want any of you in the way."

"Fuck." Dave was staring at a screen in his hand.

"What? What is it?"

Dave looked up. "It's a message from Pete. He's got some gen on Wei. He's making a move tonight. Word is he's coming over the river."

"Fucking great," said Colin. "Wei crossing the Rubicon? That's all we fucking need. All right, let's go. We've got some work to do, lads."

The others planted their empty or half-empty glasses on the table and stood up.

Colin scowled. "Let's not run into each other tonight, Nick."

They headed for the door. Nick sat and stared at his hands resting on the table.

The barman appeared, his hands poised to reach in.

"All right, Nick?" He motioned at the glasses. "Any of these dead ones?"

Nick looked up at the backs of the lads as they left the pub.

"Yeah, Jon." He sighed. "Matter of fact, I reckon they all are."

# 47
# Brilliant Mind

Darkness was falling across London. In the stratosphere fifteen miles above the city, one of many remote vehicles began the ten thousandth circuit of a loop that it had been launched into four years earlier. As the sun's rays thinned out and starved its photovoltaic skin of energy, it lowered its altitude by a few miles. The drone's wings, the length of a football pitch, flexed gently as it descended, while signals pinged off its communications equipment in a constant barrage as it tracked and guided other UAV's circling the city at lower altitudes.

Far below on the north bank of the Thames, Wrecked John was ambling along one of his regular looping paths through the heart of the city. His routes were elliptical and hard to define, and so broken up by his frequent disappearance into blank spots in the electronic surveillance net, that it was almost impossible to predict where he would be at any given time.

At this particular moment he was walking along the river's muddy shoals east of Blackfriars. At Millennium Bridge he walked up the stairs, his shoes leaving brown spots of mud on the steps and he trudged across its metal spine to the South Bank. There was a fresh wind blowing across the Thames and he shivered a little as he walked. To his left was the illuminated magnificence of Tower Bridge and the high rise of the City, but they might as well have been distant galaxies in the corner of the night sky for all the attention he paid them.

His head was filled with other thoughts. They weren't the usual kind, like the kaleidoscope that was in his head when he was stoned, but odd ideas that dropped in like urgent questions that needed an immediate answer.

*How many tonnes of carbon particles have dropped on the city since the Romans? How many gallons of blood are wandering around the streets right now? Are there still unexploded bombs deep in the foundations of the city? Does the name Thames really mean dark?*

Wrecked John reached the far side and turned left in front of the monolithic brick chimney column of the Tate Modern. He stopped and looked at his surroundings.

*I threw up there. I pissed against that wall.*

A voice spoke in his head. 'London leaves its mark on you' it said, 'but you also leave your marks on it. Not marks that everyone can see, but marks that you know are there; the vomit, the piss, the blood. What say you, John?'

"I fucking hate this!" he yelled out loud, startling passers by, then, "I fucking love it!"

He shook his head and continued east along the river, past the white shell of the Globe Theatre. People passed him by, walking or cycling, mere ghosts of the city projected onto his worn retinas.

The cyclists flashing past unnerved him a little, so he checked the stash pocket of his denim jacket to see if he had anything. There were no pills but he felt powder and the rough crumbles of something promising. He licked a finger and put it into the mixture in his pocket, moving it about. The detritus stuck to his finger and under his nails and he pulled it out and put it into his mouth. It tasted bitter and felt rough against his tongue, but he felt the kick as whatever it was found its way into his bloodstream.

He continued on through the crumbling ancient stones and new composite spires and towers that pushed up out of the artesian basin that shaped the city. Wrecked John imagined he was walking among the many teeth of some giant beast, some old and broken off, some new and sharp.

As the drugs took hold, things became choppy and confused even by Wrecked John's standards. London went by in fragments: a railway bridge, a weathered and fluorescent gargoyle face, broken bottles in the gutter, a brightly coloured boat, crumbling brickwork, the arches of Borough market, traffic lights blinking near London Bridge station, lost people circling Guys and St Thomas' Hospital, and the sharp glass blade of the Shard.

He passed out for a while in London Bridge Street in a doorway close to the Shard, slumping to the ground next to a pile of black plastic bags filled with rubbish. For hours he was oblivious to the world passing him by, and the world was equally oblivious to him.

The sound of a helicopter clattering overhead brought him back. He pushed on one of the rubbish bags to no effect, then rolled over onto his belly and pushed himself up to his knees and from there to his feet. He stumbled through the other bags, kicking them across the pavement and into the gutter. John stayed upright with the practiced skill of the habitual drug user and traipsed down the road towards the steel fingers that held the crystalline stiletto of the Shard up against the black sky.

He wove his way around the square metal columns at the base of the building, invisible to the eyes of the monied Londoners returning home from restaurants, pubs, and theatres. Their vectors took them in short straight lines from their cars to the entrance of the building. To John they were like meteors streaking across the sky, blurred trails of light that arrived and were gone almost before he knew they were there.

He wandered down St. Thomas Street, through the old brick tunnel that cut under the railway lines, and followed the line of lock-up garages in the arches down to St. Saviour's Dock. He stood there for a long time, leaning on the brick wall and staring down at the green scum that covered the water. Either side of the dock the converted warehouses stretched away to the Thames, just visible at the end.

He tried to remember whether he was supposed to go right to Mill Street or left down Shad Thames. He never seemed to pick the right one. He looked in his pockets for a coin to toss but found only a rolled up wad of cash and some old iron keys. As he put the things away, he stumbled and lurched right so he kept going in that direction and headed for Mill Street.

The street was long and narrow and bordered by old working buildings that had been made into flats and offices. John stumbled along until he reached the point where the street made a sharp turn. In the wall of the Reeds Wharf building in front of him was a low arch barred by an iron gate, and beyond it the river.

He walked up to the gate and tried to open it. It was locked. He reached into his pocket and pulled out the bunch of keys. One after another he tried them in the old lock until one of them felt right; he turned it and the lock clicked open. John went through the gate and after much effort locked it behind him.

He walked down a few steps and on to a gangway that took him out to the Downings Road Moorings. The rows of barges and lighters tied up there were quiet in the night as John walked down the tree-lined roof gardens that they shared. It felt like another world. The smell of flowers and herbs gave him a momentary memory of a cottage with a garden and the sound of children laughing. He walked past quince trees, and box hedges, and rows of poppies gone to seed.

When he arrived at a dark green barge near the eastern end, he stepped on board. He walked the length of the deck and stood looking out across the Thames. Tower Bridge spanned the river on his left and beyond it the Tower of London. On the opposite bank, the great double spiral of the Coronation Tower rose high in the night sky, the lights at the top blinking ceaselessly.

He turned around and saw with relief the hammock that was suspended between two masts. With the dexterity of long practice, John wandered through the potted plants lining the deck to the hammock, rolled over into it, and was lulled to sleep in seconds by the gentle slap of the Thames against the side of the barge.

When he awoke, it would be to a very different sound.

# *48*
# One More Thing

Nick stopped outside the underground space in the base of the Coronation Tower that housed the security for Harry's suite of offices. There was no point in listening at the steel reinforced door, so he put down the duffel bag and drew out a small cosh with one hand, his security chip with the other.

He flashed the chip at the sensor and there was a click as the door opened. Nick slipped inside and crossed the space between him and Dave in three quick steps. Dave saw Nick's ID pop on his monitor as the software registered his entrance and had just enough time to turn and say, "What the fuck?" before Nick caught him in the side of the head with the cosh. Dave lolled forward in his chair and fell to the ground.

Nick dropped the cosh and pulled out the contour polymer that he'd used in Jeremy Wells' room earlier that day. He laid it down on the control console. A few seconds passed, then Mike's voice spoke in his earpiece. "I'm in. Wait one."

Nick checked on Dave and laid him out flat on the floor. Then he grabbed his duffel bag from outside and closed the door behind him. He tied Dave's arms behind his back, and his feet together, with plasticuffs from the bag.

"All right. I have control." Mike's voice was low and even. "Cameras and locks in the suite are mine. I can't do anything about the lift since that's on a separate system. You'll show up on the building security monitors, but no one in the suite will know you're coming."

Nick spoke and the mic taped to his throat transmitted, "On my way."

He picked up the duffel bag and left the office, closing the door behind him. He strode across the parking garage to the silver lift doors and swiped his ID. The doors slid open and Nick stepped in.

He punched the top-most button and the lift shot skywards, the green dots lighting his progress. As they approached the top floor, Mike started a running commentary.

"Cameras show no one in the lobby or the office. Checking the other rooms. Empty, empty, empty, OK there they are. They're in the lounge."

"How many?"

"The big man, the Judy, two rough looking types, one bloke dressed like a Soho pimp. Total of five."

"Don't lock the doors yet, there's one missing. Take a look at the outside surveillance."

"Hang on, looking, looking. There! Another bloke outside in the gardens having a smoke."

"Figured as much. OK, lock the door from the lounge to the reception area. Leave the doors to the garden open. When he comes back in, lock those, too."

"Got it."

Nick drew his gun as the lift slowed, and the doors slid open. He stepped out into the reception. To his right was a door to the roof gardens, straight ahead was the door to the lounge, and Harry's office was on the left. He walked over to the office and the door opened for him. He went straight to Harry's desk and the clock, the monitor, the phone, the gun – the simple tools that Harry used to run his criminal empire.

Nick holstered his gun and took a device from the duffel bag that looked like a large old-fashioned calculator. He pulled the secure network cable from the old black rotary phone on Harry's desk and plugged it into the device.

"Over to you," he said.

There was a long silence while Mike worked. Nick drew his gun again and watched the door.

"Fuck."

"What's going on, Mike?"

"You aren't going to like this."

"What?" Nick almost shouted the question.

"Passwords checked out fine. But there's another layer of security we didn't know about. There's a biometric lock."

Nick looked at the empty desk chair.

"Harry."

"Yep. You'll need his eyeballs."

"I don't think he'll be too thrilled about giving them to me and I don't fancy my odds against the lot of them, plus the Judy."

"Then we're fucked."

"Yeah," Nick grimaced. "Got damn close, too. All right. I'm getting out of here. Can you cover my tracks?"

"Everything except the ride down and whatever you did to your mate in the control room."

"OK," Nick said. "I'm heading for the lift."

Then all hell broke loose.

# *49*

## Royal Free

It being an average night in London, the emergency department at the Royal Free Hospital was very busy. Hodges walked through the growing crowd on his way to see Larry in the Intensive Care Unit. He liked to take the temperature of the city from street level, and hospital emergency rooms were a good place to see and hear what was going on.

It seemed very normal so far: several drunks, a couple of car accidents, people with chills, fevers, slip and fall injuries. At the reception desk, a man with glass fragments embedded in his face and blood running down onto his shirt was answering questions from the receptionist. "Married?" she said. "Not anymore," was the gruff response. "It was my wife what done it."

Hodges walked on, past people on stretchers and benches, doctors and nurses moving around them in a complex dance whose measures were driven by the relative severity and urgency of the injuries of the patients. His badge advertised his presence to the various monitoring devices built into the doors. Laser scans read his face as he walked, and let him through to the secure area of the hospital.

He took the lift to the fourth floor ICU where Larry was being treated. His badge had alerted the staff that he was on his way up, and he was met at the door by a doctor.

"Evening, Inspector."

"Doctor."

"I hear you want to talk to Mr. Summers."

"Please."

"He hasn't been conscious for long and I don't want to put him under too much stress. His condition is very fragile, and it's something of a miracle that he's conscious at all."

"This is a personal visit. I'd just like to have a few words with him."

"Fair enough. Follow me."

They walked through the ICU, past hermetically sealed treatment rooms with transparent walls. Hodges could see the contents of each room – the machines keeping the patients alive while they were waiting for new organs to be bioprinted or for viruses to be scrubbed from their blood. In one room, human and synthetic medical personnel worked side by side, treating a patient who looked to Hodges to be short a couple of limbs.

At Larry's room the doctor used his pass to let Hodges into the airlock and left him there.

Hodges stood for a minute then opened the door into the room and looked at the shape on the bed. Judging only by the colour of his skin, he looked no worse than he had the previous night, but the tubes running discreetly from his abdomen to life support equipment, and the sterile treatment bag wrapped around the space where his right hand used to be, told a different story. Hodges knew that his spleen had been shredded and that he was in the market for both a new lung and a new kidney on his left side. He'd get his hand restored, too, as soon as he was strong enough for surgery. It would never be quite as good as it had been, but the advanced nerve grafting techniques available at the Free would make it come close.

Of all the places he might find himself in London, a hospital bedroom was where Hodges was the least comfortable. He went over to Larry's bedside.

"Larry?"

His eyes opened and he looked at Hodges.

"Larry, I'm sorry. About how things turned out. About all this."

Larry nodded and spoke, his voice a whisper. "Not your fault, 'Odge."

"We're still piecing together what happened. Damned if I know how it all fits. All I do know is that it doesn't feel over yet. It's quiet out there at the moment, but something's not right. Can't put my finger on it, but there's more trouble brewing."

"Well, you be careful out there 'Odge."

"Thanks, Larry. I got lucky last time." He held up his bandaged hand. "Just a scratch compared to you and the others."

"They're both dead, aren't they?"

Hodges nodded.

"Nick got away though?"

"Yes."

"You married?"

Hodges looked at him. "Married? All these years, Larry, and we never talked about that?" He gave a short laugh. "No, I'm not married. I was, but I gave that up a long time ago. Why do you ask?"

"You just seem like the sort of bloke 'oo ought to be married."

Hodges smiled, looked at his feet. "Thanks, Larry." He gestured behind him at the door. "Best be off. Got work to do."

"'Odge?"

"Yes?"

"If you run into Nick, give 'im a chance. All right?"

Hodges nodded. "Rest up, Larry."

He turned and left the room and the airlock hissed shut behind him. He walked down the transparent hallway and out to the lift. At the steel doors his face stared back at him, blurred and sad and tired. The doors slid open and he stepped into the lift. He swiped an icon on the touchpad and it descended, taking him back to the ground floor and the dark streets of London.

# *50*

# A Walk in the Park

As the public lift of the Coronation Towers shot up to the rotunda at the centre of the rooftop gardens, Valentin pulled out his battered paperback book. The men around him were checking their gear: weapons, harness, electronics, the usual drill.

He opened it and turned the worn pages to the epigraph. He read to himself words that he had long ago committed to memory:

*"...who are you, then?*
*I am part of that power*
*which eternally wills evil*
*and eternally works good"*

He closed the book, and ran his thumb over the familiar face of the black cat on the cover, then he opened his jacket and put it into an inside pocket. He felt its weight over his heart.

Around him he heard the metallic clicks of weapons being readied, and men talking in low voices. He felt in the air the tension, the nervous horror men feel when they know they are about to dance along the line between life and death.

The shock of Mikhail's voice in his ear broke the long silence of their incursion into the tower. "Don't fuck this up, Valentin. *Ni puha, ni pera.*"

No fluff, no feathers. Valentin couldn't restrain a smile. "*K chertu*," he said, and wondered to himself if there was a hell deep enough for people like Mikhail.

The lift was approaching the roof garden. No one said a word, but the men around Valentin moved with purpose, taking up positions so they could disperse rapidly when the doors opened. They reached the top and there was a musical chime followed by a friendly voice over the lift speakers: "Welcome to the Coronation Tower Roof Gardens, the most beautiful park in London."

The doors opened and Valentin's men burst from the confines of the lift, scattering into the park in a loose cluster, taking cover wherever it was available. To their right was the long slope down to the infinity pool and the nightscape of London. In the darkness to their left, across several hundred yards of lawn dotted with trees, fountains, sculptures, low walls, and a playground were the lights of the office suites, including Harry's. They took up firing positions facing the offices, and waited.

Valentin lifted night vision glasses to his eyes and scanned the front of Harry's office suite. There was a man standing in front of the double doors, a cigarette in his hand, staring in Valentin's direction. Unsure whether or not the man could see him in the low illumination of the rotunda path lights, Valentin froze. The man took a drag on his cigarette.

"Dimitry," hissed Valentin, his throat mic carrying his voice to the entire squad. "Target 12 o'clock."

There was a rustling in the bushes in front of Valentin, then a low voice, "I have the shot."

"Take the shot."

Valentin heard the crack as the sniper fired his rifle and almost simultaneously saw the man stagger and drop behind a low curved brick wall. He scanned the windows of the offices for any indication that the shot had been heard but there was no sign of any movement.

"Good shooting, Dimitry, now, on my signal the advance..." Valentin's sentence was cut off by the sound of a gun firing from the direction of Harry's suite. He swung his glasses back to see a head pop up above the wall and the flashes of a gun as the man fired at them again.

"Shit!" Valentin waved his men forward. "Go, go!"

Semi-automatic weapons clattered from either side of him as some of his men provided suppressing fire, while others made short sprints from cover to cover. Valentin signaled to a man carrying an RPG and pointed at the offices.

"The doors, quickly!" he yelled. Then he clipped his glasses to his belt and raised his own weapon, popping off rounds at the distant wall.

In his gut he had the feeling that this was not going to be his night.

# 51
## Look Here

The sudden sound of gunfire from the roof gardens was loud even in Harry's office. Nick froze and listened to the patterns, identifying at least three different weapons.

"Shit." He grabbed the duffel bag and headed for the door.

"Just got a building security notification," Mike said in his ear. "They're implementing SECCON2, whatever that is."

"Shutdown," said Nick. "Fuck."

He ran into the lobby in time to see the lift doors slide shut.

"What's going on, Nick?"

"Security protocol. They shut down inter-office access and that means the lift's out. Tenants make their own decisions about whether to go to lockdown or not so we still have control of the office spaces, but the building company runs everything else. Check the cameras. What's going on outside?"

"Hang on, having a butchers. Looks like a big shootout. Lots of weapon flashes, lots of shouting. Sounds foreign. Bunch of paramilitary types heading towards you from the public lifts, the ones that come up through that round building in the middle of the gardens."

"How about the lounge?"

"One of them tried the door to the lobby then went to the doors to the roof garden and now they're tooling up," Mike whistled. "Got some

213

heavy metal. Now the four lads and the Judy are taking up firing positions on either side of the doors. And they're outside shooting."

Nick heard the sound of a riot gun and several semi-automatic weapons join the cacophony on the roof gardens.

"Who's left in the lounge?"

"Just Harry."

"Armed?"

"Nope."

Nick looked at the ceiling as if seeking inspiration, then he said, "Lock the roof garden doors and open the lobby door when I say."

"This wasn't part of the plan, Nick."

"Neither was a biometric lock and a firefight."

"You're a bloody walking disaster area, you are." There was a loud sigh in Nick's ear. "All right. Ready."

Nick put the duffel bag down next to the door from the reception to the lounge. He stood at the doorway, his gun ready.

"Let's go."

There was a click as the deadlock disengaged and Nick pushed the door open and stepped in.

"Evening, Harry."

Harry turned, fast on his feet, his eyes scanning the room for the nearest weapon.

"Well, well," he said without feeling. "Nice of you to drop in."

Nick walked into the room.

"Not really a social call, Harry."

Harry's mouth smiled, but his eyes were cold.

"What do you want?"

"A minute of your time. I need you to come to the office with me."

Harry tilted his head, squinted.

"What's on your mind, Nick?"

There was a flurry of gunfire from the roof gardens.

"No time for questions, Harry. You're by yourself, and I've got the gun. Nick motioned at the door. "Let's go."

"You won't shoot me, Nick."

"I fucking will, Harry."

"What for, Nick? What's this about? Money? You need a raise, why didn't you come talk to me? We've been working together for years. We could have worked out an arrangement."

"Shut it, Harry, or I'll shoot you and fucking drag you to the office."

"You won't shoot me over money. What is it?" Harry shouted "You gone over to Wei? Is that it? You a fucking traitor, Nick?"

Nick's face twisted up. "No, you bastard, it's not about the fucking money. It's about Allie. You're the fucking traitor. You!"

Harry took a step forward, his arms open. "She tell you something was going on?"

"No she didn't bloody tell me."

"That's because there isn't anything, Nick. It's all in your imagination."

Nick leveled the gun at Harry's head.

"Don't try that shit with me, Harry. You're lucky I don't just put a bullet in you. Right about now, I'm very tempted to say fuck the money and just top you."

"There's so much you just don't get, Nick. She wouldn't have married you anyway."

Nick fired once to either side of Harry's head, then pointed the gun at him again. He motioned to the door.

Harry's eyes burned in the mask of his face as he walked with his slow measured boxer's gait over to the door. Nick stepped to one side and followed him as he went through the reception area and into his office. The gunfire outside continued in sporadic bursts.

"Stop!"

Harry waited as Nick went over to the desk and looked down at the clock, the monitor, the phone, the gun. He smiled and removed the gun from the desk then stepped back and motioned for Harry to continue.

"Sit."

Harry glared at him and sat down in the chair.

"Look at the screen."

Harry turned his basilisk gaze to the monitor.

Nick spoke in a low voice. "Ready?"

"Hah! Yeah, I'm ready. Just glad I'm on this end of things."

"Over to you," Nick said.

The monitor blinked into life and ran a laser across Harry's face. It flashed up a variety of security notifications as it read Harry's retinas.

There was a long silence, broken by the chatter of automatic weapons and the occasional explosion out on the roof gardens.

Mike's voice came over the earpiece. "Fuck me, it worked."

"It's done?"

"Millions of quids-worth of done. All clear and getting a wash cycle through Zelley's laundry service."

"Well that was easy, wasn't it?" said Nick.

"Not exactly," said Mike.

"How am I getting out of here?"

"Well, you said Plan B was through the roof gardens."

"Not a good option just at the minute. What's Plan C?"

"Working on it."

"Work faster."

"You always say that. Shut up and let me see if I can access the lifts."

His eyes on Harry, Nick started to walk backwards to the door. Harry stared at him, motionless. Nick had taken only a few steps when from behind him there was a very loud explosion and the lobby filled with debris, dust, and smoke.

# 52

## Cuckoo's Nest

Colin fired his last round, ducked down behind the wall surrounding the roof gardens, dropped the clip from his gun, and reloaded. He was crouched behind the wall with Chopper, Billy, Pete, and Cassie. Billy was bleeding from a shoulder wound, but was putting down suppression fire using an SMG that Cassie had hauled over. Chopper was using an illegal sniper's rifle to take potshots as their assailants moved from cover to cover. There were three bodies lying still on the grass out in the gardens. Gunfire flashed and echoed toward the gang from behind the cover of statuary and fountains. Off to their right was a pile of rubble where the reception door used to be.

"Someone get the fucker with the RPG!" shouted Colin, as he put his gun down and rummaged through a kitbag that he'd brought out with him.

"Who the bloody hell are they?" yelled Billy.

"They sound like Russkies," said Pete.

"I thought you said it was Wei's lot who were on the move," Chopper growled.

"That's what I heard," said Pete.

"Fucking wrong again," muttered Chopper, belting off a few more rounds.

"Don't speak too soon," said Colin, pointing to the far end of the gardens where they disappeared into the infinity pool and the illuminated skyline of London beyond.

A helicopter was tearing straight in on a fast approach. It wasn't subtle. It came in with lights blazing, exposing the men advancing through the gardens, who ran like rabbits.

"If it's Wei, he's doing us a bloody favour at the minute," called Chopper over the firing and the noise of the helicopter, and he cracked off a few rounds at a man etched in stark black relief against the searchlights. The man fell and did not move again.

The helicopter roared in over the infinity pool and slowed rapidly to a hover about twenty feet above the westernmost part of the gardens, behind the Russians. Colin pulled night goggles from his pack and put them on, then watched as ropes dropped to the ground from each side of the 'copter, and men slid down to the lawns. He counted twenty, almost all of them in body armour, and heavily armed. The last two out were different, tall and thin and weaponless. They moved faster than the others when they hit the ground, running towards the Russians, who were now sandwiched between Harry's gang and the new arrivals.

Gunfire was flying in all directions as the helicopter tilted away from the gardens, presenting its belly. From somewhere near the pavilion a rocket streaked through the sky and caught it in the tail rotor. It span around in a wild circle and came down in the pool with a terrible crash and a fountain of water.

"It's a fucking war zone!" shouted Billy.

"No shit." Colin took an assault rifle out of the kitbag, jammed in a magazine, and put the strap over his shoulders. Next he grabbed a Frisbee-sized metal disk from the bag and threw it into the air. There was a high-pitched whine, and the drone disappeared up into the black sky.

In his night vision goggles the drone's surveillance systems came online. Spiral wind patterns coming up off the tower buffeted it, but the onboard software systems provided stabilization, reduced the turbulence, and streamed a near-steady infrared image of the gardens below.

"Keep 'em occupied," he called to the others. "I'm going hunting."

Colin looked at Cassie, who had been crouched motionless behind the wall since they'd tumbled out of the lounge. "You coming?"

It turned its head in his direction.

"Then let's go."

Colin crouched low behind the wall that circled the gardens as he ran, moving to a position flanking the Russians who were pinned down near the rotunda. Cassie followed close behind, bent over and running at an angle impossible for a human.

The gunfire was near continuous now. The feed from the drone in Colin's goggles showed small groups of Russians scattered across the midsection of the gardens. The recent arrivals from the helicopter were advancing on them in a loose formation.

After he'd made a quarter circuit of the gardens, he reached a gap in the wall where a path ran into the centre. Nothing showed in his glasses so he started to cross the gap.

He'd taken two steps when he was hit hard by something that came on him fast from the gardens. He thumped against the ground with it on top of him and he felt something sharp slash across his ribs, then it was gone and he was lying on his back looking at the sky. Colin turned his head to see Cassie and one of the lean, black clad figures from the helicopter whirling and slashing at each other with wrist blades in a swift acrobatic dance. It was over in seconds. Cassie took a blade in the neck, but as she did so she punched both her blades up through the other synthetic's belly, straight into the central cortex. It doubled over and dropped to the ground.

Cassie turned immediately, set Colin up in a sitting position and put his assault rifle back in his hands. He looked from the gun to the cut in his ribs, to the synthetic jerking spasmodically on the ground, to her punctured neck.

"Thanks," he gasped.

She nodded, then froze for a few seconds. She started tearing away her clothes.

"Hey, hang on a minute," said Colin.

She dropped the last of her clothing.

Colin stared at her.

Her skin shimmered and became almost transparent.

"What's going on?" said Colin.

"Harry," she said. Then she turned and headed back to the offices her passage marked by a wavering distortion of the objects behind her.

Colin took up a firing position at the wall.

"Fucking hell," he said and began firing into the melee sweeping across the gardens.

Over at the suite Billy had eased off on the SMG since the attention of the Russians was focused on the larger force coming at them from the opposite direction. Chopper had put the rifle against the wall and was loading his personal weapon, an ornate large calibre silver handgun. Pete had his gun out, but hadn't fired a shot.

Out at the flanking position where Colin had gone with the Judy there was the sound of gunfire.

"Nice one, Col," said Billy. "The Russkies aren't going to mess with us again after tonight."

"We're not out of the woods, you plonker," Chopper cut in. "There's Wei's lot to deal with after them."

"Yeah," said Billy, "but by the time they get finished with the Russkies, the law'll be here, or the military. Reckon this is gonna turn out all right."

From behind him, Pete's voice was cold with certainty.

"You've never been more wrong, Billy."

As he opened his mouth to reply, Pete shot him in the back. Billy slumped forward over the wall, the SMG pointing skyward.

Chopper turned, raising his gun, as soon as he heard the shot. He looked into the barrel of Pete's weapon, and then his quiet smile. Chopper pulled his trigger too late; the thump of his silver hand cannon as it fired into the night sky was the last sound he ever heard.

# 53
## Sladkikh Slov

Lying on his back, his breathing ragged, Valentin tried to ignore the pain and process the events since the arrival of the helicopter. The slashes across his chest and arms hurt with an exquisite precision causing him to wonder how badly he was injured. He closed his eyes and summoned all the energy he could to focus on what had happened.

It had begun with the helicopter. The proximity alerts had sounded on his teams' combat suits and he'd turned to see the new threat flying in at the far end of the gardens, ropes dropping from the sides as it slowed. While the gunmen spilled from the helicopter, sliding to the ground, Valentin had directed most of his men to engage them, including the squad with the RPG.

They'd taken down the helicopter within seconds but not fast enough to stop the deployment and subsequent assault. Of the two threats now faced by the Bratva this new one was the most dangerous, and Valentin led a counterattack to try to contain it. He had taken up position with some members of his squad in a small stand of trees and had been about to open fire when from nowhere two lean shapes sprinted into their midst.

There had been a short, bloody close combat as the synthetics took his men apart. Valentin had managed to slap a fragmentation grenade onto the back of one of the synthetics as the frantic butchery came to an end. It had turned on him, blades swiping at his arms as he tried to protect himself, then cutting deep wounds across his chest. He'd fallen to the ground, his jacket slashed to ribbons, the bloodied pages of the book in his pocket spilling out across the grass. On his back, staring at the sky, he'd waited for the killing stroke but instead heard the fragmentation grenade go off with a loud thump. After that he'd found himself alone with the sounds of the battle raging around him.

Now, with great effort, he was able to turn his head and look to the side. In his limited field of vision were the body parts of some of his men and one of the synthetics lying face down in the grass, a large hole in its back; the other one was nowhere to be seen. The shredded pages of his beloved book were scattered over everything like so many white leaves beneath the trees.

It hadn't been his night.

# 54
# Dead Ends

Hodges let the car drive him back to Fenchurch Street and he watched the late Saturday night crowd dispersing from the pubs and bars along Haverstock Hill as they went by. When the car approached Chalk Farm Station at the bottom of the hill, he told it to slow down. They went through the traffic lights and on to Chalk Farm Road in a smooth glide.

He spoke to the computer as he looked at the darkened front windows of Turner's flat

"Turner surveillance update."

The screen flickered and Jim's face came up on the screen.

"Oh. Hi, Jim. Didn't mean to bother you."

"No worries, Inspector. Not much doing tonight in the City so thought I'd grab your call."

The car was passing the site of the confrontation with the UGV. There was a pile of scorched bricks surrounded by a bright orange construction fence but little else to show the violence that had happened there the day before.

"Nothing new on the woman. She ran errands, met a few friends for dinner, went home, and went to bed."

"I wish my days were like that," said Hodges.

"Might be if you ever took a day off, sir."

"I don't think I'd survive a holiday. I'm dependent."

"On what, sir?"

"London."

The car swung left at the Hawley Arms and did the one-way loop around the north side of Camden Town to the residential haven of Camden Street. Hodges would have preferred to be traveling Camden High Street, lined as it was with the seedy but trendy bars that were the area's trademark. They'd still be packed to the nines, and there might be something going on to alleviate the boredom.

"Dead ends," said Hodges, glancing at a small group of either drunks or druggies staggering along by the railings of St. Martins Gardens.

"What, sir?"

"Nothing but dead ends, Jim. Vanishing Russians. A dead artist. A missing gangster. Dead policemen." He sighed. "Dead ends."

"Something'll turn up, sir, it usually does."

"Yeah, but usually too late. I was thinking of pulling Harry in for questioning tomorrow. I don't expect his lawyer would let him say much, but it'd be something to do. Maybe shake things up a bit, get a reaction."

"If you like, sir. We can get the permissions ready when you get back to the station."

"Anything else going on?"

"Dead as a dodo. I was just going to put the kettle on."

"Sounds great, Jim."

Hodges was about to cut the call when his screen lit up.

"Wait a sec. Bloody hell." The alerts flared on the screen against a map of east London with the Coronation Tower at the centre. Text scrolled across the top: Multiple shots reported – Explosions and gunfire from the roof gardens – Building lockdown.

"Jim, scramble SCO19 and get every officer available to the tower. I'm on my way. Looks like we won't need those permissions."

Hodges tapped a screen icon and the car locked in the route to the tower then tightened his four point harness, pulling him back into his seat. The adaptive skin of the car flashed a pattern of emergency lights as its sirens burst into the night and it hurtled forward, tearing towards Kings Cross. The car's sensors and telemetry combined with the city route management systems to take it through London at speeds that would have been fatal with a human at the wheel.

Hodges stared for a few moments at the streets of London accelerating towards him through the windscreen. Then he closed his eyes.

# 55

# Shame about the Boat Race

"Clock's ticking, Mike," said Nick. "That was another explosion in case you didn't notice, and the shooting's getting closer. Where's my exit?"

Nick was standing in the same place he'd been when the RPG round took out the door to the lobby. He'd turned so he could keep one eye on the entrance to the office while keeping his gun trained on Harry. The two hadn't spoken a word to each other since Harry had sat down in the chair. Harry glared out through the office door.

"If this was easy, everyone'd be doing it," said Mike.

"Not laughing."

Mike's response was clipped. "Then shut up and let me get on with it."

"Fine."

Nick heard a sound from the lobby and looked over at the door. Harry pushed his chair backwards very fast, the wheels squeaking on the wooden floor. Nick turned to Harry, stabbing his gun in his direction as a warning. Then, as Pete stepped into the office, Chopper's silver handgun leveled at Nick's face, he almost had time to bring the gun back around. Almost. At this range 'almost' was the difference between life and death. Nick lowered his gun.

"About bloody time," said Harry, standing up, "Where the fuck have you been?"

"Busy," said Pete. "Drop it, Nick."

Nick tossed the gun to one side.

"And lose the comms."

"See you," Nick said, and he peeled off the microphone strip and took the earpiece out. He dropped them on the floor. Then to Harry he said, "Why don't you ask him what he's doing with Chopper's gun?"

Harry stared at Nick as if he were insane. Then he looked at the gun in Pete's hand.

"What's going on, Peter?"

"I think we all need to have a little chat," said Pete moving his gun to point first at Nick and then Harry. "Let's go to the lounge."

"What the fuck for?" said Harry.

"I fancy a drink," said Pete "and that's where the booze is."

"Don't be fucking stupid…" Harry started.

Pete pointed the gun directly at Harry. "The world just changed, Harry. See the gun? Now, stop trying to give orders and get your arse in the lounge."

Harry's body was a clenched fist, but he got up and walked around to the front of his desk.

Pete stepped back to give him room.

"Now," said Pete "Both of you hold out your right hands and grab the other like you were having a friendly shake."

Harry stared at Pete, who motioned with the gun. His mouth set, he held out his hand. Nick did the same and they held hands.

"Same with the left," said Pete.

They complied and now the two of them looked as if they were about to begin some odd dance, standing there holding hands with their arms crossed. They stared at one another as if by doing so they could somehow make the other one disappear.

"Very nice. Now, shuffle along to the lounge. Either of you let go, you're both dead."

The two set off crab-like into the reception area where the carpet was covered in broken glass, shattered wood, and dust. Nick saw that his duffel bag had been thrown against the opposite wall by the force of the explosion. Outside, through the gap where the reception door to the gardens had been, the sound of small arms fire rattled and echoed across the rooftop.

They edged through the door to the lounge passing the pool table on the left. On the right the continuing firefight was visible through the doors to the roof gardens as frequent flashes of blue and white light.

"Keep moving, keep moving. All right. I'm tempted to keep you like that, but then who's going to get my drink? Slowly let go and put your hands to your sides. Good. Harry, you can sit down."

His face a stone, Harry sat in the armchair.

"Well, gentlemen, this is a turn up, isn't it? Who's the idiot now, Nick? Never mind. Be a mate and get the drinks in, they're on me. What do you fancy, Harry?"

"Nothing."

"Funny, I thought you'd appreciate a last drink. Suit yourself. Double Scotch, Nick. Be quick about it." Pete waved his gun at the bar.

Nick looked from Pete to the bar, then back again.

"Get it your fucking self."

The sound of the gun going off was very loud. Splinters of wood flew and left a huge hole in the middle of the lounge table.

"I was hoping we could have a talk, but I'm just fine with shooting you now if that's what you'd prefer, Nick."

Nick lifted his chin as he looked sideways at Pete, then turned and walked over to the bar. He took the bottle of Scotch and two glasses and poured. He picked them up and walked over to Pete.

"Just put it on the table. Now, sit down opposite Harry. Good."

Pete walked over and picked his glass up with his free hand. He raised it in a toast.

"To the future," he said with a smile, and took a drink.

Nick slugged back half of his and put the glass on the table.

"You broke the number one rule, Nick. I know you think I ask stupid questions, but humour me. Why'd you do it?"

Nick looked for a moment as though he was going to laugh, then he frowned.

"All right, you fucking ponce, I'll tell you. I'll tell you about getting out of this stupid fucking game. What it looks like for you and me. If you're really, really lucky it's a flat on the Costa del Sol and enough readies to keep you in satellite telly and sangria. Or if you're less fortunate it's a flat in Bognor and pints of bitter at the local.

"Most of the time, though, actually almost all the time, it's a wooden box and a bunch of flowers on a grave. I don't know about you, but I'm not much impressed by the options, especially the last one. Although, I dunno, it might be better than living in Bognor, but I think you get the point. I've had enough and I need the funds to get out of this business the way I'd like to. Harry has the funds. QED."

"QE what?" said Pete. "Never mind. That's it? Money? That's why you did a deal with Wei? I don't believe that, Nick. There's got to be more to it than that. No? Must be pissing you off a bit, Harry. All those years, and this is what you get" Pete grinned. "There's no loyalty any more, is there?"

Nick picked up his glass. "What's your angle, Pete?"

"Me? I'm a...a problem solver. I've solved a problem for Mr. Wei. Or I will have in a minute." He laughed. "You can finish that drink first if you like, Nick." Pete set down his own glass and took a step back towards the reception door. He pointed the gun at Nick. "Last words?"

Behind him, silent and stealthy as a ghost, Cassie entered the room. She moved with a fast gliding step, the only trace of her the rippling of the walls seen through her adaptive camouflage. She didn't register on Pete's peripheral vision until he caught something in the look on Harry's face and he turned his head slightly. He saw the movement, turned and fired the gun in one smooth motion, shooting at the blur of her face.

If Pete had met a synthetic in combat before he would have known it was a waste of time; he would have known that the vital organs are in the chest and well armoured; he would have known that they can see and hear through sensors built in to their bodies just as well as with their eyes and ears. He would have known that in a fight at this range he was fucked.

The shot destroyed most of Cassie's face and the shock of the impact made her stagger for a second, but she came on. Pete managed to fire twice more, the rounds thunking off her armoured skin, leaving black dents in the adaptive camo, and then she was on him. She swung upwards at his neck and abdomen with the blades that projected from each of her wrists. There was no time for any final words from Pete.

He slumped to the ground, blood gushing from the puncture wound to his carotid artery and the slashing cut that had opened his belly. Cassie had followed through on the initial strike and was poised over him, his blood spraying over her torso. She plunged a blade into his heart and Pete was dead.

As the short flurry of violence erupted, Nick jumped to his feet, threw his glass in Harry's face and ran to the reception door. He stumbled across the rubble carpeting the floor, not daring to look back. Falling on to the duffel bag, he reached inside, his hands scrabbling among the various weapons and electronics that he'd bought from Scruff.

He could hear Harry roaring with rage back in the lounge – "Fuck you! Fuck you! Fuck you!" – and he imagined the grotesque, grisly mess that was Cassie turning from Pete's lifeless body to come after him. He felt a sudden cold horror as the threat of evisceration came closer to reality.

Then he found what he was looking for.

He rolled over to see the headless gory shape of Cassie almost on him, a cold monster poised to kill. He barely had time to point the smooth contoured weapon at her but it was enough. Nick pulled the trigger, the EMP generator fired its one and only charge and Cassie collapsed on to him in a jerking tumble of limbs. All the lights in the reception and lounge went out then seconds later, low level emergency lighting came on, providing just enough illumination by which to see.

Nick dropped the EMP gun and pushed the motionless synthetic off his body. Then he grabbed the duffel bag and stood up. His breath coming in short gasps, he stared at the thing on the floor. Back in the lounge Harry was yelling profanities into the darkness while outside in the night the battle continued.

Nick ran to the shattered doorway and looked out on the roof gardens. The battle had split into multiple small firefights and he had no idea who was who. At the wall to his left were the bodies of Chopper and Billy.

He dropped the duffel bag outside the door and took out a black backpack with a double harness which he pulled it over his shoulders and secured in front using the clasp. Then he reached inside once more and took out a handgun. The gun at the ready, he stepped into the night and turned to the left.

His last view of Harry was as he went past the viewing window of the lounge. His former boss was a dark shadow in the low illumination of the emergency lights. His head was hunched forward from his shoulders as he bellowed with rage, his hands raised to the ceiling, a gun in each hand.

As impossible as it seemed to find a way through the firefight, for the second night in a row, it occurred to Nick Turner that whatever awaited him outside couldn't be worse than what was inside. He ran into the darkness.

# 56
## Curtain Call

The police car cornered onto East Smithfield at an alarming speed and tore past St. Katherine's Dock on its way to the Coronation Tower. There were several other fast-moving vehicles ahead of him, and as Hodges curved onto The King's Highway outside the tower he saw many more parked around it, emergency lights splashing red and white against the concrete. Up on the roof gardens something was burning.

Hodges' car took a sharp right into Tower Plaza and screeched to a halt next to the cluster of police vehicles, ambulances, and fire engines already dispersed there. He stepped out of the car and walked straight to the command centre that had been set up outside the lobby by the lead officer from SCO19.

"Inspector."

"McKay. What's the latest?"

"Building's on lockdown. Big firefight on the roof; surveillance shows 53 known combatants. Maybe more inside the building. There's a helicopter down in the roof gardens; that's the fire you can see up there. We have the perimeter and all exits secured."

"Civilians?"

"Unknown. We don't think there are any on the roof. Good thing is, it's the weekend, so the offices are mostly closed. Building staff are all accounted for and we have the residents being tallied up over on the other side of the tower."

"Well, this is quite a mess." Hodges looked around the Plaza.

His phone rang: priority call. West Drayton ATC. He sighed and took it. The face on the screen was the last one he wanted to see at this moment.

"What?"

"Do you have any men on the roof, Inspector?"

"Why?"

"I say again. Do you have any men on the roof?"

Hodges looked at McKay. McKay shook his head.

"We have the tower perimeter secured and are proceeding with containing the situation," said Hodges. "We don't need your help, ta very much."

"Too late for that, Inspector. You've done a piss-poor job on this one, and it's out of your hands. Not only did you fail to keep me informed, you let things get out of control and now we have a full scale military incident."

"This is not a military situation!" Hodges yelled at him "This is a gang turf war!"

"There is a crashed helicopter on the roof, and drone surveillance has picked up heavy weaponry. This is now a military situation and I have assumed control. Commandos are inbound by helicopter and I am taking action to reduce the threat of civilian casualties."

"What the fuck are you talking about?"

"Stay clear, Inspector. Code 10 in progress. I say again, Code 10 in progress. Impact in 3 minutes."

"You have got to be fucking kidding!" Hodges yelled at the phone, but the call had been cut off. He looked up at McKay who was talking urgently into his throat mike. The alert had already gone out to the SCO19 team and they were hustling everyone away from the tower.

Hodges ran back to his car.

"Holy shit. Holy fucking shit!"

He looked up at the night sky above the tower.

Twelve miles above his head a surveillance drone the width of a football pitch received a signal from a controller at West Drayton ATC.

The signal was decoded and run through a verification sequence before being relayed to three smaller drones cruising at a much lower altitude.

Weapon deployment sequences fired in the electronic brains of the drones. Seconds later, precision cluster bombs dropped from their wings, and gravity pulled them inexorably towards the top of the tower.

Back at West Drayton the controller turned to his commander. "Deployment confirmed, sir."

He watched the progress of the bombs on his monitor as they fell towards the roof gardens. A few hundred metres above the tower they split into multiple bomblets and formed a deadly pattern that descended on the combatants below.

The commander watched them fall without emotion.

"It's going to be hot in the City tonight."

# 57
## Base Instinct

Nick was a little over halfway to the far end of the gardens, where the helicopter burned close to the edge of the infinity pool, when he ran into Colin. Amid the confusion and noise of the ongoing firefight he didn't see him until the last minute, crouched by a gap in the wall.

Colin, on the other hand, had seen Nick approaching on his goggle display. He didn't know who it was, and he held fire since they were coming from the direction of the suite and were probably a friendly rather than an enemy. When he saw it was Nick, he thought hard about which category he fell into.

"Hold it, Nick."

Nick dropped behind the shelter of the wall. They held their guns on each other as the ripple of small arms fire continued in the background.

"Hello, Col."

"What's going on back at the office?"

"Not good. Lots of dead people."

"Harry?"

"No. Everyone else, though."

"You kill them?"

"Oddly enough, not a one."

"What happened?"

"Pete. He was working for Wei."

"Bastard. How'd he die?"

"Look, Col, I'd love to sit and chat with you but this isn't the time or place. I need to get off the tower, so if it's all the same to you I'll be on my way."

Colin shook his head. "Can't let you go, Nick. I still work for Harry. Come back to the office with me, and let's talk it over after this little fuss has died down."

"Harry's not very interested in chatting with me at the moment."

"Still can't let you go. Where are you going anyway? Lifts are locked down. There's no way out."

"Thought I might jump off the side."

"Very funny, Nick. Not really the time for jokes."

"You sound like Allie. Look, this isn't going to end well, Col. Time's running out. Let's lower our guns, and go our different ways, all right?"

Colin didn't move an inch. "Sorry, Nick," he said, and then the world fell apart.

A cacophony of thunderous explosions deafened both of them as cluster bombs exploded all across the gardens, momentarily illuminating everything in a precise pattern of bright white flashes. A large segment of the wall against which Colin was sheltering turned to rubble and both of them were thrown to the ground.

Seconds later it was over and when it ended, so did the gunfire. The only sounds coming across the gardens now were cries and screams of pain.

Dazed, Nick got to his feet. Colin was down, half covered with rubble, but moving. Nick stumbled past him and headed for the infinity pool. He could see in the low level lighting of the gardens the bodies scattered here and there and the holes that had been blasted in the ground. Much of the ground was churned up, and the rotunda had been almost completely destroyed. No exit there.

Nick stumbled on past bodies, scattered rubble, and shattered glass. He looked back to see Colin getting to his feet and looking around. Nick picked up his pace.

He continued to follow the curved wall until it brought him round to the wrecked helicopter and the shallow infinity pool. Across the pool was the glass wall put there to stop people going over the side. The helicopter had broken through a section of it.

Nick ran into the pool, glancing over his shoulder. Colin's night vision goggles gave him the edge and, gun in hand, he was gaining on him. He fired and the bullet clanged off the side of the helicopter.

"Stop!" yelled Colin. Nick halted next to the helicopter, standing on the parapet by the smashed glass wall. He turned around; behind him was a 1500-foot drop to the plaza below and in front of him was Colin, approaching with his gun raised.

"Hands in the air, Nick."

Nick raised his hands.

"Good man. Now, come back over here. It's not like you have much of a choice." Colin waved his gun towards the suite. "Do the sensible thing."

"I'm a long way past sensible, Col" Nick said with a grin, "See ya," and he hurled himself off the parapet and disappeared down the side of the tower.

"Jesus Christ." Colin splashed through the pool to the edge of the garden and peered down. He was just in time to catch a glimpse of the upper surface of the parachute as Nick corkscrewed it out of sight around the curved frame of the tower.

"Fuck!"

Colin stood staring down at the dark streets below. For a moment or two he thought about jumping after Nick and then he turned wearily around and walked back up the path through the shattered roof gardens to the remains of Harry's suite.

# 58
## Dark Street

Wrecked John lived on the river, but it also lived in him. At night it was like a deep, dark winding artery that flowed through his consciousness and, depending on the mood, it could be filled with blood or bile. He knew the sounds it made, the smell of it, and everything that moved on it or in it. He knew the river like nothing else in his life.

This particular night, he had been awakened by sounds that were not normal for the river or the sprawling city that had grown up around it.

He had opened his eyes and looked across at Wapping. He'd heard explosions and gunfire, lots of it. The distant pop pop pop of the guns had reminded him of the fireworks display that had been held on the riverbank last November. At the top of the Coronation Tower frequent staccato flashes had illuminated the sky. He had seen a helicopter passing overhead, very loud and very fast, and shortly afterwards it had disappeared from sight near the top of the tower and there had been an explosion. John had tried to go back to sleep but he needed a piss.

Now he got up out of his hammock and walked between the potted plants to the stern of the barge where he unzipped his jeans and urinated into the Thames. The light show across the river grew more frantic, and the sounds of police sirens filled the sky. He zipped up his jeans and stood watching. Lights came on in the apartments that lined the river on each side, and a few of his fellow barge residents came out on the decks of their homes to see what the fuss was about.

The gunfire rose and fell in intensity as whatever was going on atop the tower ebbed and flowed. It became sporadic, and John was wondering whether it was about to end when the entire top of the tower erupted in vivid flashes of light. A few seconds later came a hammering of multiple explosions, one on top of the other. It was like the end of a fireworks display when all the biggest and best ones are set off in a grand finale.

He wiped his eyes and stared, wondering if there was going to be any more entertainment. A couple of minutes went by without gunfire; only the wailing of police sirens cut the darkness.

Then John saw a shape, a dark dragon in the night, come gliding down towards him from the direction of the tower. It was black against the sky, and because it was moving he knew it was real. He could see it now and again illuminated against the few lights that were on in the tall buildings on the other side of the river.

He tracked it as it soared down in gentle curves to left and right as if it was looking for something, a place to land, perhaps. He hoped that it didn't land on his boat. It didn't look at all friendly.

It turned and swept along the river in a long glide all the way down until its claws were almost touching the water; then it seemed to collapse in on itself and disappear. There was the sound of a splash.

John watched as a fast boat zipped into the river from St. Katherine's Pier and sped over to where the dragon had vanished. It slowed down when it reached the spot, and he thought he saw a dark shape climb in before the boat rushed off downstream and out of sight round the bend of the river at Rotherhithe.

All around him, John could hear the voices of the barge people and the residents of the warehouse flats chattering and shouting. He looked blankly around. Off in the distance he thought he heard the sound of more helicopters approaching. It felt like it was going to be a noisy night.

*If I'm not going to be able to get any more sleep here, I might as well go and see what all the fuss is about.*

John walked to the edge of the barge and stepped onto the walkway. He threaded his way back through the gardens towards the iron gate that would let him back out onto the streets of London.

# 59

# Cry Havoc

Colin stepped into the remains of the office, the shattered glass crunching beneath his boots. Bombs had hit the building on the side by the gardens, destroying the windows and knocking down chunks of the walls. The lounge was a wreck.

He walked through the remains of the reception area and looked into Harry's office. It wasn't as badly damaged as the other rooms and Harry was inside, his dark bulk motionless behind his desk on which a pair of guns lay beside the antique black phone. The night glow of London through the blinds cut him into strips of light and shadow.

"What's the story, Col?"

"He's gone, boss. Got away."

Harry nodded over and over again. "Right. Right."

There was a ping from the reception area and the sound of many men entering.

"Gun down, Col," Harry said.

Colin raised his eyebrows. "Come again?"

"It'll be the law."

Colin removed the clip from his gun and tossed both pieces of hardware to one side.

"Police! Anyone in there?"

"Yes. Two of us," Harry called out.

There was the sound of swift activity and low voices from the reception area.

"This is Hodges. That you, Harry?"

"Come in, Inspector," Harry called back.

Hodges walked into Harry's office. He nodded to Harry and Colin and looked round the room.

"Evening, Inspector."

"Harry."

"Busy night."

"Yeah," Hodges gave a regretful smile. "About to get busier. I'm going to have to take you in, Harry."

Harry nodded. "May I have a minute, Inspector? I'd like to make a quick phone call."

Harry looked at Colin and gestured with his head towards the door. Colin started for the lobby.

"One coming out, unarmed," Hodges called. He looked at Harry. "Be my guest. Make it quick, though would you, Harry? I think half of Special Forces are going to be landing on this roof in a minute."

Hodges turned and left the room.

Harry didn't move or make a sound for a minute, then he looked at the old-fashioned handset on his desk. He unplugged the hacking device that Nick had left behind, and plugged the network cable back into the phone. Rolling his head around on his neck like he was squaring up for a fight, he breathed in deeply through flared nostrils then he reached for the oversized black handset.

He worked his fingers round the rotary dial in slow, deliberate arcs. The only sounds in the room were the tick-tick of the clock and the purr as the dial rotated counterclockwise after each number. Harry finished dialing and after a short pause there was a distant ringing and then a click as the call was picked up at the other end.

"Martin? Harry. I've got a lot of work for you."

# 60
# Morning Chorus

The first faint glimmer of dawn illuminated the inside of Wei's private suite at the top of the Shard. It provided enough contrast across the city to define the shapes of the tall buildings of Wapping, outlining them as black columns, punctuated by occasional squares of light shining through the windows of flats and offices.

The Coronation Tower was lit up from top to bottom. Every light in the building was on, and had been on, since the rooftop battle had ended in the small hours of the morning. The top of the tower was dotted with the spotlights of approaching and departing helicopters. Curling threads of smoke rose from many places, curving away to the south as the wind took them.

Wei sat, as he had all night, at the window, his impassive gaze fixed on the events unfolding at the tower. Now, as the dawn continued to bloom like a pale orange flower, and London began to take shape below in the gathering light, he looked around for the first time and smiled.

# *61*
# A Glass Half Full

It was busy at Fenchurch Street Police Station. Officers, members of SCO19, and the occasional commando moved busily back and forth. Every screen was a riot of colour, flashing alerts, and scrolling news streams, and there was a constant background noise of urgent voices sorting out the night's events.

Inspector Hodges sat at his desk, sipping at his tea.

"Another hour, Jim, and I think you can knock off," he said to the duty sergeant.

"Right-o, sir," he gave Hodges a stern look "You too, sir."

Hodges nodded and smiled. "Yes, all right. Me too."

"Lots of people going down for a long stretch after last night," said Jim. "The ones that aren't dead, anyway."

Hodges nodded; there was nothing to add.

"Just the big fish left to sort out then, sir. Valentin's an easy one, once he gets out of intensive care, anyway, but what are we going to get Harry on? He's banging on to anyone who goes by his cell about how he's the victim in all this."

Hodges laughed. "Possession of an illegal synthetic. Accessory to killings by said synthetic. Possession of illegal weaponry. I think we've got enough to put Harry away for a decent stretch."

"Fair enough. That just leaves Wei."

Hodges sighed.

"And there, my friend, we have nothing. Nothing that'll stick, anyway. No one left alive out of that bunch of mercenaries is talking, and we can be sure they won't. Wei is nothing if not thorough. No, Jim, I'm afraid that Mr. Wei's reckoning will have to wait for another day."

Jim nodded. "S'pose so, sir. Anything else I can sort out before we finish up?"

"Yeah, what's the story with Turner's girlfriend?"

"Surveillance shows she was asleep the whole time, but I had a woman officer interview her anyway. She was very shocked and asked after Nick and Harry. That was it."

"Keep her under a watch until we're sure that Turner's really gone, would you?"

"Will do, sir."

"Oh, and one more thing, Jim."

"What's that, sir?"

"Any chance of another cuppa?"

# 62
## Unfinished Business

After the police officer had left, Allie shut the door behind her and went to the kitchen to make some tea. The dawn was beginning to show; there were no clouds in the sky and it looked like it might turn into a nice day.

She put on the kettle and thought about Nick and Harry.

It looked like Nick was gone for good from what the police had told her; left the country on a boat or a plane. Harry was probably going to prison, and his gangland empire was in ruins. Things were a mess. She wasn't sure how she felt after the last two days. Part of her felt like if Nick walked into the flat right this minute and said, 'Let's make a go of it, what do you think?' she might just say yes.

She put a teabag into a cup and stood while the kettle boiled, thinking nothing in particular. After a little while the kettle clicked off and she poured water on the tea, thinking that it was funny how in the end life always came down to the small things. Last night there was a pitched battle on the roof of one of London's most prestigious buildings and she was a person of interest to the police. This morning she was making tea by herself in her flat.

Allie finished up making the tea and took the cup out to the living room. She sat down in the chair Nick had sat in not much more than a day ago. When she went to put the cup down she moved the coaster and found a note under it.

Nick's handwriting, she realized, a chill in her heart. She put the cup down and picked it up the note. Her heart beat a little faster.

*'Allie – I'm sorry how all this ended up. When you turned me down, the one thing I'd thought would never change in my life went away. I know I wasn't everything you wanted, but I thought perhaps I was close enough. Obviously not. I've tried to understand about Harry – not understand, I mean that I've tried to figure it out.*

*I can't handle it. That's as honest as I can be. Things are not going to end well between me and him. That's not your fault, that's just how it is. After years of having both of you in my life, now I have neither.*

*I have a few more things to do, then I'm going away. I can't tell you where because I don't feel like I can trust that you'll keep it from Harry. Better that you don't know. Somewhere warmer than London, that's about all I can tell you.*

*I'd like you to know this, though. If I ever get back, if I ever see you again, then...'*

The note ended.

She read it several times, tears in her eyes. Then she put it down and cried.

A few minutes later she picked up her cup and drank some tea.

She got up and walked to the bedroom and looked out the window at the people starting to fill the streets of Camden Town. The sun was coming up. A new day was dawning over London.

# 63
## Albion

The door to the Albion quivered as Mike heaved it open and he walked in and looked around at the busy lunchtime crowd. Something melodic and retro was playing over the speakers. Over at the back he saw Tom sitting as always with his pint of Guinness. Sam and her apparent new best mate Louise had a table over in the corner. Sam looked fantastic, as she usually did, in some sort of silver top, her hair spilling out over her shoulders, a vast improvement on the last time Mike had seen her, at the New Clarendon.

Mike waved to them and pointed at the bar. He made a drinking gesture with his right hand and raised his eyebrows. They both shook their heads so he went over to the bar where Bob was pulling a pint for someone else.

"What the hell is this, Bob, more musical archaeology?"

"Psychedelic Furs," said Bob, without looking up. "I'm not even going to try to explain."

"Bit melodic for you."

"I slum it every now and then." He finished pulling the pint and put it on the bar. He looked up and caught sight of the bruises on Mike's face. "Bloody hell. What happened after the gig last night, Mike? You look awful. Well, you know, more awful than usual."

"Someone worked me over."

"Heard you playing, did they?"

Mike laughed. "Actually, Bob, you've no idea how close to the truth that is."

"Pint of the usual?"

"Might as well."

Mike rummaged in his pockets while Bob pulled the pint, then pulled out a memory cube which he put on the bar. "Got you a recording of last night's show."

"Will it make me want to beat you up?" Bob put the pint on a beer mat and picked up the cube.

"Quite possibly."

Bob threw the cube on a shelf behind the counter. He turned to serve someone else further down the bar. "Yes, mate?"

Mike took his pint over to where Sam and Louise were sitting, put his drink on the scarred round table top, and sat down on a chair.

"Hello, girls."

"Hi, Mike." said Sam, "Face is a bit rough."

"Thanks. I'm working on a new look. You look great, though."

"Doesn't she?" said Louise, with a meaningful arch of her eyebrows.

Mike looked from one to the other. "What am I missing?"

"Louise is helping me get sorted out. I'm gonna try to do without the drugs for a bit. Without Zelley too."

Mike laughed. "That's excellent. There's a perverse symmetry about this; one of us dumps him and the other gets back together with him"

"What do you mean?"

"I'll tell you later. It's a long story." He raised his glass. "Your very good health," and he took a drink.

He saw Scruff come in to the pub, a shambling mound of hair and denim.

"'Scuse me. Need a quick word with someone"

Mike put down his pint and went over to the bar.

"Scruff."

"Ah, Mike. You look bloody awful."

"I'm getting that quite a lot. What's the story?"

"He made it to France."

"Great. I got the signal from the boat after he got on board, but nothing since."

"That's the way it's supposed to be."

"Yeah, suppose it is. Cheers then, Scruff. It's been lively."

"Yep. Certainly has; taking a low profile for a bit now, mate. How're you staying out of the limelight?"

"Zelley's people are shifting my gear as we speak. I'm moving into the company compound. Nice flat, high visible security, plus a few other measures I can't mention."

"Rent free living? Nice one, Mike."

"There's no money changing hands, but it still comes at a cost, Scruff."

"Right," Scruff nodded. "Well then, see you after the dust settles."

"Amen."

Mike left him at the bar and walked back to see Tom.

"Tom."

"Mike."

"Thanks for the work on the song. Turned out brilliant."

"Told you it was big."

"You did. Anyway, it was amazing working with you."

There was an awkward silence as Tom picked up his tobacco pouch and started to roll a cigarette. Mike stood there and watched him.

"Just one thing I was wondering about your music, Mike." He finished laying out the tobacco and raised the paper to his lips to lick the edge.

"Yeah? What's that, Tom?"

He finished rolling his cigarette, and looked up at Mike from under his beret.

"What else you got?"

# 64

# A Rude Awakening

In a suite in the most fashionable part of London, Zelley woke up on one side of his bed and looked at himself lying next to him.

He blinked and sat up.

"Well, that must have been quite a night."

The other Zelley opened its eyes and looked at him.

"It's always 'quite a night' when I'm there."

"Don't get carried away, my dear boy, you were adequate, nothing more."

The other Zelley feigned shock. "You ought to be looking in a mirror when you say that, old thing."

The first Zelley sighed. "One of us really has got to go."

# *65*
## Flotsam

Wrecked John stumbled along the thin strip of mud beach on the Wapping shoreline. The tide would soon cover it over, but he had time to make it to the steps at the far end. His shoes were caked in the brown mud, and his feet were soaking wet but he didn't notice.

He found it soothing to walk along here. Things moved slowly and predictably along the river, and there were no sudden appearances to disturb his mood. In the small hours of the morning he'd run into an old acquaintance in the streets around the Coronation Tower, and he'd been able to refill his stash pocket with pills. Since then, he'd half emptied it again.

He looked across the river to the green barge at the moorings and remembered something from last night. The dragon. It had swooped down from the tower and disappeared into the river. He wondered if it had been a dream; it was so hard to tell these days. His eyes roved from the barge to the mud at his feet where he saw a piece of rope snaking into the water. It was heavy in his hands when he picked it up, but it came out of the river as he pulled.

Black cloth appeared, and a tangle of rope, and he heaved more and more of it out of the river. Staring at the wet shape on the beach he knew that it hadn't been a dream. He'd found the dragon's wings.

John looked down the river. The dragon was gone. He wondered if it was coming back. He decided to keep its wings safe, just in case. He hauled on the rope and began the slow walk home along the beach.

# 66
# Epilogue

Nick stopped in the shade of a palm tree, the sun hot and high in the sky above. Before him was a strip of sand and glittering blue sea. Behind him was dense jungle.

He ran his hands through his thick head of grey hair and breathed in deeply. His beard was prickly with sweat.

It had been a long and complicated journey. He'd made flights on ramshackle third world aircraft, a series of interminable bus rides, hikes across difficult terrain, and a long voyage across open water on a small decrepit boat that stank of diesel, rust, and piss.

Finally there had been the trek through the trail-less jungle, his only companions the monkeys moving silently in the trees and the spiders that waited patiently in the giant webs they had spun between the branches overhead and the jungle floor.

Off to his right in the trees behind the beach was a low wooden A-frame hut, open at the sides. Nick walked over, unshouldered his pack and put it down. Below the angled roof of the hut was an upturned canoe. Beneath that, Nick knew, there was a fishing net, a paddle for the canoe, a bucket and a shovel. Buried in the earth below all of these was a metal storage locker that held other things he would need in the weeks ahead.

He walked back to the empty beach. He wouldn't be able to relax his guard. Not for some time. Not until he felt that the trail was cold. He had no idea how long that would take but one day he would know.

He surveyed the restless ocean beyond the tree line. This wouldn't be a bad place to wait.

# The End of Dark Streets
### Book One of the Dark Futures series

### The sequel
## Dark Cities
### will be available June 2015

Visit www.andyravenscroft.com
for news and updates

## Other stories by the same writer:

### The Facebook Genocide
(as Andy Ravenscroft)

**Visit Karen (editing):** artstuckinmyeye.wordpress.com
**Visit Mary (graphic design):** www.marymusker.com

www.ingramcontent.com/pod-product-compliance
Lightning Source LLC
Chambersburg PA
CBHW060130130626
46556CB00006B/2295